BLOOD
OF
QUEENS

TO ℰMILY,

For being my sister in blood and soul and creativity. Thank you for always being there, and for understanding my hunger to makes my dream a reality.

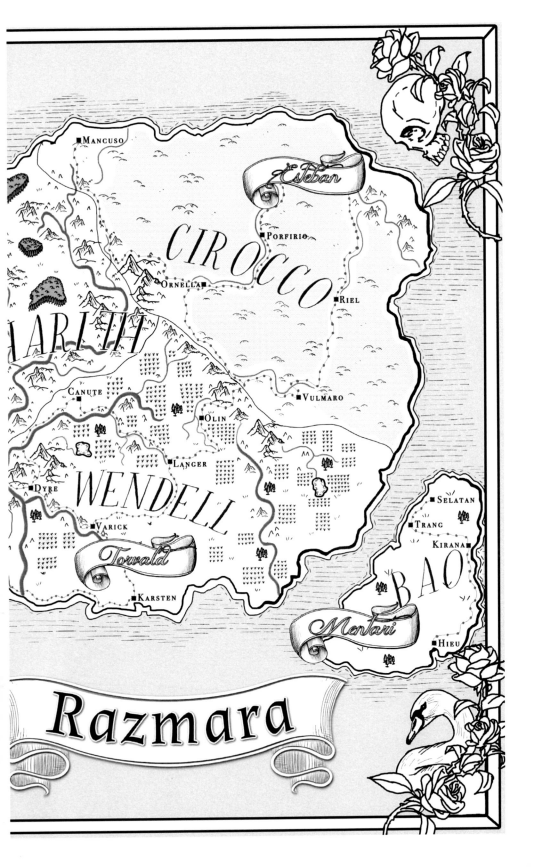

PROLOGUE
MIRIAM DARNELL

The city burned.

The scent of fire clogged the air as Miriam Darnell emerged onto her balcony to find Marinel bathed in smoke and flame. The low ringing of the bells alerted the city to what Miriam already suspected—they were under attack. Cold dread washed over her as she wrapped her shawl tighter around her thin form. She had foreseen this, yet the event coming to pass did nothing to ease the sheer terror that enveloped her now.

Gathering her wits about her, Miriam strode back into her room, knees trembling as she shook her husband awake. The King of Basium jerked out of slumber, blinking rapidly as he registered his wife's silhouette. They didn't need to share words—the suffocating stench of fire had Patrick Darnell out of his bed in an instant, hands reaching for his swan-hilted sword.

"I saw this." Miriam's words were little more than a hoarse whisper as she watched Patrick ease himself to his feet, the glint of his blade and the ferocity in his eyes starkly contrasting the grey of his hair and the slowness of his gait. "I told you of a future in flame, our capital burning to the ground, yet you would not listen."

Patrick planted a kiss to her forehead. "Find the children."

Miriam swept from the room without another word. For as foolish as Patrick had been to ignore her, he was right—the Warmonger would come for their grandchildren as certainly as night followed day. Her heart thudded a frantic pace in her chest. The castle could already be overrun, and a man as cruel as their enemy wouldn't hesitate to threaten their family.

Visions plagued Miriam frequently. As one of Basium's most treasured

Imperium, her gifts of foresight and healing could just as easily become curses. She had seen the fire consuming the capital, but she had not been prepared for the screams that resonated throughout the castle. Horror renewed her resolve and quickened her feet. She needed to find her son and his children.

Miriam's fingers shook as they tightened around the brass handle of her youngest grandson's room, the metal icy to the touch. What would she find when she opened the door? Would Sebastian be hiding under his bed, like any child attempting to escape a nightmare? The thought of her grandson trembling in such terror made Miriam wrench the door open—and immediately she pressed a hand over her mouth, tears welling in her eyes.

Of course the Warmonger's men had arrived first. Imogen lay dead on the ground, a gory red gash carved across her throat, her crimson blood staining the stone floor. So much blood.

Imogen had been all that Miriam could ever have asked for of a daughter-in-law. She was kind, graceful, and she had loved her husband and children dearly. A knife was inches away from Imogen's bloodstained fingers. A vision flashed through Miriam's mind, Imogen fighting like a feral animal to protect her youngest child, teeth gritted and steel bared though she was not a warrior. Miriam's brow pinched. Where was Sebastian?

"We didn't want to kill her."

Miriam spun around at the remorseful, unfamiliar voice. It belonged to a boy of about seventeen, whose jackal-crested armour and silver-and-black livery marked him as a member of House Morrow. Miriam stepped forward, hands clenching into fists, but the soldiers who flanked the boy seized her by the arms. This boy must be the Warmonger's own son, Jacen Morrow. A spoiled prince experiencing war for the first time. She wondered how he liked the taste.

"I don't want to hurt you. My father wishes for me to bring you to the gardens, along with the others."

"Others?" Miriam let optimism get the better of her. Perhaps, despite Imogen's tragic demise, some of her family was still alive. She truly hoped that Patrick had not done anything rash. He was not as young as he once had been and had a habit of forgetting that.

That fragile thread of hope let Miriam be marched down the corridors of her own palace and into the gardens without a fight. They could salvage the situation — Marinel might not yet be lost.

Then she saw *him*.

The Warmonger. Cobryn Morrow. King of Genera. There were a whole host of names for the tall man with the fair colouring and cruel eyes who regarded Miriam with something like amusement as she was forced to her knees on the wet grass. A quick glance at the other kneeling prisoners indicated at least some other survivors: Miriam's son Frederick, his middle son Peregrine, and his only daughter Carissa.

"This is what happens to those who defy me." Cobryn stepped forward, examining the remnants of House Darnell with contempt. Behind him, the sky glowed a deep orange tainted with billowing grey smoke. "We could have been allies, but instead you chose the path of resistance. Now, you will learn what becomes of my enemies."

"Where are the others?" Frederick demanded. Miriam wished he would remain silent, hoping Cobryn's wrath would not silence him next. "My wife Imogen and my other sons, where are they?"

Jacen had gone to stand beside his father, but he did not share Cobryn's triumph. Pale and shaken, his gaze raked over the frightened faces of their prisoners. If anyone would save their lives, Miriam knew it would be that boy.

"Imogen is dead." Cobryn waved a careless hand, but the malice in his eyes belied his attempt at disinterest. "She died protecting your youngest—Sebastian, is it? The boy made it as far as the tunnels before we collapsed them onto him."

Cobryn tossed a ring to the ground in front of Frederick, one all too familiar—a silver ring with the symbol of a swan, House Darnell's sigil. It had been given to Sebastian on his last birthday, his twelfth. Her stomach twisted and churned, chills of horror running up the length of her spine.

Frederick unleashed a scream. Beside him, Carissa sobbed openly. Tears blurred Miriam's vision. She would never see Sebastian again. Never scold him for stealing tarts from the kitchens or hear his mischievous laugh as he pranked his siblings. How much had Cobryn ripped away from them? How much would he still take?

"Brother." A brown-haired man strode over to Cobryn. Slighter in build than his older brother, the resemblance lingered in the glint of his hazel eyes. Miriam went cold all over. If the sight of Cobryn Morrow was enough to inspire fear, seeing Deacon produced nothing less than sheer terror. He carried something under his arm, eyes raking over the royal family on their knees.

Deacon gave them all a wicked smile before tossing something at Frederick's knees. Carissa reeled back with a sharp cry, and Frederick paled as he examined the bloody head of his son and heir, Theodore.

"He was a good fighter," Deacon said, with all the casual cruelty of his older brother. "A shame he lost."

Cobryn glanced at him. "What of the King?"

Miriam sucked in her breath as she waited for word of Patrick. She knew she would most likely be met with disappointment, yet she could not believe her husband was dead until she knew for certain.

Deacon shrugged. "Saw him near the battlements with five arrows in him."

Those five arrows pierced Miriam instead. Hot tears leaked down her cheeks as the pain of her loss struck her down. It would rent her apart. Two of her grandsons, her daughter-in-law…now her husband as well. What did the Morrow family want? How far would they go before the suffering and humiliation of House Darnell was enough?

"You'll pay!" Peregrine bared his teeth and lunged, but Cobryn's sword pierced his chest before he even made it to his feet. Carissa screamed and Frederick pressed his face into his hands to avoid watching the last of his sons die. The metallic tang of blood clogged her nose as Cobryn withdrew his sword, leaving Peregrine to die on the ground, convulsing. Horrifying gurgling noises escaped his lips.

"What do you want?" Carissa cried, voice shaking with sobs and desperation. "Just tell us what you want, and we'll do it."

The Warmonger's attention fell on the girl, and a sense of dread Miriam couldn't explain washed over her as Cobryn looked over Carissa. His gaze was cold and calculating. Deacon looked at her too, a smirk across his lips and something sinister in his eyes.

"I want Basium, child."

Trepidation seized Miriam by the throat. She looked to her son, her only child, just as Cobryn swung his bloody sword forth once again and cut off Frederick's head. Carissa dissolved into tears, her face and dress spattered with her father's blood.

Miriam closed her eyes, but she would hear the dull thump of her son's head hitting the grass for as long as she lived. She remembered the moment she'd held Frederick in her arms as a babe, the swell of love she'd felt for him, her only child to reach adulthood. She had never thought she would see her son die so violently right in front of her. Part of her wanted to die, too.

"You'll never have Basium." Miriam's voice was low and venomous as her eyes snapped open. "You're a fool if you think my people would ever bow to you."

"Oh, I know they wouldn't bow to me." Cobryn's gaze flicked to Carissa once again. "Yet they would for their rightful Queen."

Miriam realised then that the murders of her family had not been senseless violence in the least. Her husband, her son, her grandsons... All of them had to die to pave way for Carissa's ascent to the throne. This had been Cobryn's plan all along. She feared the circumstances that would come with her granddaughter's coronation.

"What...what do you mean?" Carissa choked out the words, voice hoarse.

A grin lit up Deacon's face as he stepped forward. "Cobryn..."

The Warmonger flung out an arm in front of his younger brother, using his free hand to beckon his son. Jacen's eyes flew wide as he stepped forward, head tilting askance to the side.

"Father?"

"Every Queen needs a King." The words were soft and ominous. The fear in Carissa's violet-blue eyes indicated she understood the implications all too well. Miriam did not miss the tense set of Deacon's jaw and resentful look that came over his face. She thanked the goddess it would be Cobryn's son and not his brother, yet either way, Carissa would be forced into her wedding bed with a man who participated in the slaughter of her family.

"She is a child," Miriam hissed, her voice rising in anger. "She is fourteen years old!"

"There have been younger wives and Queens." Cobryn shrugged his powerful shoulders, before he turned his attention on Carissa. "Tomorrow, you will be crowned, and then you will wed my son."

"Father," Jacen protested, sounding as though he liked this idea almost as little as Miriam and Carissa.

Why am I still alive? Miriam wanted to ask the question, yet she dare not in case Cobryn changed his mind. She would not leave Carissa alone to suffer the humiliation the Warmonger had in store for her. Perhaps it was because Miriam was but a woman. Perhaps it was because her abilities as an Imperium granted her no fighting skills, no secret weapons she might use against them.

Instead, Miriam moved to embrace her traumatised granddaughter. Carissa had seen enough violence and bloodshed this night. Miriam's heart ached, her entire body crumbled trying to hold back the anguish at all the needless murders. If she broke down, Carissa would fall apart. The poor girl had suffered much—and Miriam knew that if Cobryn had his way, she would suffer far more.

The royal family had once been called 'goddess blessed'. Legend had it the ancestors of House Darnell had been from the bloodline of the goddess Elethea herself. Yet such rumour had surely been quashed with the realisation of how swiftly the enemy had torn them down. Almost all of the Darnell family was dead, with Miriam and Carissa subjugated by Cobryn Morrow. Now, Miriam heard the whispers through the half-burned capital. They called them 'goddess cursed'.

Marinel still smoked the day Carissa Darnell's coronation took place, but the dark clouds looming overhead threatened a storm. Miriam had said her prayers for rain, yet she doubted they'd be heard. Where was Elethea when her son had been decapitated in front of her? Where had she been when they collapsed the tunnels on her sweet little grandson? Such terrible memories brought her dangerously close to tears. She could not afford to cry, not when Carissa relied on her strength.

It was Miriam's role to prepare Carissa for the coronation ceremony. No servants could be found. Another cruel jab from the Warmonger. Miriam already powdered Carissa's face, her lips painted crimson red. She wore the deep crimson robe of her forefathers, yet it swamped her small and slender frame. Although Carissa attempted to act older than her age, head held high, it only reminded Miriam how painfully young her granddaughter still was.

"There." Miriam fitted the last of the hair pins to Carissa's glossy black tresses. "All done. You're ready for your coronation."

The bells pealed again, a more cheerful tone this time. Their joy didn't deceive Miriam—there could be no rejoicing throughout Basium, not when almost all of House Darnell had been butchered and the young Princess was a prisoner within her own capital, forced to take up her grandfather's throne.

"What if I can't do this?" Carissa spun to face her grandmother, eyes wide and fearful. "I know they want to use me as a puppet, Grandmother. How could I ever rule our people knowing that?"

"Because you are strong." Miriam gripped her shoulders, squeezing lightly. "One day, we will have Basium back. They've won the battle, but not the war. We will obey for now, as they expect us to. Any hint of defiance, and they'd kill us both."

Carissa swallowed and nodded fervently. The girl had always been clever—shy and a little slow to warm to others, but observant. Under Miriam's guidance, she would play the role of Basium's child Queen. It had been mere days since the fall of Marinel. Carissa was learning and adapting quickly.

The door opened and Carissa took a deep breath, squaring her shoulders and walking down the purple carpet that stretched the length of the chapel. Miriam followed a few steps behind, completely aware of the Morrow family in the front pew. Jacen was staring at his feet like he wished he could be anywhere else.

The archbishop was nowhere in sight. Many believed he had been killed during the battle. Instead a priest came to officiate the ceremony, a man that Miriam did not recognise. He was a member of the Priesthood that had been installed into a position of power on the basis of serving the Morrows. The thought made her lip curl in distaste. There would be more to grovel, to promise servitude to the Warmonger in exchange for power.

Carissa adjusted the heavy robes and knelt before the priest as Miriam took her place at the foot of the steps. Patrick's golden swan-adorned crown—a ceremonial item that he'd only ever worn during celebrations and special events—looked as though it would be far too heavy for Carissa's head.

The coronation ceremony was a predominantly silent one. It had been many years since Patrick's, but Miriam still remembered it clearly. It had been a far less solemn occasion, and the chapel had been full of cheer. She had never believed she'd be alive for the coronation of a grandchild.

No words were spoken, and the chapel was quiet as the priest anointed Carissa's forehead with the holy oil before setting the crown of House Darnell upon her head. The girl's shoulders trembled as she rose, but when she turned to face the crowd, her expression was fiercely resolute.

Pride swelled within Miriam for her granddaughter, in the fact that

7

Carissa took this difficult situation and did the best she could with it. Then she noticed that Carissa's nails dug into her palms, so hard that drops of blood trickled down her fingers. No one else in the room, except those with magic in them, could have sensed what Miriam did—and it chilled her to the bone.

Carissa moved down the steps with the grace of her mother and the strength of her father. Stern violet-blue eyes cast across the chapel. The assembled crowd, including Miriam, knelt before the Queen. Even the Morrow family bent the knee, although amusement decorated Deacon and Cobryn's faces. This was a joke to them, but it was deadly serious to Miriam.

Miriam stared at her granddaughter with a mixture of horror and wonder. She had always sensed the magic in Carissa's blood—in the Darnell family, women predominantly held magic more than men. Miriam had thought one day Carissa might become a powerful Imperium to rival herself, but this...

Goddess above, they have crowned a Maleficium as our Queen.

A royal wedding turned Miriam's mind from the matter of her granddaughter's dark magic, due to how busy it kept her. Cobryn was keen to see his son wed to Basium's new Queen, and only a few days stretched between Carissa's coronation and her wedding.

Miriam recalled her own wedding to Patrick with heartbroken fondness. She had been nineteen years old at the time and so very in love with the prince who courted her. It was a love that had only grown and strengthened throughout the years, despite the trials of Miriam's many miscarriages and stillbirths. Even though Patrick had his flaws, Miriam had loved her husband very much.

Now he's dead.

The consummation had been the most embarrassing part of all, yet it had been gentle and compassionate on both sides. Miriam had known it was her duty as a wife. Patrick had treated her with kindness, and all her fear of the moment she had been dreading for some time had dissipated.

Unfortunately, she was under no illusion of what would happen to Carissa. Cobryn was a violent man who knew only conquest, and that extended to women. His marriage to a Harithian princess—his second, as his first wife had died some years prior—was a loveless one. Miriam did not know Jacen well enough to pass judgement but assumed he would be facing pressure from his father. If that pressure meant Carissa's pain and humiliation, Miriam didn't think it would matter to the boy.

Miriam never spoke of consummation with her granddaughter. She did not want to lie, yet she also didn't want to expose the girl to such an ugly truth. Carissa was already too young for the burden being thrust upon her. Best that she went into the situation ignorant of how awful it might be, and that Miriam's prayers for mercy would be heard by the goddess.

While the coronation robes of her ancestors had made Carissa seem like a small child dressing up in her parent's clothes, her wedding dress was another matter entirely. It hugged the subtle curves of her slender body and reminded Miriam that, to the enemy, her granddaughter was not a little girl. Carissa fussed over the lace-coloured ivory white dress, over the intricately braided mass that made up her black hair.

Miriam stayed quiet until the maids left, when she could speak with Carissa alone. Did her granddaughter suspect the power that coursed through her veins? Perhaps, but Miriam didn't think Carissa knew darkness dwelled within her. Approaching the girl, Miriam cupped her face in her hands and smiled sadly.

"You look beautiful."

"I don't want this," Carissa protested, her vulnerabilities painfully obvious now that only the two of them remained. Her bright, fierce eyes met her grandmother's. "I can't do it. I'd rather carve out my own heart!"

"Darling, don't say that." Miriam pulled her into a tight embrace, rubbing Carissa's back as the dark-haired girl sobbed openly. "Listen to me. I don't know much about Jacen Morrow, but he is hesitant about this too."

When Miriam drew back, Carissa's brow creased into a confused frown.

"Do you think I could find happiness with him? The son of the man who murdered my family?"

"No." Miriam gripped Carissa's hands tightly. "But you could find a path to vengeance. There's a power in you. I felt it during your coronation. The same magic that flows through my blood is in yours."

"Mother said that Imperium traits might become obvious once I bled, but..."

"Imperium?" Miriam shook her head slowly. There was no point in lying to the girl and giving her false hopes. "No, child. You are Maleficium."

Carissa's eyes widened with horror and she opened her mouth, but Deacon strode through the door before she could voice her thoughts. Miriam clenched her hands into fists at the sight of him.

Cobryn was a famed warrior, but Deacon was an Imperium—what the Generans referred as a Primordial. According to the rumours, Deacon had the power to make rivers flood cities, to turn water into ice at his mere touch. Miriam did not know how much truth those rumours held, yet she knew better than to underestimate someone like Deacon.

The way Deacon looked at Carissa made Miriam's skin crawl. It was clear he believed he should be marrying her instead of Jacen. He wanted the title of Basium's King, and it had not been granted to him. Certainly a man to be wary of, and Miriam did not trust him around her granddaughter in the slightest.

"Come." Deacon offered his arm. "In the absence of your father, I'll be walking you down the aisle."

Carissa clenched her jaw, but lifted her chin and took Deacon's arm, eyes fixed straight ahead of her. Miriam moved behind to hold Carissa's train. How she wished she could find joy in this wedding. She saw it for what it was—Carissa would forever become a prisoner of the Morrow family.

Jacen was dressed as splendidly as Carissa. He wore a black and silver doublet with a jackal, the symbol of House Morrow, sewn into the breast. Misery was etched across his face as he observed the girl who took her place beside him, hardly daring to look at him. Miriam pitied them—two children forced into a match neither of them wanted. The same priest who had crowned Carissa led the ceremony, and even his expression was grim as he began.

"Ladies and gentlemen, we are gathered here today..."

Miriam took her place in the front pew. Only days before, Carissa had been crowned in this chapel, and now she would lose all that power and become a man's possession. Tears spilled down the girl's cheeks despite her attempts to hold herself steadfast. No one in the chapel did anything, despite the guarded expressions of many lords and ladies.

"Jacen Morrow, do you take Carissa Darnell to be your wife?"

The boy clenched his jaw and offered a curt nod. When the priest raised his brow expectantly, Jacen spoke hoarsely.

"I do."

"Carissa Darnell, do you take Jacen Morrow to be your husband?"

The girl looked to Miriam, silently pleading for her grandmother to find another way. Miriam nodded, encouraging Carissa to go forth with the vows that would bind her to Jacen—until death did them part.

"I do."

"Then I pronounce you husband and wife."

Jacen leaned in and placed a chaste kiss on Carissa's lips. The girl stood frozen like a statue, her shoulders tense. There they stood, Basium's King and Queen—two miserable teenagers who never wanted this burden thrust upon them. Cobryn smiled, but Deacon's expression remained cold. Jacen took his wife's hand and led her back down the aisle. Carissa reached up to quickly wipe away her tears. Jacen looked anywhere but at her.

The wedding feast would commence soon. After that would be the bedding, where Jacen and Carissa would have to consummate the marriage for it to be legitimate and binding. Miriam pressed a hand over her mouth at the knowledge that despite everything she'd been through—her family murdered, her humiliation at being made a puppet Queen—Carissa would have to endure rape tonight to make Cobryn's son their King.

One day, we will bring it all down. We will burn their fucking empire to ash.

THE PUPPET QUEEN
CARISSA DARNELL

The gardens were peaceful during winter. Carissa found herself spending much of her spare time there, surrounded by serenity. The royal gardens had become her personal refuge for some time now. She knelt amidst the daisies, inhaling their sweet scent combined with the grounding smell of damp earth. Her fingers worked at adjusting a particularly stubborn daisy that had not responded to the sunlight filtering through the leaves of the oak tree hanging overhead.

During spring and autumn, many of the court would often marvel at the beauty of the flowers and plants that grew. No beauty could be found there in winter, when the trees shed their leaves. Winter was also the season during which several members of House Darnell had been brutally murdered in the very same gardens.

Carissa withdrew her hands from the soil with a satisfied smile. Every year since the Conquest, she came to these gardens on the anniversary of her family's deaths to honour their sacrifice. She enjoyed gardening, the earth beneath her fingers. Miriam had always told her that a monarch must have a passion or craft to keep them level-headed with everything else they were dealing with, and so gardening had become Carissa's escape.

Spending time with Vida and Bellona helped as well. It had never occurred to Carissa, when she had first accepted the burden of rulership, that she might befriend the Warmonger's eldest daughter. Vida was the same age as Carissa and had arrived in Marinel soon after the Conquest. Carissa suspected that Cobryn wanted a Basiumite marriage for Vida, but nothing had ever been set in stone.

Carissa pushed herself to her feet, wiping her dirty hands on her smock. No one had ever outright called gardening an unladylike pursuit, but the looks of disapproval on the faces of some courtiers said more than words. At first, Carissa had relied upon validation from her lords and ladies, young and self-conscious that she wasn't a good enough monarch. Miriam had later taught her that while advice from the court mattered, their personal opinions did not. Carissa had slowly learned to stop taking criticism to heart.

"Your Majesty!"

Carissa recognised the voice all too well, and she cringed at the sound of it. Deacon Morrow strode through the gardens with one of his usual smug smiles on his face. Vida was not the only member of the Morrow family to reside permanently in Marinel—since Cobryn and Jacen's departure mere days after Carissa and Jacen's wedding, Deacon had remained as regent. Carissa knew how much he must enjoy overseeing everything, but he worked on borrowed time. When Jacen returned...

But when would Jacen return? It had been close to four years. Carissa could not say she missed her husband—she barely knew him. His abrupt withdrawal from Basium left several matters that needed attending to, some that would have to wait until his return. Deacon didn't talk much about what happened, but Carissa heard the news.

The Generan islands of Severino and Philemon had attempted to secede from the kingdom immediately following the Conquest. While taking Marinel and massacring the Darnell family had proved easy for Cobryn, it seemed that retaining the islands had not, if the nearly four years Jacen had been away were anything to judge by.

"Can I help you, Lord Morrow?" Carissa's voice was dry. The years had proved what kind of person Deacon was, and Miriam's initial dislike and mistrust of him were well-placed. Deacon was a snake, slithering around to whisper in ears and gain whatever information he thought would best serve him.

Although Carissa might be the Queen, Deacon held the true power in Basium. The threat to Miriam constantly hung over Carissa's head. She despised the games of court—the gilded truths, the painted lies. But it was a game she had to learn to play. She had no other choice.

Deacon reached Carissa and sank into a bow. A mocking smile played about his lips as he rose. Every reference to her position was a jab, a reminder that she was a puppet Queen and he pulled the strings. He inspected her dirt-splattered smock with disdain.

"I would suggest you change into something more befitting of your station. There is much to be discussed."

"Can we not discuss it here and now?" Carissa folded her arms over her chest. The garden was her sanctuary and although she didn't approve of Deacon being here and wanting to speak with her, if they were to have a conversation, she'd prefer it to be on her grounds. Little victories, Miriam called them. The rare occasions when Carissa felt she had some form of success.

"There is to be a council meeting, Majesty." Deacon raised his eyebrows as he looked over her. "Surely you cannot be attending dressed as such."

"Of course not." Carissa forced a smile. "I will go and change into something more appropriate. Which other council members can I expect at the meeting?"

It was no secret that Deacon aspired to be more than the mere regent in his nephew's absence. If Deacon could have chosen, he would have married Carissa instead and reigned Basium as its rightful King. She could think of nothing worse. If Deacon was King, she would become nothing more than his property. The thought terrified her, particularly as Deacon had made several insinuations that he regretted the fact she married Jacen.

He could never know that Jacen and Carissa had never consummated their marriage.

It had seemed a relief, at the time. Carissa remembered her wedding night vividly, shivering in her paper-thin nightdress. She had not known what to expect from her new husband and she knew little about Jacen, other than that he hadn't wanted the marriage either. She remembered lying back against the pillows and blinking away tears, praying that if Jacen forced himself on her, he would just *do it*.

I can't. Those had been his first words to her, the only words he spoke that night. When she'd looked at him, his hazel eyes had been wide in horror. They both knew their duty, but neither of them could commit to it. Jacen had lain beside her on the bed and never once touched her that night, or in the following scant week before he'd departed Marinel. The matter was never mentioned again, so Carissa suspected Jacen had lied to his family about what happened.

Deacon couldn't know that Carissa's marriage was a sham. It could easily be dissolved without the consummation. Carissa doubted Deacon would show her the same mercy Jacen had. The idea made revulsion crawl up her spine. She may not know Jacen, yet she suspected knowing Deacon was worse.

Deacon often excluded Miriam from proceedings, which frustrated Carissa but was unfortunately valid. As the Queen's advisor, Miriam was not required to be present in all council meetings, particularly now that Carissa approached the age of majority. Something else Deacon feared, no doubt—once Carissa turned eighteen, he would have to step down. He would find other ways to control her. Everyone in Basium knew the Generan royal family truly ruled their realm.

"I have not yet confirmed with the noble families who'll be in attendance. Your advisor won't be required."

Carissa gave a stiff nod. She was not a girl with a temper—sometimes she wondered how much worse she would fare if she was—but Deacon always had a way of rousing her ire. She wished she could speak to him the way she truly wanted to, but with actions came consequences. So, Carissa continued to play the role of the easily manipulated puppet. Miriam had warned Carissa if the Morrow family even suspected resistance from her, she would pay dearly for it.

She strode from the gardens, aware of Deacon's eyes on her. Once, she'd imagined what her life might be like if they'd never taken over, if her grandfather Patrick still ruled, if her parents and brothers still lived. She hadn't been able to picture it. She'd crushed any such fantasies. No point in making herself miserable dwelling on what might have been. She had long since accepted her fate. Carissa couldn't change her past—only her future.

Carissa considered herself lucky to have two best friends, even if one of them was the enemy's daughter. When Carissa returned to her chambers to redress, Vida Morrow already stood there waiting for her. Despite Carissa's initial misgivings, Vida had proven to be harmless—she had all of her uncle Deacon's charisma yet none of his spite. Her interests befitted her station as a noblewoman: trying on pretty dresses, gossiping about handsome courtiers, and admiring jewellery.

Carissa's other best friend could not be more different. Bellona Lenore also waited with Vida, pacing restlessly. The only child of the Lord of Theron, Bellona was more inclined to swinging swords and nocking arrows. Although such behaviour was highly frowned upon considering her station and gender,

Kato Lenore could never deny his daughter anything. The way he doted on Bellona made Carissa's heart ache, wishing there was a place in her life for paternal affection.

The room Carissa called her own had once belonged to her grandparents. Many nights as she lay awake in the four-poster bed, she would trace her fingers over the peeling cream wallpaper, the golden swans that adorned it fading more each year after the summer sun. During pleasant weather, she would bring a book—typically a historical volume—and a mug of chamomile tea to sit on the balcony.

"Uncle Deacon's called a council meeting, hasn't he?" Vida rolled her eyes. She shared the same golden hair as many of the other members of the Morrow family. She had a small, pointed nose and big, doe-like hazel eyes. Taller than both Carissa and Bellona, she had little in the way of curves. Whereas Jacen had a chiselled jawline and sharp, striking features, his sister was delicate and poised.

The casualness with which she spoke of Deacon was never shared by the other girls. To Vida he might be her endearing uncle, but to Carissa he would always be the manipulative monster who'd participated in the slaughter of her family.

"Do you know what it's about?" Bellona's tone was more cautious. Small and freckled with a shock of ginger hair, she was not the sort of girl one would've picked for an aspiring archer. She had bright, pale green eyes and moved with a feline grace, calculating and assured.

She had also experienced loss during the Conquest—and could often turn her bitterness onto Vida due to the blonde girl's sheer naivety. One day, she would go on to become Lady of Theron, and as such her short temper had been curbed many times over the years.

"I have no idea," Carissa admitted, walking into her chambers and heaving a frustrated sigh at the prospect of choosing a more glamorous dress for the meeting. Fortunately, Vida swept over and rifled through her things, saving her the trouble. Very few things excited Carissa about being Queen, but having her best friends as her ladies in waiting was certainly one of them.

"Have you heard word from your father?" Bellona asked, directing her attention to Vida.

Although the three girls were all close, Bellona and Carissa had certain restraints and reservations when discussing the Morrow family. Vida was clearly devoted to her relatives. Whether she thought the Conquest was justified or turned a blind eye, she'd never spoken against it. Bellona and Carissa could speak more freely when it was just the pair of them. Vida's presence restricted conversation that could have been considered mutinous.

"Not yet, but I assume he's extremely busy with the Island Wars." Vida laid out a violet dress on the bed, smoothing it out. The dress was one of Carissa's favourites—it flattered the curves of her figure and the silk ran smooth beneath her fingertips "This would go wonderfully with your eyes, Carissa."

Carissa sighed and pried off her dirt-splattered smock. She understood having to don suitable dresses for various occasions was part of her role. Sometimes, she even enjoyed the chance to dress up. But today she wished she could have stayed in her smock in the gardens. Nonetheless, she remained still as Vida and Bellona helped her change into the violet dress.

"Have you been asked to attend the meeting?" Carissa glanced at Bellona. The noble lords and ladies customarily had a proxy—usually a family member—attend council meetings if they were unable. Kato did not like leaving Theron, nor did he enjoy leaving his only child in the capital alone. If Kato did not come, Bellona would sit in on the meetings instead.

"I was." Bellona finished the laces of the dress, stepping back. "Deacon doesn't seem to trust your grandmother."

Deacon suspected Miriam was less of a frail old woman than she let on. He was right—not that Carissa would admit to it. Miriam moved carefully, knowing that Deacon had the power to dispose of her should she step out of line. Carissa didn't know what she would do without her grandmother's counsel.

"It doesn't matter, I don't need her there." Carissa would relay everything she discovered to Miriam and seek her advice later on. She extended her arm to Bellona. "Come. We shouldn't keep them waiting, no doubt most of the others are already there."

The girls departed the sanctuary of Carissa's room for the wide halls beyond. Vida bid them a cheerful farewell as they headed down the corridor. Bellona glanced over her shoulder, before tightening her arm in Carissa's. Bellona's restlessness caused Carissa to raise her eyebrows.

"Are you alright?"

Bellona heaved a sigh. "I wish we knew if we could trust her."

Carissa threaded her fingers through Bellona's. The only comfort she held in being a prisoner in her own palace was that there were others like her, that she did not suffer alone. She did not wish the pain and trauma of the Conquest upon anyone, but it helped having people who understood. Bellona was one of those people—she had lost her mother during the Conquest. Carissa bestowed her trust upon only a handful of people. Vida was not yet one of them.

"We can trust no one but each other."

The council meeting consisted of all representatives from the core five noble houses rather than the lords and ladies themselves. Carissa could not help but find this amusing. The insinuation that Deacon was not worth the time of the reigning lords and ladies of Basium was a small but allowable defiance.

Many of the heads of the five prestigious noble families simply did not have time to reside at Marinel and attend court whenever they wished. Carissa didn't think she had seen Lord Cyprian Ambrose of Emlen at all since the Conquest. Bellona lounged in her seat, playing with the end of her braid. The other house representatives appeared just as uninterested.

Carissa sat at the head of the table, hands clasped in front of her. She remembered running into this room as a child, interrupting her grandfather's meetings because of a squabble she had with one of her brothers. Patrick always had the patience to calm her before continuing on, and the nobles had accepted this. She'd never imagined sitting in the same mahogany chair that her grandfather once did, looking around the brightly lit room at people who were both her subjects and her most valuable resources.

She inhaled the comforting scent of old parchment and worn leather, mixed with the tang of the sandalwood candles that burned bright across the table. As a child, this had been a forbidden and magical place. The rectangular table that stretched across the middle of the room provided for fantastic hiding places. She had often pilfered books from the shelves embedded in the walls, reading them into the early hours of the morning by waning candlelight.

The door creaked open and Deacon strode in. Around the table, the postures of the representatives had gone tense—their shoulders tight, backs stiff and upright. None of them had ever been at ease around Deacon.

"I've called this meeting because I've just received news from Genera." Deacon sat directly beside Carissa, as befitted his position as regent. "The Island

Wars are over. Philemon and Severino have signed peace treaties. Cobryn has returned to our capital of Nicodemus. Jacen is heading to Marinel as we speak."

"Jacen?" Carissa repeated as she processed what Deacon had just said, her stomach plummeting. Eventually her husband was bound to return to Basium. Although almost four years was no short time span, she found herself at a loss of how to react. She and her husband had barely spoken, barely spent any time together before he'd left. How was she supposed to interact with a man who was a stranger to her?

"Yes, Your Majesty." There was no mirth in Deacon's eyes, just hardness. Carissa knew why—his nephew returning meant that he would no longer hold the same power. "He should reach the capital in a matter of days."

Carissa's heart rate accelerated rapidly, and she exchanged a look with Bellona, who had ceased examining the tangled ends of her hair. Her friend appeared just as stunned by the news. It also brought forward the issue Carissa had avoided since her wedding night—the consummation of their marriage.

Jacen had likely fought in the Island Wars with his father. What sort of man would her husband return as? Would he be as terrible as Cobryn and Deacon, or would he have some of Vida's softness? Would he still be the same person who'd shown her compassion that night?

"This…is good news," she murmured. The chair dug into her spine, the wood hard and unforgiving against her back, holding her ramrod straight.

"It is indeed." Claudio Tamarice, younger brother to the Lord of Isadore, spoke. "We do require a royal heir, and that's usually easiest when the King and Queen are in one location."

Carissa's cheeks flared with heat. Although there could be doubt that Claudio was right—without any immediate family members, Carissa did not have a direct heir—it was forward of him to say such a thing. Bellona leaned forward in her seat, eyes narrowed.

"I don't believe that's any of your concern, Sir Claudio."

"Forgive me, Majesty." Claudio raked a hand through his unkempt hair, blinking rapidly at Bellona's sharp words. "It was not my place. Certainly, though, it should be good to have the King return to Basium."

The tension in the room was palpable. Claudio's implications were clear—they would prefer Jacen back at their Queen's side rather than Deacon pulling the strings. None of them wanted a Morrow on the throne in any regard, but they had little say in it. At least with Jacen in Basium, Carissa might have a firmer hand in how her own realm was ruled.

They played a game of chance. She could only hope her husband would return a better man than his father and uncle. She didn't think she could stomach him being any worse. War could make and break people. Carissa could only pray that the Island Wars had shaped Jacen into someone she could tolerate.

THE UNWANTED KING
JACEN MORROW

Three and a half years ago, Marinel had been up in flames. Dismounting his horse, Jacen cast a critical eye over the capital city. It seemed to have recovered from the Conquest. Jacen didn't know the city well enough to be able to tell what had changed—he'd been in Marinel barely a few weeks before the Island Wars had commenced.

Nonetheless, Jacen observed what was certainly a formidable capital city. Marinel's towers stretched higher than any city he had visited. The houses were built similarly, storey upon storey stacked on top of one another. From the castle parapet, Jacen remembered glimpsing the ocean, glittering like oil under the full moon. On the city's other side, beyond the walls, the woods loomed in the distance blanketed by a thick cloud of mist.

A small crowd assembled out in the castle's front courtyard, at the foot of the palace steps. Some of the faces Jacen knew well—his uncle, Deacon, his sister, Vida. Others were not as familiar to him, yet as Basium's King, he would be expected to learn. Raking his dishevelled, dark blonde hair from his eyes, he examined the lesser known members of the crowd.

The old woman with greying brown hair and a terse frown was the former Queen, Miriam Darnell. She looked as though she had aged ten years instead of almost four, although Jacen supposed he couldn't blame her—she'd lost a lot during the Conquest. Nonetheless she held herself with a regal bearing that indicated she had not forgotten her former status, nor would she.

Jacen's stomach twisted as he examined the young woman beside her. The golden crown with a swan at its front and her extravagant cream and gold dress gave her identity away immediately. Queen Carissa Darnell—his wife.

Swallowing hard, Jacen approached her. She'd been a young girl when they'd wed, but now her body flared out into subtle hourglass curves, and her heart-shaped face was slimmer. Her raven-black hair almost reached her waist. Far paler than his sun-kissed skin, Carissa's skin held a creamy complexion. Clearing his throat, Jacen took her hand and kissed the back of it.

"Lady wife."

Cool violet-blue eyes examined him imperiously. "Jacen."

He hoped the rest of the assembly couldn't sense the tension between them, but he suspected they could. Carissa was no longer the young girl she had been on their wedding day. Perhaps as his years in the Island Wars had changed him, her years as Basium's Queen had changed her too. She drew her hand from his, letting it fall to her side.

"Nephew." Deacon stepped forward to embrace him, grinning widely. Jacen clapped his uncle on the back. The years had treated him kindly—casual and confident as opposed to Carissa's rigidness. Knowing Deacon, he had a heavy hand in Basiumite politics.

"Good to see you, Uncle Deacon."

"Jacen!" Vida threw her arms enthusiastically around his neck, and he refrained from picking her up and spinning her as he might have in their childhood. Over her shoulder, he could see the disapproving looks of Miriam and Carissa. If it were up to them, he wouldn't be here at all.

Jacen Morrow, the King Basium didn't want.

Releasing his sister, Jacen offered his wife his arm. Carissa pressed her lips into a thin line but took it. Casting a glance over his shoulder at the others, Jacen adopted an easy-going smile he certainly didn't feel.

"I hope you don't mind if I borrow my wife for a few minutes."

Miriam looked as though she might object, but it was Carissa who spoke up first.

"I must show you what I've done with the gardens in your absence. They're positively thriving."

Tightening her arm through Jacen's, she led the way up the stairs and through the winding corridors into the gardens in the centre of the castle. Jacen remembered vividly what had happened in these gardens years before. He doubted that Carissa brought him here out of spite. She hadn't been lying when she said there had been work done in the gardens—for a place that had seen violence and death, there was loveliness.

Jacen took a good look at his wife. She had become a beautiful young woman, yet there was an indifference to her. Carissa had little interest in getting to know him, or she was wary of doing so. She withdrew her arm from his and leaned down to admire some of the flowers before glancing sharply at him.

"So, you have returned. Permanently?"

He nodded. "That is my intention."

"You haven't told anyone that…" Carissa's cheeks flared with colour and she turned her attention back on the flowers, unable to meet his eyes.

He knew precisely what she meant and heaved a sigh. "No. Of course not. You know that would render our marriage invalid."

"Isn't that what you want?" she asked. Confusion coloured her tone, the expected accusation missing. Neither of them had been particularly enthused about the match. Declaring a lack of consummation would enable the marriage to be annulled. He'd considered it, yet Jacen suspected doing so wouldn't go well for either of them. If he admitted the truth now, his father would be livid.

Cobryn had, of course, pushed his son to consummate the marriage. When Jacen had seen how fragile and miserable his young bride was, revulsion washed over him at the thought of raping her. While Cobryn may have no qualms about the idea, Jacen liked to believe he had *some* morals. He hadn't touched Carissa, not that night or any other night in the brief week he'd been in Marinel. Everything about it was wrong.

"I thought that was what *you* wanted."

Although he'd initially assumed Carissa may attempt to get out of the marriage by revealing the lack of consummation, Jacen knew his father well enough to know that for the Queen of Basium, there was no escape. Cobryn would force them to consummate it in front of witnesses if that was what it took to have his son legitimately on the country's throne. It was common practice in Genera. The thought brought a sour taste to Jacen's mouth.

"Believe it or not, no." Carissa rubbed her arms, her formerly imperious stance fading into vulnerability. "Our marriage being considered legitimate protects me."

Jacen frowned. "From what?"

"Men that would take advantage of a young, unmarried Queen needing a husband to control her."

23

Her fierce eyes contradicted her soft tone. When Jacen had left, he'd seen her as a girl dominated by his father's will and persuaded by her grandmother's counsel. While Carissa may have little real power under Deacon's close supervision, she was no longer lost and reliant on others for guidance. Some still saw her as a little lamb and circled like wolves.

"Which men?"

"Men who would see me carrying an heir before a year has passed." Carissa shivered, but did not mention any names. Before Jacen could pry any further, she changed the subject. "I hear that Severino and Philemon are back under your father's control."

"Indeed." Jacen had not thought she wanted to hear of it. Certainly it would remind her of what she'd lost. "The insurrection was crushed, and its leaders replaced with new houses, ones loyal to my father. The old ones wished to secede and rule in their own right, but Cobryn would have none of it. It took almost four years, but as usual, he got his way."

Bitterness flooded Jacen's voice. Cobryn was a bully. He couldn't remember a time when his father hadn't gotten what he wanted. Although he respected Cobryn's achievements, their relationship was complicated. He disagreed with many of his father's methods, not that he would admit such a conflict to Carissa. Let her see the doggedly loyal son she wanted to believe him to be.

"I suppose you were quite involved in the fighting."

"I was. Father wanted me to get a feel for it all."

Cobryn had been adamant that Jacen take up a position of command. It had been difficult at times. He had not wanted to execute the old lords, but they had been unwilling to cooperate. Cobryn had needed to send a message: look what happens if you disobey. Jacen had been the messenger.

"I can imagine he did." The tightness in Carissa's voice indicated precisely what she thought of Cobryn. Jacen couldn't blame her—his father had orchestrated the deaths of almost her entire family. Yet what would that hatred gain her, when Cobryn and Deacon controlled everything?

"Come." Jacen offered his arm again. "If we linger too long, your grandmother will likely suspect the worst."

Jacen was surprised—and suspicious—that Deacon insisted his first dinner in Marinel become a family affair. Apparently, family did not extend to Carissa. Jacen found himself picking at his food, disappointed with only Deacon and Vida for company. Vida's bubbly demeanour never diminished despite the arrangement. Deacon watched Jacen like a hawk.

Jacen knew precisely the type of man his uncle was and had been for years. While Cobryn liked physical displays of power, brute force and open threats, Deacon was subtle. He enjoyed mind games and gilded lies. The fact that Jacen had returned to Basium as its rightful King probably displeased him—he had successfully maintained control of the realm for the past four years in his nephew's absence.

The dining hall stretched larger than the one in Nicodemus, more open and inviting with a large window on one side and a roaring hearth on the other. The dining table allowed for ample space, the cedar wood smooth to the touch. Above the hearth's mantelpiece sat the cream-and-gold swan sigil of House Darnell, mildly surprising Jacen. He assumed Cobryn or Deacon would have taken it down.

The food was delicious. After being on the roads for weeks from Genera's capital city of Nicodemus, Jacen had mostly partaken in overcooked rabbit and many hastily prepared salad dishes. He had eaten with no complaint—during the Island Wars, he had often seen days without any food at all—but he had missed marinated lamb and spiced pork, the richness of a cream sauce and the heat of mulled wine. Tonight's meal consisted of herbed potatoes and a honeyed chicken that melted on Jacen's tongue.

"You and Carissa seem to be friends, Vida." Jacen turned his gaze upon his sister. It hadn't escaped his notice that the two young women were at least on amicable terms. It pleased Jacen, both that his wife had a friend her own age, and that Vida didn't feel too displaced in Basium. She could have returned to Genera if she had wanted, yet she had made the choice to remain here.

"The Queen and I have become close." Vida took a sip of her white wine, a playfulness winking in her hazel eyes. "I would suggest you do the same, brother."

"Indeed, you should." Deacon finished cutting his meat, setting his knife and fork down. "Your wife was a little young before, but she's a ripe age now for childbearing. Basium needs an heir, as I'm sure both of you are aware."

Jacen restrained the urge to groan. He had this conversation before with Cobryn. His father had even written back to Deacon to determine whether Carissa might be with child from the mere days she and her husband had been in the same city. It had been a challenge not to laugh at the time, knowing his wife was just as pure as she had been before their marriage. When the Island Wars ended, Cobryn had again pressed the importance of an heir upon Jacen. Now he seemed to have to endure the same commentary from his uncle.

"Is that really the most pressing concern?"

"It should be one of them." Deacon arched his eyebrows. "Considering the Queen has no direct heir, having a child—preferably a son—is paramount. Perhaps such conversation irks you, but it needs to be had."

Jacen glanced at Vida, who rolled her eyes. She didn't object though, most likely knowing her interjection would simply lead to a conversation about why she should be getting married in the near future. As Cobryn's eldest daughter, it would become just as important for Vida to marry to secure an alliance as it had been for Jacen to become Basium's King.

"I'd prefer to hear about what you've been doing to help in my absence, Uncle Deacon." Jacen's tone was cool enough to indicate that he could turn the tables just as quickly. If they wanted to discuss progress then Deacon surely must have something to offer as well.

Vida unsuccessfully attempted to hide a smile behind her hand as she glanced between her brother and her uncle, amused at Deacon's surprised expression.

"Whatever do you mean?"

"Well, as you have been regent while I've been away, I'm certain you've been making beneficial decisions on my behalf."

"The noble families have come to terms with the situation." Deacon reached for his goblet of wine, taking a sip before continuing. As a powerful Primordial, he would have little trouble in maintaining an uneasy peace. "We have kept many of the realm's traditions the same, such as the noble families attending council meetings in regards to important decisions. Their religion remains the same as well."

"I'd see no reason why it wouldn't." Jacen leaned back in his chair. "We might be their rulers, but we can't strip down all their beliefs and force our own on them. I've heard they believe in the goddess Elethea. They should be entitled to pray to whoever they like."

Cobryn certainly liked to assert his authority everywhere, but if he wanted Jacen to be an effective King of Basium, he couldn't make it a second

Genera. They had already taken much from these people, and the last thing they needed was a rebellion on their hands. The Basiumite public had been quiet over the last few years.

Deacon's expression was terse before he turned his attention back to his meal. Jacen exchanged another look with Vida. Only three years apart and the only children of Cobryn's to share a mother, they'd been incredibly close. Vida had been quite the tomboy when she had been younger, but it seemed she had learned courtly manners in Jacen's absence. Her mischievous nature was the same as ever, yet Jacen questioned how much his sister had changed under Deacon's influence.

"What political decisions have you made, to benefit the people?" Jacen demanded. Cobryn had always raved about what a spectacular job Deacon did governing Basium, but Jacen only saw a realm that resented Deacon's presence.

His uncle's smile was wolfish. "Maleficium are no longer outlawed."

Maleficium. It had been some time since Jacen had heard the word, but he recognised it. Generans used the term Primordial for any person with magical abilities, but Maleficium was the Basiumite term for dark mages. Dark magic had been banned under King Patrick. His brow furrowed as he attempted to discern what benefit this could have been to Basium.

"Dark magic is good for the people?"

"*Balance* is good for the people," Deacon corrected him, pointing his fork in his nephew's direction. "Patrick was a doddering old fool who thought light magic was benign and dark magic was evil. We have introduced several Imperium and Maleficium within the court since Carissa became Queen."

Jacen remembered that many Imperium had fled Marinel after the Conquest, terrified their abilities would be seen as a threat. Those who had pledged loyalty to the Morrow family had been permitted to stay, and it would appear the promise of being able to legally use magic had drawn some Maleficium from the woodwork as well.

Fear was a powerful tool, one Deacon had wielded effectively throughout his time as steward. Jacen had to admit that his uncle had been clever in legalising dark magic—although he wondered what the council had to say about that matter.

"What did the Queen have to say about that?"

"She agreed to it." Deacon shrugged his shoulders. "With a little persuasion. She can be sensible when she wants to be."

It irked Jacen that his uncle knew Carissa better than he did. It was unavoidable, considering the years they had spent apart. He hoped he would get the chance to know her just as well, if not better. Deacon knew Carissa's strengths and weaknesses, whereas Jacen knew…very little. Knowing that she had said yes to legalising dark magic made him believe she must be fairly forward-thinking.

It suddenly struck Jacen that this would be the first night he and his wife would be sharing a bed since his departure. An odd idea, particularly considering they hadn't consummated the marriage. They would need to do so soon, but he wouldn't pressure her, not when they'd both agreed to keep it a secret for the time being.

That didn't mean they had all the time in the world. Some time spent with his wife, getting to know her or at least making sure she relaxed around him, could prove useful. The nervousness that came over him, making his palms clammy and his knees unsteady, was unexpected and unwelcome. How could one girl make him feel like he had no idea what he was doing?

"If you'll excuse me." Jacen got to his feet, the chair scraping noisily as he stood. "It's been a long journey back to Marinel, and I intend to get some rest."

"Very well." The hint of a smile played about Deacon's lips. "Goodnight, Nephew."

Jacen needed directions from a servant to find his way to the royal bedchamber. He awkwardly rapped his knuckles against the oak before entering, a stranger to his own room. He remembered the wallpaper vividly—fading gold swans on a cream background. The rest of the colouring in the room matched, including Carissa herself, sitting cross-legged on the bed in a cream nightdress.

It must have been difficult for Carissa the first time they had shared this room. The room that had once belonged to her grandparents, the room where she hadn't known if her husband would force himself on her. He couldn't even imagine the sort of terror she had felt on their wedding night.

Carissa slipped off the bed with resolution etched across her face at her husband's appearance. She appeared at ease in this room now. Sharing the bed again was likely a discomfort for both of them, yet she handled the company well. Tossing her black hair over her shoulder, Carissa's fingers reached up for the laces of her nightdress.

"Would you prefer the candles lit, or did you want to do this in the dark?"

Jacen understood her intentions and masked his astonishment. He had expected Carissa to protest the idea of consummation, not offer herself on their first night back together. Cool determination filtered through her eyes. The lack of any sort of desire told Jacen she saw this as a duty, not something she wanted to do. As Queen, Carissa had likely learned many duties over the years, including that she would eventually have to give herself to her husband upon his return.

In absence of Jacen's answer, Carissa heaved a sigh and eased herself back against the pillows. Forcing himself into motion, Jacen crossed over and tugged off his boots, his movements mechanical. She wouldn't be the first woman he had, yet that didn't dispel any of the awkwardness as he crawled on top of her.

He took a few moments to study his wife, the way the waning candlelight threw shadows across her face, the curves of her body barely concealed in her thin nightdress. She was beautiful. Warm desire stirred in the pit of his stomach. So why was this so hard?

Carissa craned her neck up and kissed him, winding her fingers through his hair. The clumsy, uncertain motion gave indication of her inexperience in this. Jacen kissed back, letting himself ease into her.

Carissa's slender fingers drifted from his hair down his back. He let her hands explore as he deepened the kiss, pressing closer to her. The feeling of her fingers traversing his arms caused his actions to become more heated, lips trailing down her neck. Carissa let her head fall back, dark hair spreading like oil across the golden and cream pillows.

Emboldened by her reciprocation, Jacen raised one hand to touch her breast through the fabric of her nightdress. Carissa gasped sharply and then relaxed as Jacen fondled her, marvelling at the fullness of her breasts. The way she bit down on her lip and arched her head back stirred something inside of him. His hands roamed her curves with more urgency than before.

When Carissa opened her eyes, he still saw the same determination there as before. The complete lack of passion or heat made Jacen draw back. Carissa would permit this, but it didn't mean she'd like it. Although he understood the crucial need for them to have sex, he couldn't bring himself to do it. She frowned as he took his hands off her, sucking in a deep breath to calm himself.

"No."

"No?" Carissa repeated, eyes narrowing. "What's the problem?"

Jacen shook his head fervently. "I don't want this."

She glanced pointedly at the bulge in his pants. "It certainly seems like you do."

Jacen didn't know how to explain it to her. He knew his stepmother Lilith had married Cobryn under circumstances similar to how he'd ended up marrying Carissa. He was under no delusion that his father forced himself on Lilith had she not proved willing.

I'm not my father. I'm not Cobryn.

"I won't do it when I know you can barely stand the thought of it."

Carissa flinched, but he was right. It seemed her willingness to make sacrifices meant offering herself, body and soul, to the enemy. Jacen's family had already stripped Carissa of enough. He wouldn't strip her of any pride she might have left. Carissa clenched her jaw and rolled onto her side, her back to him.

Jacen blew out the candles and flopped beside his wife, wondering if all marriages were so difficult. He remembered the rare occasions when his father had smiled. It had been when his mother Annaliese had been alive. After she died, such affection was rare and came with conditions. The Warmonger doted on his children from time to time, but they all had their purposes. Nothing came from Cobryn without an ulterior motive, an agenda.

Carissa's breathing evened out, indicating she'd fallen asleep. Every now and then, she would toss over restlessly, murmuring under her breath. Did she still dream of the Conquest, of the fires that had burned throughout Marinel that fateful night? He did. He often woke in a cold sweat, having found the mangled pieces and disfigured head of the youngest prince, Sebastian. They'd found the ring and several parts of him, but parts of the boy would always be buried under those rocks they'd brought down on him.

Jacen couldn't wait forever for Carissa to truly want the consummation. Deacon would sense something amiss, particularly when they stayed so stiff and formal around each other in public. If Jacen could give her a short breathing space, a chance to adjust to his presence…well, he hoped that it would be enough.

THE SECRETIVE QUEEN
CARISSA DARNELL

"Concentrate."

Carissa hated that word. No matter how much she focused, Miriam always said it. Concentrate. Ever since Carissa had discovered she was a Maleficium four years prior, Carissa submitted to her grandmother's guidance. Miriam was one of the most powerful Imperium in Basium, although her abilities were strictly defensive—hence why Cobryn hadn't felt the need to kill her.

Years passed, yet still Carissa's power lingered beneath her skin, her calling undiscovered. Miriam said it could take a while for mages to hone their craft and figure out which area they were most proficient in, but it didn't stop Carissa from being annoyed. Her magic seemed to strengthen and weaken, although she could not begin to understand why. Knowing she possessed powerful dark magic but not being able to control it irritated her to no end.

When they had first begun practising, Miriam had pressed the importance of secrecy. If the Morrow family discovered Carissa had abilities of her own, it would change everything. Besides, having a secret weapon to use against their oppressors could only help in the future. One day, Carissa would ruin them the way they'd ruined her family. She would take back Basium and rule of her own accord, not as someone's puppet.

She had often questioned how Miriam knew so much about dark magic for an Imperium, but her grandmother was long ago closed off to that line of interrogation. Today, Carissa read the bones, an ancient dark art that had been one of many forbidden under her grandfather's rule. Since the legalisation of dark magic, few practises were outlawed. Miriam had taken some time to get used to the idea, though even she admitted there were benefits to such magic.

Carissa's fingers traced over the bones, her eyes firmly closed. She found herself distracted, her mind on Jacen's abrupt return rather than focusing on what the bones told her. Unable to discern anything, Carissa opened her eyes, scowling.

"I can't focus."

The room smelled of lavender and sandalwood, two of her favourite scents. Even the calming aroma couldn't coax Carissa into relaxing enough to call her magic forth.

Miriam sat beside her granddaughter. "Have you consummated the marriage yet?"

Carissa bit her lip and shook her head, twining her fingers together to disguise her anxiety. Her grandmother had been the only one she had entrusted with the knowledge she and Jacen hadn't had sex. Mostly because Miriam believed was a monster who'd raped her granddaughter until Carissa assured her that wasn't the case.

"You must." Miriam caught Carissa's hands in her own, stopping her fidgeting. "As soon as possible."

Carissa frowned. This came from the woman who had constantly cautioned patience, yet she understood Miriam's concerns, for Carissa shared them. Jacen had little idea, but the longer he stayed in Basium the sooner he would realise he was not the only Morrow man to feel he had a claim to Carissa.

"If this is about Deacon…"

"You know what would happen if he learned the truth." Miriam turned away. With the candles burning all around the room, she walked over to the balcony, smoke obscuring her figure.

Carissa busied herself putting the bones back into the cloth bag. Deacon had made insinuations for some time that he should have wed Carissa, that he should be Basium's King. If he knew Jacen and Carissa hadn't consummated the marriage, he would want her for himself and he wouldn't show the same restraint his nephew had. The thought made her nauseous as she slipped the bag of bones back into the drawer.

"I'd die before I'd let that happen," Carissa declared passionately, following her grandmother through the smoke and leaning against the stone wall of the balcony.

From any balcony in the castle, she could look over most of the city below.

It had scared her at first, realising just how many people she ruled—not just in Marinel, but throughout the entirety of Basium. In her early days as Queen, she remembered watching her people from her balcony for long periods of time, studying how they interacted, a sense of claustrophobia taking hold of her. They roamed freely. The castle trapped Carissa.

"I am not letting you die." Miriam's voice was sharp as steel, drawing Carissa's gaze from the city. "I have already lost too much. I won't lose you too. I swear to you that Deacon will never touch you, but you need to set things into motion with Jacen."

"I tried." Carissa toyed with the end of her braid, remembering what had occurred in the darkness of her room. "The first night he was back. I attempted to initiate, but…"

Such frank discussion would have had her turning crimson once upon a time, yet that was another thing Miriam had taught her: a Queen's life was never secret. People wanted to know what she was doing, who she was with. When she became pregnant, they'd want to know all about the baby. Queens got very little privacy, even less so when they were constantly in the presence of Generan spies.

Miriam frowned. Deep lines etched across her brow, around her mouth. It was obvious to Carissa that her grandmother had been attractive in her youth— Miriam still had a certain elegance to her now. Being robbed of her family had aged her.

"But what?"

"He didn't want me." Carissa met her grandmother's eyes, overcome by a sense of guilt and frustrated confusion at Jacen's actions. "He doesn't want to consummate, not until I stop treating it like a duty. I don't understand him. I thought he would have been pleased to just get it done with."

"Perhaps your husband is a man with more morals than his father." Miriam spoke cautiously, as if uncertain if she would be proven wrong.

A humourless smile graced Carissa's lips. So far, Jacen had surprised her. He didn't seem to be much like Cobryn or Deacon, yet she didn't know him well enough to establish the sort of person he was. She could only pray to the goddess that he didn't turn out to be something worse than the monsters who already surrounded her, circling like vultures over a rotting carcass, waiting for the moment to strike.

Despite her husband's sudden return, Carissa was determined to keep to her routine as much as possible. Part of that routine was tending to the plants in her garden. If necessary, she would argue with Jacen until she turned blue in the face so he could understand its importance. Dressed in her plainest smock with her fingers buried in the soil gave Carissa a sense of tranquillity, and she wouldn't have anyone take that away from her.

Her garden times seemed cursed to be constantly interrupted. Deacon strode over to her and she stifled a scowl. Fighting back the urge to tell him she didn't want to be bothered, Carissa remained where she knelt amidst her plants, squinting into the sunlight at his approach.

"Deacon."

"I thought we might speak, Your Majesty." He offered a hand, which Carissa pointedly ignored as she rose from the dirt.

"Yes?" The edge beneath her polite tone hopefully indicated to Deacon she would rather be left alone.

"I just wondered how you were feeling about Jacen's return."

The question caught Carissa off guard, and she found herself uncertain how to respond to such a personal inquiry. Not once had she ever treated Deacon as a confidante over the years, so the question came as rather forward considering their interactions had been civil at best.

"I…I am glad to see my husband back in Basium."

"Are you?" Deacon arched an eyebrow. "He's a man you hardly know. You were only married a few days before he left. Yet you maintain that you're pleased by the return of a near stranger?"

"Forgive me, Deacon." Carissa's voice took on a steely note, fingers gripping her smock to stop her fidgeting. "But I hardly see how this is relevant."

"Of course it's relevant, my dear." Deacon stepped closer. Carissa tensed but didn't move away, despite desperately wanting to. "Your realm needs a united front, a King and Queen who can work together. I am just hoping that you and Jacen are capable of doing so."

"I believe we can," Carissa responded, realising just how much her hands shook at Deacon's close proximity. She craned her neck to look up at him. "You are right in saying I do not know my husband well, yet he seems to be a reasonable man."

"I wonder what may have happened, had things gone differently." Deacon's eyes raked over Carissa's form in a way that made her deeply uncomfortable. She remained still and silent, despite every fibre of her being wanting to turn and run. Her father had always told her that some predators found the chase to be thrilling, and she had no doubt the same could be said for Deacon.

"Differently how?"

"Well, if I had married you instead of my nephew." Deacon's voice remained light, but something dark and menacing shadowed his eyes, something that terrified Carissa. She had suspected of late that Deacon's intentions toward her were not quite appropriate but realising her husband's uncle desired her left a foul taste in her mouth.

"What would that have changed?" Carissa asked.

"A fair deal, I would imagine." Deacon reached out and traced a finger down her cheek, unperturbed by the way she flinched at his touch. "Jacen's absence has left almost four years of wasted potential that, had you been married to me, would have been a great deal more productive."

Carissa turned her face, but Deacon gripped her chin, forcing her to look at him. Her heart hammered frantically. Her stomach roiled, bile clawing at the back of her throat. The odd comment here and there previously had been bearable. His touch made her want to scrub her skin raw. Miriam claimed she had not foreseen anything, yet even she suspected that Deacon lusted after her granddaughter. At first, Carissa had thought it was only status he coveted—that he wished to be King of Basium. Her certainty wavered now.

"You have become a beautiful woman, Carissa," he said, his voice dangerously soft. "If you and I had married, I can only imagine how powerful we'd have become. We'd likely even have an heir by now."

A cold stone dropped in her stomach, but she stood her ground, attempting to ignore the fact that her body shook in trepidation. Whatever Deacon's fantasies, she wanted no part in them. She was not his wife. She never would be.

"Let me go."

"Is there something going on that I should be aware of?"

Deacon released Carissa at the sound of the familiar voice, taking a step back and glancing at his nephew as Jacen approached with a suspicious expression.

"Jacen. Carissa and I were merely—"

"I'd like to speak with my wife, alone." Jacen interrupted Deacon, completely shutting down whatever smooth excuse he'd been about to utter. The older man appeared startled at being cut off, but he pressed his lips together in a thin line and inclined his head. Carissa glanced at Jacen as Deacon departed the gardens. Her husband did not appear thrilled by the apparent intimacy of what he just witnessed.

"You and my uncle?"

"No!" Carissa exclaimed. Disgust riddled her at the thought, but terror quickly replaced it at the idea that Jacen might misinterpret what he walked into. "Never. I would *never* be his."

Jacen raked a hand through his hair, closing his eyes and taking a deep breath. Carissa wrung her hands, awaiting his verdict. Would Jacen verbally lash out at her, accuse her of being some sort of temptress? Would he not believe her story? Distress ran through her at the thought she may have lost the chance to gain ground with her husband when he'd barely been back a few days.

"When you mentioned men that would want to take control of you, men who'd want you to bear them an heir if you and I were not married..."

"Yes." Carissa knew what he tried to ask, and her response was little more than a whisper. She didn't want to be responsible for making Jacen choose between her and Deacon, but he deserved to know what sort of man his uncle was. Perhaps he already suspected.

"Has he ever laid hands on you?" Jacen demanded.

"Not until now." Carissa rubbed her arms, shivering for reasons that had nothing to do with the cold. "He was ruminating on what it may have been like should he and I have been married instead."

She did not mention the fact that she hoped her magic might one day match Deacon's. That would involve admitting that she was Maleficium, and Miriam had urged the importance of keeping her abilities secret for as long as possible. Carissa did not even know if she could trust Jacen yet.

"He needs to remember his place." Jacen's brow furrowed. "I am the King of Basium, not him. Thinking that things could have gone any differently is a dangerous game for him to play."

Carissa hoped Jacen understood now why she had been so quick to want to consummate their marriage. If there was any doubt as to whether it was legitimate, Deacon would take full advantage of the fact. Any chance to become

King and he would seize it, swiftly and without mercy. When his gaze returned to his wife, Jacen took in her dirt-splattered smock.

"When you said that you had work done with the gardens, I didn't realise you were the one doing it."

"I enjoy it." Carissa shrugged her shoulders, wondering if he would chastise her. Jacen seemed more curious than anything. "It gives me space and privacy."

He sighed. "I feel that I've intruded."

"Not at all." If he hadn't shown up, Carissa didn't know what would have happened. She doubted Deacon would have done anything too inappropriate, yet she couldn't know for sure. Power, and the idea of more power, seemed to do strange things to men.

Bellona paced Carissa's room like a caged animal, brows knitted close together as she processed everything the Queen had told her about Deacon. Carissa knew her friend had never liked the regent yet had refrained from commenting out of respect for Vida. Whatever the man was like, he had a good relationship with his niece. Without their friend present, Bellona could speak her mind freely.

"I wish that I could say I'm shocked, but I'm not." Bellona ceased her pacing and walked over to Carissa. The Queen sat on the bed in silence, trying to process everything that had happened—particularly the fact that it seemed Jacen had taken her side. The redhead knelt in front of her friend, taking Carissa's shaking hands in her own. "Are you alright?"

"I'll be fine." Carissa couldn't help but smile, as appreciative as ever of Bellona's fierce loyalty. In truth, Jacen's reaction to the situation had given her some hope. If he had defended Deacon's actions and attempted to frame Carissa as a temptress, they would have had problems. Deacon's intention had been to intimidate her. She could not let him see that it had worked.

"I am glad your husband defended you, at least." Bellona tossed her hair back. It had been obvious to Carissa that her friend did not approve of Jacen, and she could not say she blamed Bellona. After everything that had happened, Bellona had every right not to readily accept Jacen, especially as Carissa did not even fully trust him herself.

A knock on the door made both girls pause. Bellona glanced at Carissa, and the Queen cleared her throat.

"Enter."

The door swung open and a tall, ginger-bearded man strode into the room. Kato Lenore bowed deeply before his Queen before looking between her and his daughter. A relieved smile broke out across Bellona's face. She crossed the room and embraced her father tightly. Carissa had not been expecting the Lord of Theron in Marinel, yet as one of her biggest supporters and a trusted friend of Miriam's, Kato was always a welcome sight at court.

"Lord Lenore." Carissa eased herself to her feet, attempting to model effortless grace but knowing she merely looked exhausted. "It's a pleasure to see you, although I must admit I am surprised. I know you do not usually frequent the capital."

"I come bearing urgent news." Kato extricated himself from his daughter's arms, and Bellona dutifully returned to Carissa's side. "I rode with haste in the hope that you would hear it first from me, although I am not sure that's the case."

Carissa frowned, panic searing through her. "What news?"

Kato raked a hand through his thinning hair. "There is rebellion rising in Emlen."

Carissa's stomach twisted as Bellona shot her an alarmed look. Emlen—the Basiumite city where everything first began. She should have known that she could only maintain control over her country for so long, especially when most believed her to be little more than a pawn for her Generan in-laws. She pressed a hand over her mouth, lapsing deep into thought.

Almost five years ago, Cobryn Morrow had approached Patrick Darnell regarding Emlen. Renowned as the most effective and productive forge in Basium, and perhaps the continent, it lured in the Warmonger's greedy gaze. Knowing the talent of the blacksmiths there, Cobryn had attempted to strike a deal with Patrick—food and supplies from Genera in exchange for weapons from Basium. Knowing Cobryn's reputation, and the fact that he had already conquered the country of Harith, Patrick had refused.

Then came the Conquest—the fall of House Darnell, and the decimation of Carissa's entire family. All in retaliation for denying Cobryn something he wanted. Emlen should have been the first city Carissa expected to rise, yet in truth she had anticipated her position as Queen—a member of the Darnell family still alive and ruling—to have calmed such resistance. Apparently, she was wrong.

"What do you mean?" Carissa asked. She had a deep, uneasy feeling. If this resistance did not die down, Cobryn would snuff it out. The King of Genera was ruthless and would not enjoy his son's power in Basium being challenged.

"Lord Ambrose has made his dislike of the Morrow family particularly clear." Kato pressed his lips into a thin line. Although the nobility made subtle nods toward their hatred regarding the Conquest and the Generan occupation following, none had openly rebelled. Cyprian Ambrose doing so risked war, and the annihilation of Emlen, the city that Cobryn had once coveted.

"Is there anything that can be done?" Carissa didn't wish to consider the more unpleasant options, including the possibility of silencing Lord Ambrose should he continue to speak out.

This could get serious quickly, and she would have to act in the best interest of her people. Deep down, she wondered if Lord Ambrose's outspokenness and Emlen's potential for resistance could be the catalyst she needed to break free of her own chains.

"This must be kept quiet for as long as possible." Kato folded his arms. "It was the reason I came to you in haste. The other members of the council cannot know."

He doesn't trust them. Carissa couldn't blame him. The uneasy peace and being subject to Deacon's rule in all but name meant there could be no telling who he'd managed to get on his side, and who only feigned loyalty to protect their city. Carissa rubbed her temples, a headache building. She needed Miriam's guidance in this troubling matter. Being Queen of a nation under Cobryn's thumb presented ever-changing problems.

Carissa nodded. "Of course."

"There's more." Kato's expression became more solemn, and Carissa braced herself for another onslaught of bad news. Certainly, it could not be any worse than the potential uprising.

"Yes, Lord Lenore?"

"It's your husband's twenty-first birthday soon. The event will be cause for celebration." He paused, glancing at his daughter before meeting the Queen's questioning gaze. "It's Cobryn Morrow. He rides for Marinel."

Carissa's knees trembled and gave out beneath her. She sat down heavily on the end of her bed, fingers tightly gripping the wooden frame. Jacen returning to Basium, she could understand. Deacon's presence, she could tolerate. But the man who had authorised the murders of her entire family coming to the capital, while she faked a smile and polite greetings? She didn't know if she could stand it.

"How long?" Her voice escaped as little more than a whisper, filled with dread.

"He should be here in a matter of days," Kato said, his tone apologetic. He knew, as everyone did, just how much the Queen hated Cobryn. Unfortunately for them all, court politics called for civility. Carissa wondered how much longer she could wear the mask of the polite and gracious Queen, how far she could bend before she broke.

THE COWARD KING
JACEN MORROW

Cobryn arrived in Marinel on the coldest day of winter. The idea of his father coming to Basium didn't thrill Jacen, even for the logical reason of attending his son's birthday celebrations. That was not Cobryn's sole purpose. His father wanted to see the progress that had been made. He wanted to see an obedient and subservient Queen in Carissa.

Carissa stood resplendent in cream furs, arms folded over her chest as the royal carriage drew to a halt in the same courtyard in which she'd first greeted Jacen. There was a deep unhappiness in her eyes. Neither of them had spoken about Cobryn's arrival, but he had never expected his wife to show enthusiasm. Whatever Cobryn was to him, to Carissa he would only ever be the Warmonger.

Jacen sighed heavily, his breath misting out before him as Cobryn stepped out of the carriage. He was not alone—his wife Lilith and their daughter Ayesha, Jacen's half-sister, exited the carriage as well. As Cobryn made his way towards them, Carissa gripped Jacen's wrist tightly. He glanced at her, but her eyes weren't on him. Her focus stayed on Cobryn, her jaw set in contrast to the Warmonger's dazzling smile.

"All hail King Cobryn!"

Jacen did not know who sounded the cry but he hated them for it. Deacon shot a meaningful look at his nephew before sinking to one knee. The rest of the assembly reluctantly followed his lead. No matter if Cobryn was equal in rank to Jacen and Carissa, they would be expected to show their respect by bending the knee. Looking around, Jacen noted that even Miriam had unbent her pride enough to kneel before Cobryn.

Carissa's violet-blue eyes gleamed with anger. Jacen took advantage of her grip on his wrist to squeeze her hand hard. He glanced sharply at her as he knelt, keeping his eyes on her, hoping that his wife would follow his lead. *If you do not bend the knee, he will make you suffer for it.*

Carissa sank down onto one knee, keeping her fingers linked through her husband's. Jacen did not know if she wanted support or to maintain the illusion of a civil married couple, yet he felt utter relief at her decision to mimic him. She kept her head bowed. He knew there would be fury on her face, a rage she determinably masked. Carissa was good at keeping her emotions in check, from what he had seen. Seeing Cobryn would bring back traumatic memories—the violent deaths of her family, her rushed coronation, and the forced marriage.

"Rise." Cobryn sounded amused, and when Jacen rose to see his father right in front of him, he indeed grinned. He immediately released Carissa's hand as Cobryn drew him into a tight embrace. "My son. It's good to see you again, and in your rightful role as King of Basium no less."

Before Jacen could respond, Cobryn turned his attention upon Carissa. She had managed to regain her composure, lips upturned into a pleasant smile. She was no doubt practised at this by now. The King of Genera leaned in to plant a kiss on his daughter-in-law's cheek. Carissa remained motionless, but Jacen noted that her hands balled into fists.

"How you have grown, Carissa." Cobryn did not even do her the courtesy of addressing her by her title. "My son is indeed fortunate to have such a beautiful wife. My brother tells me you have been most adept at ruling since we saw you crowned."

"I am a Darnell." Carissa's voice was cool, her smile tightening. "I have had guidance from my grandmother. She has helped to shape me into a better ruler than I could have seen myself becoming."

"Miriam!" Cobryn exclaimed, walking over to Carissa's grandmother as if they were old friends. "You are looking well."

Jacen marvelled at just how strong these two women were. If he faced someone who had taken all that he held dear, he didn't think he could have behaved with such remarkable restraint. Miriam smiled and allowed Cobryn to plant a kiss on the back of her hand with a grace the Warmonger certainly didn't deserve. Cobryn's attention turned to Vida, who appeared delighted to have her father here.

"Jacen!" Ayesha bounded over, disregarding dignity and flinging herself into her brother's arms. His tension melted and he picked up his little sister and spun her around until she shrieked. Placing her back on her feet, he ruffled her dark ringlets affectionately.

"I've missed you so much."

"Mother says that you might have a baby soon, so I'd be an aunt." Ayesha's dark eyes widened hopefully. "Do you think you will?"

"Ayesha," Lilith chided, her eyes locking with Jacen's. He had never been especially close with his stepmother. A solemn, dark-skinned woman who did not care for feasts and social occasions, she chose to keep to herself where possible. Lilith had been married to Cobryn for a decade now, but Jacen hardly knew her at all. She haunted Cobryn's side like a ghost.

Carissa watched Jacen and Ayesha's interaction with curiosity, and Jacen wondered how much she knew about Cobryn's second wife, about the way Harith had fallen even harder than Basium. It was the first country Cobryn had conquered. The history books could only teach so much. Jacen had been a mere child at the time, yet old enough to remember a lot of it. Lilith had been a similar age to what Carissa was now, a trembling girl to whom the gods had dealt a harsh hand.

Jacen looked to his father. Cobryn spoke quietly with Deacon, something that made him uneasy. Deacon had always been good with words, and Cobryn heeded his counsel. Although he was still getting to know his wife, Jacen hoped Deacon wasn't filling his brother's head with false tales. Men who had been spurned were often the most dangerous of all, and Deacon was already deadly.

"Come." Cobryn's voice boomed out across the courtyard. "I am weary from my travels. Tonight, I will dine with my family."

Jacen cringed, unable to think of anything worse. He knew that he would be interrogated about his relationship with Carissa, and he had to be ready with a response. Cobryn was a blunt man—he would have no qualms in discussing his son's sex life, especially when it seemed everyone pushed for Jacen and Carissa to have a child as soon as possible. Jacen almost thought the Island Wars were easier than being a husband and King.

The banquet hall had once been reserved for the Darnell family, but the remaining members had been banished for the night. Jacen still adjusted to the castle, to the golden swans that seemed to stare down with reproachful eyes. In the centre of the banquet hall was a long cedar table with swans carved intricately into the wood. Tonight, a tablecloth had been thrown haphazardly over it, an easy way to disguise that this had once been Darnell territory.

It had been years since the Morrows had all sat down to dinner, and Jacen had to confess it was not something he missed. He couldn't say he had much of an appetite.

"How are you finding Basium so far?" Cobryn looked up from his meal and across at his son. He had constantly expected thanks from Jacen, as if being gifted a broken and bloody country complete with a traumatised young bride had been an honour.

"I have only been here a few short weeks." Jacen shrugged his shoulders, taking a sip of his white wine. "I am still adjusting to it."

"You do not seem overly close with your wife," Cobryn commented, leaning further forward. "A good relationship with Carissa is fundamental to your reign. We need her to maintain control over her people. Without her, they will rise up and bay for blood."

"Like your good relationship?" Jacen retorted, causing Lilith to avert her eyes and Vida to scowl. His father's eyes narrowed and Jacen wondered if he would strike him right here, in front of the whole family. Emboldened by his title, Jacen challenged his father with little concern for repercussions.

"It's imperative that you produce an heir."

"Deacon and I have already had this discussion." Jacen waved a dismissive hand. "I'm not having it again. I know what my duties are, Father. You were the one who placed me in this position. You need to trust me in it."

Not so long ago, Jacen would never have dreamed of speaking to Cobryn in such a manner. However, the Island Wars had hardened him. He had seen the destruction and greed that his father was capable of, and how far he would bring down those he thought had wronged him. Perhaps Carissa had to tread carefully, but Jacen did not.

"I believe Carissa is a Primordial."

Deacon's calm drawl made them all turn to look at him incredulously. It was quite the outrageous statement, considering that Jacen had seen no evidence to suggest such a thing. He placed his goblet down and leaned back. Was this an attempt by his uncle to paint Carissa as dangerous in retribution for her rejecting his advances? Jacen would not put it past him to behave in such a petty manner.

"What makes you say so?"

Deacon shrugged his shoulders. "I am a Primordial. I can sense things that others don't. I have felt magic within the girl. She is powerful, perhaps even more so than her grandmother."

Jacen frowned. Though likely a ruse by Deacon, a part of him had to wonder whether a grain of truth hid there. It had long been said that the women in the Darnell family had powerful magic coursing through their veins. If Carissa did have such magic, she most likely would not share that fact.

"I don't think so," Vida piped up, tossing her blonde hair back and revelling in the attention that turned her way. "I know Carissa best, better than any of you. If she did have such magic, I'd certainly know about it. In fact, she has often lamented about wishing she could possess the same light magic as Miriam."

Jacen hid a smirk as he sipped his wine again. His opinion would hold little value due to the fact he'd only been back in Basium for such a short amount of time, but Vida had been a close friend of Carissa's for several years now. If Carissa confided in anyone, it would be her.

Deacon shifted in his chair. "I have sensed—"

"Perhaps her magic is dormant." Vida cut her uncle off, voice firm and head tilted to the side as she examined Deacon. "It wouldn't be the first case of someone with magic in their blood that has simply never made an appearance. Besides, if the Queen had powerful magic as you say, she would definitely have used it by now."

"I must say, I agree with Vida," Cobryn stated. "There is no doubt in my mind that if Carissa had magic, she would have turned it on us. She is powerless, and she knows it well."

"I take it you've already heard about Emlen." Deacon leaned back in his seat, raising his eyebrows. Cobryn's jaw set tight in response. Jacen had also heard the news—the fortress city threatened dissent. For now, it was a rumour of resistance, but that could lead to trouble. If Emlen did not fall back in line—and quickly—they would suffer the consequences.

"They will desist in these futile attempts to rebel, or they will learn the lesson the hard way."

"What exactly are they doing?" Jacen asked. He'd heard talk about resistance, but he'd never been told what was happening in Emlen.

"There is talk of mass weapon production, for reasons Lord Ambrose will not clarify." Deacon's expression became smug as he looked to his nephew. "Surely as Basium's King, you should be aware of such matters."

Jacen glared but had no response. He *should* have knowledge of what happened throughout his country. Informants were so used to bringing their news to Deacon that they continued to do so—or Deacon had ensured it stayed that way. Nonetheless, Jacen could not be a passive ruler, not in Basium. When Cobryn died and he took the Generan throne, his position would be secure. Here and now, with their marriage not even legitimate, things were more tumultuous.

"You're right, Deacon. I am the King here, not you. You forget yourself."

A nerve twitched in his uncle's cheek, yet he refrained from replying, something Jacen considered quite an achievement considering Deacon loved having the final word. Deacon resented the fact that Jacen had been placed in this position instead of him. If Deacon believed he could lay some kind of claim on Carissa, he was sorely mistaken.

"Enough squabbling, both of you." Cobryn pushed his chair back from the table, straightening up. "I tire of it. I bid you all goodnight."

Jacen finished his wine as his father departed without another word. Lilith followed moments later, silent and solemn. When he glanced across the table at Vida, she fixed him with a stern look. Unused to such a look coming from his typically carefree sister, he sighed heavily.

"Yes?"

"You two need to sort things out." Vida turned her reproachful gaze upon Deacon as well. "There is no point in fighting when there are more pressing issues, like Emlen. If these people think they can tear us down from within, then they will."

Jacen got to his feet. In no mood to be reprimanded, he marched from the hall with a rising sense of frustration. Vida was right—they should not argue amongst themselves. Yet Deacon vying to retain control after Jacen's return would likely make things difficult.

THE HAUNTED QUEEN
CARISSA DARNELL

Miriam pressed for Carissa to practise her magic more now that Cobryn had arrived in Marinel. Carissa had to admit she found it vexing—she did not know her calling. She had telekinesis, but it grew stronger and weaker without any apparent reason. Her fickle abilities would do her no good if she could not use them against her enemies.

"I don't know why we continue this." Carissa set down the small knife she used to cut herbs. Creating potions had been something that fascinated her, yet she still struggled to learn the art. "I am not you, Grandmother. I am not strong."

"Yes, you are." Miriam crossed over and knelt in front of her granddaughter, taking up the knife. "In fact, I have been theorising on the nature of your magic. We know that you have no particular area of strength, and that your magic is capricious. Hold out your hand."

A dozen doubts crossed Carissa's mind as she did as her grandmother asked. Could Miriam have unlocked the secret to her magic, after almost four years of the unknown? Her hand trembled as Miriam turned the knife and sliced the blade across Carissa's palm. The Queen yelped in surprise, staring at the shallow cut that stung along the edges.

"Reach into your magic." Miriam dropped the knife, clasping hands with Carissa as blood dripped down from her granddaughter's palm. "Tell me what you feel."

What had previously proved a struggle immediately became easy. Carissa closed her eyes and concentrated, her magic flooding to her with the force of a raging river. It answered her call without any resistance whatsoever. When Carissa opened her eyes, she saw the herbs she cut levitating above their heads. It was her. She did this.

Revelling in her sudden power, Carissa pushed herself to her feet, withdrawing her hands from Miriam's. The feeling of her magic being so easily accessible, so responsive…it intoxicated her. The knife that Miriam had used to slice her palm spun in circles on the ground before lifting and hurtling into the wall. Carissa imagined that it was Cobryn's head when it embedded in there, and it brought her vicious satisfaction.

I could kill him. It would be done in the blink of an eye.

"Carissa!" The urgency in Miriam's tone grounded her. The herbs dropped neatly back into the stone mortar Carissa had mixed them in. The elated sensation drained away from her as she examined the knife embedded in the wall, her bloody palm. The fear in Miriam's brown eyes stung more than the cut. Carissa had been so caught up in the glory of power that she hadn't even questioned what brought it on. She stared down at her scarlet palm, then at Miriam.

"What am I?" she asked hoarsely. Deep down, she had the horrible feeling she already knew the answer.

Miriam rose to tuck a strand of Carissa's dark hair behind her ear. "You are a blood mage."

Carissa pressed her clean hand over her mouth. The darkest of all Maleficium, blood mages relied on spilling blood to call forth and enhance their magic. Although immensely powerful, their magic could be intoxicating.

The last well-known blood Maleficium had been Jameson Burnett, who had lived in her great-grandfather's time. The story had gone that Jameson had become so addicted to blood magic, to the high it gave him, that he used human sacrifice to call on his abilities. Jameson had become a madman, a monster. It had been his own daughter, just a girl at the time, who had been his destruction. An Imperium of great power, she'd led him into the trap that had claimed his life.

"I…I can't be." Carissa shook her head fervently. Although she knew her grandmother spoke the truth, how could Carissa accept something that had been strictly outlawed under her grandfather? How could she use her magic without feeling like she could succumb to it at any point in time?

"Your magic is strongest when you have your monthly bleeding, correct?" Miriam stroked her hair as Carissa nodded mutely, taken aback by the link to her power. "I sensed your dark magic the day you were crowned. You struggled to control it then. You have had your struggles since, but now at least you know the sort of power you are fighting to contain."

"Could I use it?" Carissa didn't know if she asked for permission, or guidance. Realising now the nature of her magic gave her hope that she could be formidable. Emlen's uprising, the knowledge she was a blood Maleficium...the pieces all began to come together. What would she have to become in order to defeat Cobryn and the Morrow family once and for all?

"That depends on you." Miriam drew back to tug the knife out of the wall, setting it down beside the mortar and pestle. "You are a woman now, Carissa. You have my support as always, but these are choices you must make yourself."

"I could become Jameson Burnett." Carissa choked the words out, cold terror washing over her, and Miriam winced.

"Perhaps." Miriam's voice was soft. "But you could also go on to prove that being a Maleficium does not make you cruel or vindictive. I can teach you restraint. I can teach you control. But you need to want it."

"I do." Carissa's voice filled with a strength she didn't feel. "More than anything."

They'd searched for a way to destroy Cobryn and his family for years, and this was the first big step. Carissa would have to take them all down—but the more she got to know Jacen, the more she realised he did not take after his father or uncle. Neither did Vida, and Lilith and Ayesha were innocent in all of it.

How much damage would she have to do? How much havoc would she have to wreak to ensure no one ever rose against her and her family again? She shied away from an inevitable truth—no matter what, the Basiumite people would never accept a Generan King.

Winter trailed to its end when the celebrations for Jacen's twenty-first birthday commenced. Vida had pushed for a masquerade ball, and of course none of the men in the Morrow family could deny her anything. Whilst Vida oversaw the preparation, Carissa asked Bellona to assist her in getting ready. Both girls had decided to go as their house's sigils—a fox for Bellona and a swan for Carissa.

In Carissa's case, it was a risky move. The act could easily be interpreted as one of defiance. The swan reminded them that no matter who she had married, she would always be a Darnell. Her heart hammered in her chest as Bellona tied the swan mask tightly at the back of her head. While Carissa had donned a beautiful cream dress for the occasion, with layers of tulle and intricate beading, Bellona's green gown was simple in comparison, pure silk with no ornament. When the Queen spun to face her, Bellona grinned.

"You look radiant, your Majesty."

Perhaps Jacen will think so. The thought felt treacherous, as though she betrayed her dead family by hoping her husband would consummate their marriage tonight. The weeks had dragged into over a month now. Carissa had hoped Deacon's forwardness would help Jacen realise the urgency of the matter, but it had made little difference. Maybe she surrendered, in some form. Carissa knew it had to be done, to protect both of them.

"Thank you, Bellona."

Carissa had noticed that since Cobryn's arrival, Kato had remained at court, unwilling to leave his daughter alone with the man who had orchestrated the Conquest. She couldn't blame him. Any father would want to protect their child from the Warmonger, especially when Bellona was unmarried and her father's only heir.

Linking her arm through her friend's, Carissa made her way toward the great hall. She could already hear the lively music and laughter. Part of her wondered what everyone would be masked as, but another part of her hated the idea of a masquerade. They all wore masks of civility in any case. Not to mention that parties cost an exorbitant amount of money, money that should have gone to better use than funding her husband's birthday. The frivolous use of the treasury would have to change.

The great hall had not been used for festivities in some time. Across the far end, in front of windows that stretched from the floor to the ceiling, were the twin thrones—high-backed, golden, and ornate with cream cushions in each seat. There had often been music and laughter in this hall when she had been a child, when she had escaped the stifling small talk to paddle in the fountain with Peregrine and Bellona.

"A swan, your Majesty?" A man in a wolf mask approached. Deacon. He caught her wrist and kissed the back of her hand. Bellona remained close to her friend, eyes narrowed behind her own mask. "How unsubtle. I was hoping you would be a little more creative."

"A wolf, Deacon?" Carissa imitated his tone, pure venom in her voice. Momentarily, she was fearless. "Fitting, considering the predator you are."

Tugging her hand from his grasp, she moved away from him. What had afforded her such confidence? She usually would never have spoken to Deacon in that manner. She hadn't touched a single glass of wine yet. Was it the knowledge that she had the power to destroy him, despite his own dangerous magic? Was it Cobryn's presence, the idea that he favoured his son over his brother? Beside her, Bellona let out a short burst of laughter.

"I have never heard you speak to Deacon that way before!"

"If you'll excuse me, Bellona." Carissa extricated her arm from her friend's. "I should find my husband and wish him a happy birthday."

Easier said than done in a sea of colourful masks. She did not know Jacen well enough to guess what he might be masked as. She froze on the spot when she saw her grandfather's crown atop the blond head of a man in a plain black mask who stood alone at the drinks table. It took all of her self-restraint not to march over and rip the crown off his head. Instead she approached with caution, touching her husband's arm to catch his attention.

"I had no idea you had a fondness for crowns." She spat the words, struggling to rein in her emotions at seeing a Morrow with a Darnell crown on his head. It didn't belong there. She barely felt it belonged to her, but she certainly had more of a right to it than Jacen.

"Carissa." Jacen reached up and immediately took the crown off his head, placing it atop hers instead. "I apologise. My father insisted that—"

"That you wear my grandfather's crown, *my* crown?" Carissa demanded, folding her arms over her chest. "Have I not been humiliated enough? Now he wants to make me watch as he parades you around in a swan crown? Do you listen to everything that your father tells you?"

"Clearly not, or you wouldn't be a virgin."

The quiet, vicious words slapped her. She had been quick to assume that Jacen was not like Cobryn or Deacon, but such poisonous words made her reconsider. How quickly his apology had faded into something more sinister. How would he behave if she angered him? Did she want to know the answer? They had been civil thus far, but Carissa wondered now if they could continue to remain so.

"Watch your words, *husband*. They implicate you as surely as they do me."

"I did not want some masquerade celebration." Jacen raked a hand through his hair, casting around as if looking for someone who might spirit him away. "I didn't want that crown. I didn't want you."

The words burned like the cut Miriam had slashed across her palm, yet Carissa chose to ignore the fact that they hurt. Why should she care if Jacen wanted her or not? Part of her did, and she hated that part of herself. As his wife and Queen, she may one day soon bear him a child. But she would never love him. She could never let herself love the son of the Warmonger.

"Then why not tell your father 'no'?"

Jacen gave a mirthless laugh. "No one tells Cobryn Morrow 'no', not without consequences. You know that better than most."

"You're his only son," Carissa argued, brows knitting together behind her swan mask.

"Especially not his son."

"Then have this small sliver of freedom." She stepped aside, gesturing toward the dancing and celebrations taking place across the room. "Tonight is for you. Make it yours, take off your mask if you like. You are King in your own right now. Cobryn cannot take that away from you."

They both thought there was a better use for Basiumite funds than the ball, though Cobryn had put his foot down.

No one tells Cobryn Morrow 'no'.

"Your Majesty?" It was a man in a jackal mask—the sigil of House Morrow. Certainly not Deacon or Cobryn. Perhaps a relative; he had a slighter frame and paler eyes. "I wondered if I might ask you for a dance."

"Of course." Carissa stepped forward to take his proffered hand, before glancing over her shoulder at Jacen. "Enjoy the festivities, dear husband."

She allowed herself to be led out to dance on the cream-and-gold chequered tiles of the great hall. The first dance of the night should have been with Jacen, but she was in no mindset to tolerate his current mood. If he allowed himself to, he might just have fun, as she intended to.

"Might I ask your name?" Carissa questioned, tilting her head to the side to afford her a better look at the person behind the mask. "I'm afraid I haven't the slightest idea who you are."

"Isn't that the point?" The man in the jackal mask—she suspected he was more of a boy—offered her a wide smile. "I could be anyone, or anything. Your best friend, your worst enemy."

Carissa felt calluses on his palms, but he still knew the right moments in the music to dip her and twirl her. Potentially nobility, someone who had worked hard despite his knowledge of how to dance at a celebration.

"A swan mask, a swan crown; you truly have dressed the part of a Darnell tonight."

"I *am* a Darnell," Carissa corrected him with a tight smile. "I may be married, but I will always bear the name of my forefathers. I hope to honour them in doing so."

"Do you know what I see in this hall?" Startlingly familiar bright blue eyes locked onto hers. "I look around and I see Genera pretending this is still Basium. I see the real powers here, and a young woman who is content in her position as a puppet. A fallacy of a Queen."

Carissa attempted to pull away, startled by the boy's words and the acidity of his tone. No member of House Morrow hid behind that mask. In fact, she highly doubted he was Generan, but more likely one of her own people. The boy gripped her wrist tightly and tugged her close enough to whisper in her ear.

"Emlen never forgets, Majesty."

Releasing her abruptly, the boy stepped back and executed a mocking bow before disappearing into the crowd. Overcome by panic, Carissa nudged past the other guests, but the boy in the jackal mask was nowhere to be found. Who was he? She assumed he lived in Emlen judging by his words, yet he had seemed so familiar to her. Perhaps his family had resided in the palace before the Conquest. His words had been so hateful, his eyes angry. Whoever the boy was, he despised her.

Someone grabbed her arm and she started. Bellona examined her friend with a concerned frown, Vida trailing just behind her with a glass of wine.

"Carissa? Are you alright? You look as though you've seen a ghost."

"Maybe I have," Carissa whispered. Her chest constricted, like her dress was too tight. A heavy weight sat on her, and she couldn't push it off.

Bellona took her friend's arm and gestured for Vida to follow. The three of them made their way out into the gardens, and the first breath of cool fresh air was a welcome relief to Carissa. She inhaled deeply, glad to be away from the crowded great hall. She sat on one of the stone benches, Bellona and Vida taking their places on either side of her. Vida gripped her hand tightly, while Bellona rubbed soothing circles on her back.

"Are you feeling unwell? Have you perhaps had too much wine?"

"I haven't had any," Carissa admitted. Her current state of being had nothing to do with alcohol and everything to do with the tensions rising around her. The nature of her magic, the growing rebellion in Emlen… If the boy's words had been anything to judge by, things were more serious than she'd anticipated. Emlen would not back down, not if they planned on war.

"It could be the crowd." Vida sounded sympathetic. "I know you don't much like throngs of people."

"Yes, I suppose," Carissa murmured. How could she tell her friends what she had seen, what she had heard? They wouldn't understand why she had been so shocked, why the boy had felt familiar. Better to act as though the crowd had been the overwhelming factor in tonight's celebrations.

"Should I fetch Jacen?" Vida asked.

"No." She shook her head vigorously. Jacen was one of the last people that Carissa wanted to see right now. "I just need to be here, with you two. In the gardens."

If Emlen did rise up, what would happen then? Would Carissa have to bear the burden of crushing one of her country's most powerful cities? She'd never be able to bring herself to do so. If Emlen resisted, then it would be time for her to rise up too. They all called her a puppet—and it was the truth. Yet she would be a puppet no longer. Cobryn had unwittingly given her the cards, and it was time to play them.

THE DEVOTED KING
JACEN MORROW

Jacen woke the morning after his birthday celebration to a throbbing head and soft whispering across the room. Rubbing his eyes, he rolled onto his side to see Carissa kneeling on the floor, seven candles burning bright on the table in front of her. With her hands clasped in front of her, her head remained bent, eyes closed in intense concentration.

Jacen sat slowly, suddenly curious. He hadn't stayed in Basium long enough to learn their traditions, their religion. No doubt Carissa murmured prayers to their goddess, Elethea, if he remembered correctly. Why was she praying?

Getting out of bed, Jacen grabbed a shirt and tugged it on, reaching up to rub his temples. He indulged in too much alcohol, an attempt to make the masquerade in his honour more tolerable. Despite the fact he had not gone to bed until the early hours of the morning, Carissa had arrived after him. When he looked at her again, she watched him intently. The tears in her eyes startled him.

"Are you alright?" he asked, suddenly concerned. "Was it Deacon? Did he…?"

"It's nothing to do with Deacon." Carissa blew out the candles on the table, standing up. "My prayers are for the goddess alone."

"Does she answer them?" Jacen asked. The Generans had three gods—collectively known as the Trinity. Aurum, god of the skies. Terram, god of the earth. Hydron, god of the seas. He didn't think the Trinity had once answered his prayers.

"The people used to call my family 'goddess blessed." Carissa poured him a glass of water and thrust it into his hand. "It was said that we were descended from the sons of Elethea. After the Conquest, they call us 'goddess cursed'. Does that answer your question?"

"Let's walk." Jacen downed the water in a few deep gulps, setting the glass down on the table beside the candles. "I'd very much like to go through your gardens again. Besides, I believe I owe you an apology for last night."

Carissa's brow creased momentarily before she accepted her husband's arm. A pleasant shiver raced through his body at the contact of her skin on his. The two remained silent as they made their way through the palace corridors toward the gardens. Carissa didn't have to lead him the entire way, thankfully. The labyrinth of the castle started to make sense to him.

When they reached the gardens, Jacen had to marvel at their beauty once again. Years before, this had been the scene of gruesome death, where a family had been destroyed. He glanced at his wife, puzzled as to how she could feel such calm in a place where her father and brother had been murdered.

"I thought this place would only bring you pain."

"It did, at first." Carissa released Jacen's arm to sit down in front of deep purple flowers with bright white spots. As she watched them, he examined her, his stomach suddenly full of butterflies. "Then I realised that this garden was what I made of it. I didn't want it to be a place of sorrow and tragedy. I took a place full of death and brought life into it again."

Jacen admired her. Watching her trace the white-dotted purple petals of the flowers in front of her, he saw a true Queen. Instead of being overcome by the things she had endured, Carissa had risen above them. When he'd returned to Marinel, he'd anticipated a broken, fragile creature as his wife. Carissa had shattered those expectations and proven herself as resilient as the flowers planted in soil soaked with Darnell blood.

Jacen examined her face, the gentle slope of her nose, her full bottom lip, the unusual shade of her eyes. Perhaps the reason he cared so much about her opinion was because he cared about her.

"I was unkind to you last night." Jacen sat beside Carissa. His hand stretched towards her but he paused. Would she pull away at his touch? His arm fell back to his side. "I am sorry. I lashed out. That was not right. My frustrations are not with you."

Jacen's hand brushed against hers without meaning to, and tingles raced up his spine. He was close enough to see how dark and thick her eyelashes were.

Her breath smelled like peppermint as it fanned across his cheek, making his stomach flip. She was so beautiful and so brave, and he found himself melting like candle wax over a fire around her.

"We were both unkind," Carissa admitted, tearing her gaze away from the flowers to examine him. "I was at fault too. But your family is right in saying one thing—if we don't learn to work together, we can never be a strong King and Queen. I need you, Jacen, and you need me."

Cobryn had dismissed the Darnells as a proud family, a family who would die before they allowed themselves to be subjugated. Carissa proved him wrong, proved herself to be a survivor. She would do whatever it took to be a good Queen, despite the circumstances that had led to her being put on the throne. Jacen admired her, but more importantly, he respected her.

Jacen leaned in and kissed her. It was not born of duty, but genuine passion. He did not love this girl, but he cared about what happened to her. Carissa responded with enthusiasm, taking Jacen's face in her hands and kissing him deeply in return. She smiled against his lips. She wanted this, too. When he drew back, there was something in her eyes that he never expected to be the cause of: happiness.

"Together," he agreed, clasping his hands in hers. In that moment, they were all that mattered, a young King and Queen beginning to heal the rift that his family had caused.

Deacon paced the meeting room, hands clasped behind his back. Jacen lounged in a seat, calmly watching his uncle's agitation grow. The dying fire flickered feebly in the hearth as Deacon spun to face his nephew.

Ever since they received a letter from Lord Ambrose of Emlen, Deacon had been on edge. Lord Ambrose did not recognise Carissa and Jacen as his monarchs, and he declared Emlen self-governing. While the letter's contents also concerned Jacen, he kept his feelings to himself.

"We cannot take this lightly." Deacon waved around the offending piece of parchment. "This is a threat, Jacen. To your rule, to our family. If Emlen does not become subservient, then the rest of Basium will follow their lead and rise up."

"I thought you were secure in our reign." Jacen raised his eyebrows, leaning forward in his chair as Deacon gritted his teeth. "Certainly if we have

Carissa address the issue, then they will step down. They can see us as conquerors, but she's a Darnell."

In truth, Jacen expected more of an outcry when Deacon had been regent. At least Jacen's title held through marriage—Deacon was not connected to the Queen at all, despite the fact he hoped they could be close. His uncle's magic could have intimidated them, especially if he'd cleverly brought Imperium and Maleficium into the fold. The dynamics of court still perplexed him, and he still couldn't sort friend from foe.

"Don't be a fool, Jacen," Deacon snapped. For a man usually so calm and collected, he certainly did lose his temper when he had no control. "Some of these people will never accept you, no matter who you're married to. The trick is to make them think it's in their best interests."

Tricking his subjects left Jacen uneasy, knowing it would earn disapproval from his wife. Carissa desperately wanted to be loved by her people, to be accepted as their Queen and not seen as a pawn. He couldn't help but pity her, and he wondered if that could truly be the case. Nonetheless, he did not want to be a tyrant like Cobryn, or reign through manipulation and scare tactics like Deacon.

"I think I should decide what to do about this situation." Jacen stood, folding his arms over his chest. "I don't believe telling people what their best interest is will do me any favours. They like to have a voice, a say in how they're being governed."

Deacon scoffed, waving a dismissive hand. "Many of them don't know what they're talking about or about how government even works. You're too soft, Jacen. I've been telling your father so for years, and it seems he's finally beginning to listen."

Jacen clenched his jaw. Since his arrival, he'd sensed that he and Deacon would clash. It would have been easy for his uncle to return home to Genera, yet he seemed to relish the power he'd acquired here in Basium, unwilling to give it up even when his nephew returned. Jacen was not the sort of King who wanted a man like Deacon doing all the work for him. Basium had been given to him. He needed to earn his title.

"I would have words with the Emlen representative on the council."

Deacon laughed. "Bryce Ambrose? Cyprian's younger brother? He is a man of the blade, not words."

"Regardless, I would like to speak to him and see if we can resolve this matter here in court."

Deacon's mirth faded as quickly as it came. Had he thought his nephew would be easy to control, to manoeuvre? Carissa had threats hanging over her head, but Jacen did not. There was only one member of the Morrow family Jacen felt obligated to listen to, and it was not Deacon.

"Very well," Deacon said, tone curt. "I am uncertain how much contact Sir Bryce has had with his brother, however—"

"That doesn't matter." Jacen cut him off. "He will see that I am reasonable enough when we speak."

Deacon's smile turned sour. "Or he will see you as you are, still a boy desperately trying to prove himself a man."

"I tire of your poison, Uncle." Jacen crossed over to the door, fingers tightening around the handle. He would not stand here and allow Deacon to insult him. The lack of control made his uncle upset, but Jacen didn't have control either. He had no intention of manipulating anything. He wished to come to a peaceful resolution that didn't involve bloodshed. He had seen enough of violence in the Island Wars. He had no wish to see more of it in Emlen, not if he could help it.

The chill of winter surrendered to the brightness of spring. The wind no longer howled and rattled at the shutters like an angry ghost seeking vengeance. Only a bite of cold lingered over pleasantly warm days. Basium's temperate climate welcomed him, a complete contrast to the Generan mountains and cities coated in thick sheets of ice.

Carissa's eighteenth birthday approached. Jacen he did not know his wife as well as he'd like, so when it came to the idea of getting her a gift she would like, he was clueless as to where he'd begin. Fortunately, he knew the right person to ask.

Laughter sounded as Jacen entered the gardens, making him smile. Two girls splashed around in the large fountain in the centre of the greenery, ducking and swirling around the stone swans placed here and there as decoration. One of them Jacen recognised all too well—Vida, with her golden blonde hair and tall, slim frame. The other was a girl he had seen with Carissa many a time, a petite redhead with a freckled complexion. Lord Lenore's daughter, though he could not recall her name.

"I am surprised the Queen is not with you."

The girls paused, giggles ceasing. Vida stepped out of the fountain, her usual gracefulness impeded by the saturated hem of her dress. She swept her damp hair out of her eyes.

"Dear brother. Unfortunately, your wife has other duties. She is with Miriam this afternoon and won't be joining us."

"It's you I've come to see." Jacen glanced at the ginger-haired girl, who stayed in the fountain. Vida turned and beckoned her, and she cautiously waded out of the water. "Apologies, lady. I forget your name."

"Bellona Lenore," she said, voice cool as she regarded Jacen warily. He remembered the name now—Vida said that Bellona and Carissa had been friends since early childhood. Bellona was protective of the Queen.

"I know Carissa's birthday is soon. I came for advice on what she may like as a gift."

Vida nudged him in the ribs. "For shame, Jacen. You've been back in Basium three months now, and you do not know your wife enough to present her with something she may enjoy?"

A double meaning ran under the mischievous lilt of her words. Jacen sighed and shook his head. He liked to think he could confide in Vida, yet he also knew that she and Deacon were close.

Who can I trust in this gods forsaken court?

"Don't be crude, sister. I mean it—I'd like to get my wife something that she would like."

"The Queen is lonely," Bellona piped up, her tone a lot less teasing than Vida's. "Perhaps something like a pet would keep her happy. She has little company her own age aside from us. She already has all the jewels and dresses she could ever need."

"Bellona," Vida chastised.

"I suppose it is true." Jacen raked his fingers through his hair. "I'd like her to have something meaningful, not just something expensive for the sake of it. I know enough to realise Carissa is not frivolous."

The idea of giving his wife a gift was more nerve-inducing than it should be. He wished he could hand her a peaceful country, the city of Emlen taking back their uprising. Unfortunately, he could not magically procure those things—his conversation with Bryce Ambrose had not been productive in the slightest. He hated that Deacon had been right when he'd said Bryce was a man who preferred the jousts and tourneys to the games of court.

Turning his mind from his failure at maintaining the peace in Emlen, Jacen wondered if gifting his wife a pet might be a good idea. He had a hound during his childhood, and although the creature had eventually vanished into the woods without a trace, he had been marvellous to have around during the trials and tribulations of Jacen's youth.

"You have known the Queen for many years?" Jacen asked Bellona, to which the ginger girl responded with a curt nod.

"I was promised to her middle brother, Peregrine, before…"

Jacen pointedly looked away, although Bellona never shifted her gaze from him. There had been many in court, and throughout Basium, who had suffered the consequences of the Conquest. Even if Carissa didn't hold who he was against him, there would be others like Bellona who would never let him forget how much pain and tragedy his family had caused that day.

"Then I trust your judgement in this matter."

The finality of Jacen's tone caused Vida to step back into the fountain. However, Bellona walked over to the King and caught him by the arm. When he turned to face her, her green eyes were fierce.

"A word of warning, Majesty. You have not been here over the past four years, but I have. I have witnessed how much the Queen has endured. If you were to harm her, realise that I would give my life to protect her, and any wrong committed against her I would repay a hundredfold."

Bellona's cold words sent shivers down Jacen's spine. How loyal this young woman was to Carissa, how far she would go to ensure her friend suffered no more humiliation or tragedy. He wanted to protest that he would never do such a thing, but had everyone not heard that story many times before? He must prove himself through actions, not words. Bellona bestowed an icy smile upon him, sweeping up her wet skirts as she curtsied before him.

"Your Majesty."

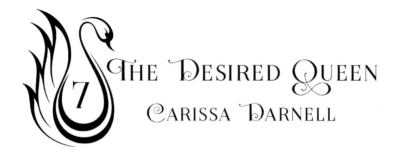

THE DESIRED QUEEN
CARISSA DARNELL

Carissa never enjoyed her birthday. It brought back memories of her childhood, of things she would rather forget, leaving her with an anxiety that settled over her like a cloud. Her brothers and their incessant teasing, her mother's gentle smile and her father's doting. Most of her family would never see another year, mangled remains buried beneath the earth. This year was particularly painful—as she turned eighteen, she would now be the same age as Peregrine when he died.

She had not wanted much of a celebration but agreed to a small garden party. With the weather warming, Carissa would have found it a shame to celebrate indoors. Her dress had once belonged to her mother—a pale blue gown that had looked far better on Imogen than it did on her. It had been the dress her mother had worn when her father had asked her to marry him, and Carissa felt close to Imogen when she wore her old gowns, stowed in the back of the cupboard and forgotten about except on these occasions.

She hated plenty about her birthday, but perhaps the worst came in the large stock of meaningless gifts that she managed to acquire, nobles who rarely paid her much attention flocking to wish her a happy birthday. Carissa attempted to stray from them, but they followed her everywhere. It took a few glasses of wine for her to slip past her well-wishers and sit by the fountain, pleasantly dizzy with a half-finished goblet in hand.

"My Queen." Celestine Renatus, the Lady of Seneca, resplendent in a deep purple gown, strode her way. She approached and curtsied before Carissa, the smile on her lips never reaching her eyes. Although Carissa dearly wished to be left alone, she understood being social was a fundamental part of her position.

"Lady Renatus. It's a pleasure to see you. I'm glad that you could make it to the capital for the celebrations."

"I also wished to speak." Celestine took a seat beside Carissa. When she was younger, Carissa had always been in awe of her—beautiful blonde Lady Renatus, so graceful and effortlessly elegant. She had married a man who adored her and had given birth to a gorgeous child loved by all. Then Celestine had lost her son and heir during the Conquest, and Carissa realised perhaps the Lady of Seneca's life was not so perfect after all.

"I am more than willing to listen." Carissa took another sip of wine. She had never liked the taste, yet she found herself growing accustomed to it. Besides, she enjoyed the sensation of light dizziness that came over her when she partook in alcohol.

"I take it you've heard all about what's happening in Emlen." Celestine's tone became serious, and Carissa tilted her head back to look at the twinkling stars, wishing they discussed anything else. "Lord Ambrose is…deeply unsatisfied with things."

"You mean with the fact that Basium has a Morrow King." While Lord Ambrose had little issue with her, he also seemed to have no respect for her. "I did not choose to marry Jacen, but certainly he is a wiser choice than a man like Deacon. I understand Lord Ambrose's concerns, yet he chooses to hide away in Emlen when he could meet with us."

"It seems he has already made up his mind." Celestine shrugged her shoulders.

"The other nobles?" Carissa was almost afraid to ask. Once one of the noble houses rose in protest, others would begin to do the same. Perhaps Celestine would know where the others stood.

"Undecided." Celestine paused. "I respect you, Majesty. You have been through more than most girls your age. You must understand, Lord Ambrose's position is not intended as a slight. There are simply those among us who feel that you would be better off without a Morrow at your side."

Carissa's fingers tightened around her goblet. "Does Lord Ambrose plot my husband's death?"

Celestine's smile turned tight. She did not respond to the question, instead taking a sip from her own goblet. Rising to her feet, she curtsied deeply before Carissa once more, inspecting the young Queen with some sadness.

"Your mother Imogen was a close friend to me. She would be proud of the woman you have become."

She wasn't getting any more answers out of Celestine—or perhaps Celestine didn't know. Heaving a sigh as Celestine walked over to greet other nobles, Carissa realised she would need to work hard to gain the support of the several large noble houses. Perhaps wanting her people to love her was pathetic when she had only ever proven herself a victim.

"Your Majesty." Deacon sauntered over and seated himself beside Carissa. She stiffened. "You are looking radiant this evening."

"I'm aware," Carissa said coolly. She hoped her cool indifference would shut the conversation down, and quickly. "Although I do not see why you aren't participating in the festivities. Bellona has even arranged fire-breathers."

From her perch on the edge of the fountain, Carissa could see the fire billowing up into the darkening sky, hear the laughter and gasps of the court as they watched with wary fascination. There had been fire in Marinel during the Conquest too, and no one had been laughing then. She cast her gaze around for Jacen but could not see her husband. She fought back a wave of disappointment, wondering what explanation he had for his absence.

"No doubt your husband has his own plans for celebration tonight."

Deacon's suggestive tone made Carissa scowl and take another gulp of her wine. She knew precisely what he insinuated and didn't appreciate it in the slightest. She set her goblet down and glowered at Deacon.

"Don't be ridiculous. Jacen would never be so crude. We haven't even…"

Her inebriated mind caught on to what her lips were saying and Carissa lapsed into horrified silence as she realised what she had done. A victorious smile curved the corners of Deacon's lips. She thought he must have suspected as much and hoped to catch her off guard. Carissa prayed that he may not have caught on, but Deacon had always been clever.

"Are you meaning to say that the marriage remains unconsummated?"

"That would make it illegitimate," Carissa responded sharply. Why couldn't she bring herself to lie? Why couldn't she just pretend it had been consummated? Was she afraid that Deacon would catch her out in a falsehood? Devastated by her inability to keep her mouth shut and the danger she had placed both herself and Jacen in, Carissa pushed herself to her feet.

"It's no secret that neither of you ever wanted this marriage." Deacon sounded amused. "It would be easy enough to dissolve it, have you remarried to someone else. I wouldn't mind being your King."

This time, he wasn't even subtle about it. Nausea rose in her stomach and desperation clawed at her skin. She needed to find Jacen. If Deacon started talking about what he learned before she could tell her husband what occurred, they would be in a dire situation indeed. Forsaking her goblet of wine, Carissa moved through the gardens with haste, her stomach coiling into knots. No, she had not wanted this marriage, but she feared the annulment of it—the consequences of her and Jacen's inaction.

"Why didn't you lie?"

Jacen closed the door to their bedroom, watching Carissa as she curled in front of the hearth. He understood the urgency of the situation, yet she could tell he was annoyed with her. His brows knitted together, arms folding over his chest as she glanced over her shoulder.

"I don't know. I wasn't thinking, it just…slipped out."

"A slip that could cost us both dearly." Jacen stepped toward her, hazel eyes bright. "You do realise the stakes, don't you? What you told Deacon tonight could ruin us both."

"Perhaps." The tears welled in her eyes and she eased herself up off the rug. She knew what she had to do—what they had to do. Jacen planned to wait until she truly wanted to, but that was no longer an option. Whatever their desires had been, it didn't matter. Acutely aware that this slip was on her, she was prepared to pay the price.

Jacen frowned. "What do you mean?"

"You know exactly what I mean." Carissa moved closer, tossing her dark hair over her shoulder as she looked up at him, chin tilted defiantly upwards. "There is nothing that Deacon can do if we consummate the marriage."

"Carissa…" Jacen looked taken aback.

Tears spilled down Carissa's cheeks, but she smiled grimly. "Either he wins, or we do. I know which I'd prefer."

This wasn't how she had wanted it to happen, a rushed union caused by her own inability to keep her mouth shut. She and Jacen deserved better. What choice did they have now? If they didn't, Deacon would see their marriage dissolved, and marry Carissa in his nephew's place. He wouldn't have the same restraint as Jacen. The thought of Deacon having her turned Carissa's stomach.

Marriage is not a romance. Miriam had always reminded her of that. It was a contract and having sex with her husband sealed such a contract. Without waiting for Jacen's protests, Carissa wrapped her arms around his neck and pressed her lips to his. She might not love Jacen, but she didn't hate him. She hoped that would make this ordeal easier.

Jacen slid his arms around her waist, backing her against the bed. Hesitation riddled his body rigid, but he relaxed, hands slipping up from her waist to tug at the laces of her dress. Carissa shivered as his fingers brushed against her skin, but she allowed him to undo the laces. When he paused, Carissa took initiative, prying her dress and undergarments off. She ignored the burning in her cheeks as she stood before him, completely bare.

Jacen's gaze raked over her body, eyes brightening with lust as he examined her. The bulge in his pants indicated he was pleased with what he saw. As Carissa flopped back onto the mattress, he pulled his shirt over his head, tossing it to the floor alongside her dress. The weight of his body was heavy atop hers as he crawled onto her, but not uncomfortable. He pressed his lips to hers again, with more hunger this time.

Jacen's hands roamed Carissa's body, sliding down from her breasts to her thighs. The softness of his fingers against her skin made her shiver, the certainty of his touch made her sure he'd done this before. She pushed that thought to the back of her mind. Perhaps it was better that one of them had some kind of experience in this area.

Jacen's lips trailed down her jaw, brushing against the sensitive skin of her neck and making her gasp. As she relaxed beneath him, he slipped a finger inside her. At first, she tensed, unaccustomed to the sensation. But Jacen's kisses became more heated, more insistent. As his lips traversed her collarbone, she fell limp against the pillows. When he moved his finger, slowly at first, she couldn't help but choke out another gasp.

"I don't want to hurt you," Jacen said, voice hoarse, his breath hot against her skin.

Carissa reached down to undo his pants. This was about duty, not desire. She would do what had been expected of her since the day she'd married Jacen, what she'd failed to do. All women had to endure this, and it was certainly worse for some than it would be for her. She tried not to think about poor Lilith as she pulled Jacen's pants off completely.

Would she lose control of her magic during this, exposing what she was? It was something she hadn't thought about. It was a risk she'd have to take. The idea that her husband might see her darkness filled her with trepidation, but so did the idea of what they were about to do.

"You won't." Carissa reached up to touch his cheek, hoping her tenderness would be reassuring for him. In this moment, just the two of them existed, and her hesitations and barriers came crumbling down. She left herself vulnerable and yet, she had never been more alive. Her heart raced, though she wasn't afraid. It might just have been desire that she felt for him, but it was enough for now.

They lay breathless and tangled amidst the sheets, the silence stretching on past comfort. A light sheen of sweat covered her whole body, her dark hair tangled. Although she wouldn't have called the experience pleasurable, it had certainly not been as painful as she dreaded. Wrapping the sheets more tightly around her chest, she rolled onto her side to observe Jacen.

"I told you that you wouldn't hurt me."

"I didn't want you to feel forced into the consummation." Jacen sighed, sitting up slowly. Carissa allowed her eyes to rake over his muscular physique, before averting her gaze when her husband looked at her.

"The consummation isn't an act of passion, Jacen. It's sealing a contract. We've both known this was coming."

Now that it was done, one less terrible thing loomed over Carissa's head. Her marriage was now legitimate, and knowing Deacon could do nothing about it left her smug. She'd sealed her fate—she was truly Jacen's wife. She could only pray to the goddess that he was the decent man he appeared to be, and that it hadn't simply been an act to gain her cooperation.

In the waning light of the fire, Carissa examined her husband. He was an attractive man—a good bit over six feet tall, broad-shouldered, fair-haired. He might have been everything she ever wanted in a husband, had he not been Cobryn's son. When it came down to it, Carissa knew he would choose his family over her. She could understand that, but it didn't stop the thought leaving a bitter taste in her mouth.

Carissa could trust very few people in Marinel. Miriam had warned her to be careful—befriend many, but keep her cards close to her chest. Betrayal never came from the enemy, but from those closest to you. A lesson Carissa had always taken very seriously. In another life, a life where her family hadn't been murdered, she wouldn't have to be so cautious. But that was a fantasy, and the reality stated she was under the control of House Morrow.

"Is there any word on Emlen?" Carissa traced her fingers down Jacen's arm, watching him closely to ascertain his reaction. He heaved a sigh, flopping back against the pillows.

"It's not good. That's all I know. They don't want to acknowledge either of us as their rightful rulers."

Carissa considered this in silence. She understood her people not wanting to acknowledge Jacen. He was the Warmonger's son. Yet did they not realise how much she had suffered, how hard she worked to be a good Queen? She had put forth her support when Deacon legalised dark magic, regardless of the fact that she had ulterior motives. Carissa had been an active participant in many council decisions. Surely Lord Ambrose realised that.

"I got you a present." The words made Carissa look warily to her husband, wondering what sort of gift he'd gotten to impress her. "I don't have it with me now, but I should by tomorrow."

"What is it?" Carissa asked, her mind immediately drifting to expensive jewels they mined in the Generan mountains.

"A surprise." Jacen flashed her a boyish grin that startled her enough to elicit a smile in response.

Curling on her side with a smile upon her own lips, Carissa wondered, for the first time in many years, if she might find contentment. Jacen certainly did a wonderful job in being reassuring, though she didn't think her paranoia would go away any time soon. Her husband still had a lot to prove if they truly intended to become a combined, driven force of nature.

"You are in an unusually good mood." Miriam sounded amused and suspicious at her granddaughter's patience in dealing with magical matters that typically irritated her. Carissa looked up from her bleeding palm, lost in thoughts of the night before.

"I had a good birthday." She paused, remembering that this was Miriam, and she could trust her grandmother with anything. "Jacen and I also consummated the marriage."

"So, he has won you over." A hint of bitterness coloured Miriam's tone.

Carissa frowned and lowered the jewellery she levitated. Her power grew stronger and more controlled every time she used her magic, but the temptation lingered, losing control and letting the blood magic overcome her a seductive allure. It was something she could never do. Power and destruction too often went hand in hand.

"Isn't that what you wanted?" Carissa's brow furrowed. "I don't understand why coming to an understanding with my husband is suddenly a bad thing."

"My sweet, you are young still." Miriam gave her a sad smile, her eyes tired as she reached out to caress her granddaughter's cheek. "Jacen can give you everything you desire; he can treat you like the goddess herself. But you must never forget he is a Morrow. You may not see his ulterior motives now, but in time, he will make them clear."

Carissa scowled, prickled by her grandmother's words. Miriam had every right to hate the Morrow family—they robbed her of almost everything she held dear. Yet she had sensed the hesitation in Jacen. How could she still say Jacen and Vida were terrible people, when they had never shown Carissa any cruelty? She did not trust them, for it would be foolish to fall into a false sense of security. That didn't mean she had to condemn them for simply being Cobryn's children.

"Jacen is not a bad man, Grandmother. You know that."

"We don't know what he is." Miriam shook her head slowly. "He has only been here a few short months. Don't be ensnared by him. The worst cages are the ones you step into unknowingly."

"But I know I'm in a cage." Carissa pushed herself to her feet, her temper rising with the swirl of dark magic within her alongside it. "I've been in a cage since I was fourteen years old, and I know I'm there now. That's what we're fighting for—to be free. I have no illusions about my position."

"You have illusions about Jacen." Miriam's sharp tone pricked at her skin. "You see him as a potential equal, someone who could help free you from your shackles. He will only fasten them tighter the moment you resist. He is not your liberator, Carissa."

"Should it have been Deacon, Grandmother?" Carissa didn't bother to keep the anger from her voice. "Should it have been a man who'd have raped me when I was a child, who would have forced an heir on me years before now? Would it have helped if it was a man I could only ever see as a monster?"

Miriam flinched at the bluntness of her words. They both knew that it could have been worse for Carissa. She'd been saved some pain with Jacen, but

Carissa had not forgotten the Conquest. Those horrific murders would be etched into her mind for as long as she lived. It would always hurt to think of them.

"Of course not. I only meant that you must be careful to put your duty before your desire. Basium is still under Cobryn and Deacon's control. They allow you to pass laws they find fitting, but we've not yet cut the strings they pull."

The dark magic in Carissa wanted her to lash out. Not at Miriam, never at her. She wanted to break something, an inanimate object, to take out her frustrations. She knew that would only be the beginning of a far more terrible path. If she lost control now, it would be that much harder to rein her magic in. Instead, Carissa turned and marched from the room, ignoring Miriam's protests.

Miriam endured so many losses, damaging her very soul, that she no longer remembered what it was like to want some sort of connection to people. Carissa had been lonely over the past few years, with only small spots of light like Bellona and Vida to guide her through the darkness. Now she had Jacen too. He might not know her intention to free Basium from his family's control, their happiness might not be meant to last, but she craved it, even if doing so was selfish.

THE WRATHFUL KING
JACEN MORROW

Jacen anticipated Deacon calling a meeting with Cobryn before the King of Genera returned home to Nicodemus. He would have told his father what had happened in private, but he wanted to see the look on Deacon's face when he realised that he didn't hold anything over Jacen and Carissa. He sprawled in a chair and waited for Deacon to enter, raising his eyebrows at the smug expression on his uncle's face.

"What is it now, Deacon?" Cobryn sounded utterly bored, as he usually did when his younger brother attempted to stir up unnecessary drama. Now that the festivities of both Jacen and Carissa's birthdays ended and Cobryn had witnessed for himself that the Morrow family still held power here, he wished to return home and plan his next war.

"You should ask your son." A smirk twisted the corners of Deacon's lips as he jabbed an accusatory finger in Jacen's direction. "How can one be a legitimate King if one does not have a legitimate marriage?"

"What are you talking about?" Cobryn sat up straighter. No doubt he wouldn't take the chance of losing all legal control over Basium lightly.

"Jacen and Carissa have not consummated their marriage." Deacon's eyes glittered with triumph. "Even if we turn a blind eye to the fact that they were married only a few days before the Island Wars began, he has been back in Marinel for months now. If he was going to do the right thing, he would have. In light of the illegitimacy of the marriage, I request that I marry her instead. I have been overseeing—"

"You've always wanted her for yourself, Deacon." Jacen stood abruptly, narrowing his eyes at his uncle. "You have a lust for Carissa and the power that

71

marrying her would grant you, and you would do anything to acquire it."

"Carissa confessed to me at her birthday celebrations that you had not yet consummated the marriage." Deacon folded his arms over his chest, eyes gleaming. "Are you calling your wife a liar?"

"Bring her here and ask her now." Jacen couldn't help the victorious grin that spread across his face as he cherished this rare moment. "We consummated the marriage last night. I can assure you that I was very thorough in my attention to doing the right thing."

The complacency wiped right off of Deacon's face. They had not consummated the marriage on the wedding night, but now the marriage was legitimate. Cobryn's brow creased in deep displeasure as he looked between his brother and his son. Jacen's triumphant glee vanished with the realisation that while he might have won this round against Deacon, he still had Cobryn's wrath to contend with.

"You did what?"

"I had sex with her, Deacon." Jacen tilted his head to the side. "I assume you still recall what that is."

"Enough," Cobryn barked, causing both men to lapse into silence. The Warmonger got up, glaring between the pair of them. "Deacon, leave us. I will speak to my son about this matter in private."

Seething, Deacon spun on his heel and marched from the room. The conversation had not gone at all the way he wanted it to. Regardless of the fact that Jacen and Carissa's marriage was secure, Jacen's current position with his father was tenuous at best. He swallowed hard as his father stalked over to him.

"Is this the truth? You did not consummate your marriage to the Darnell girl until *last night*?"

There was no point in lying. "Yes, Father."

Cobryn's hand cracked across Jacen's face with enough force to make him stumble. He reached up to touch his throbbing cheek. It was not the first time his father had struck him, but it had been some time since he'd made Cobryn angry enough for him to strike out. Jacen rubbed his cheek ruefully, awaiting his father's furious tirade.

"You could have ruined everything for us. Do you not realise that? If anyone within the court had known that your marriage was not legitimate, our control over this country could have been lost."

"You would just have given her to Deacon the moment you realised."

"Perhaps I should have done that in the first place!"

"So Deacon could rape a traumatised young girl?" Jacen's voice rose in disgusted rage. He knew that he would get into further trouble for this, but he'd had enough of suppressing his feelings on the matter. "Like you wanted me to do? Like you did to Lilith?"

"*Boy*," Cobryn hissed.

"I don't care what you say, or what Deacon says. I did what I thought was the right thing. If I'd hurt her on our wedding night, I wouldn't have been able to live with myself, knowing I'd broken her even more than you did."

He would regret his words later, but right now, they liberated him. Everything he ever wanted to say to Cobryn now sat before him, no longer bottled up inside. He was frustrated at being pushed about his marriage to Carissa, about fathering a child with her. His father and his uncle saw him as too soft, yet Jacen preferred that to being a beast. Ambition turned men to monsters—especially when that ambition involved women.

Carissa called the cat Jacen got her Soot. He had been pleased by the way the kitten elicited rare smiles from the young Queen, and sometimes those smiles aimed towards him. Their relationship had improved drastically since her birthday. Perhaps she had been hesitant about him, not knowing how he would treat her during their consummation.

Despite his tense standing with Cobryn, Jacen had found some happiness in his marriage. After consummating their marriage, it seemed Carissa found she enjoyed making love to him. It became a regular occurrence, not that Jacen was complaining. They may not care for one another deeply enough for it to be love, but the lust between them never ran short.

Unfortunately, Jacen's time with his wife came to a halt when Cobryn summoned him. The pair had not spoken for days following their argument about the consummation. Jacen knew his father would return to Genera sooner rather than later—his eyes always drifted to the next place he could conquer, and it seemed he'd found his target.

At first it had seemed odd to Jacen that the fall of Basium had been so vastly different to when Harith had been taken—Cobryn had never murdered Harith's entire royal family—but as he grew older, he realised that his father was a spiteful man, and that House Marwan had never angered Cobryn like House Darnell had. The Queen of Harith had been permitted to live because she had grovelled, never having wronged Cobryn in the first place. Patrick had all but spat in Cobryn's face, and that meant certain death—for him and his family.

"My son." By the way Cobryn gripped Jacen's shoulders with paternal affection, he had forgiven any sour words they previously exchanged. "I must return to Genera. With the Island Wars won, we must turn our attention on the next potential threat."

"What threat might that be?" Jacen asked.

"Wendell." Cobryn's lips twisted into a frown. "There have been incursions into Harith, more frequently over the past few months."

You want to put the entire continent of Razmara in its place, Jacen thought bitterly. He'd inherited Genera. He'd taken Harith and Basium. He wondered where his father's greed ended, but he supposed he already knew the answer.

"So, you will crush them too."

"You have much work to do here." Cobryn's brow furrowed as he examined his son. He put so much stock in Jacen, and Jacen often found it difficult to live up to his father's expectations. Vida strived so hard for Cobryn's blessing, while Jacen was granted it almost effortlessly.

"I know, I know." Jacen sighed, knowing where this conversation headed and not wanting to discuss the topic again. "We need a child."

"Not just that." Cobryn folded his arms over his chest. "These rumours of rebellion in Emlen will not do. Perhaps it may be one city for now, but others will follow. I have discussed the matter at length with Deacon."

Of course he had. Surely his uncle's input wasn't required. Couldn't Deacon be of more use in Harith?

"I don't care what Deacon has to say. He isn't King. I am."

"You would do well to heed your uncle's advice," Cobryn admonished, jabbing a stern finger in his son's direction. "We are both concerned about what this resistance could mean. I expect that you will go to Emlen and snuff out this insurrection, just as you did so well during the Island Wars."

Jacen grimaced, turning away. He remembered his role in the Island Wars all too well and hoped it would never need repeating.

"This is what being King is," Cobryn growled. "You douse one fire only for another to ignite. It's never easy. It's not meant to be."

Carissa would never approve of ruthless execution of rebels, but Jacen doubted that his father and uncle cared what she thought. They would silence her protests by whatever means necessary—likely using Miriam, if Deacon did the silencing. While the Queen's grandmother lived, she would be at the mercy of a Morrow.

"I will make sure things don't get out of hand." Jacen raked a hand through his hair. "You can trust me, Father. You did during the Island Wars. It took some time, but I still accomplished the tasks you gave me."

"You are a loyal son." Cobryn pulled him into a tight embrace. "I trust you to maintain the peace here."

"I will not fail you."

As Cobryn nodded, turning to depart the room, Jacen found himself wondering who he would ultimately have to betray. There would come a time when he would have to choose between his wife and his family. Whatever he chose, whatever path he took, he would forever shatter someone's trust in him. Troubled, Jacen sat down heavily and ruminated on the very real possibility that all of this would end in disaster.

It had been a while since Jacen spent a good deal of time with Vida. His sister would soon return to Genera, considering Cobryn planned to wed her to Meryn Pyralis, son and heir of the newly installed Lord Jericho Pyralis of Severino. Jacen could see his sister helping in controlling the Generan islands, and the match with Meryn was a smart one. However, Vida insisted that she intended to stay in Basium until her wedding.

"Carissa has told me the two of you are getting on very well." A knowing smirk played about Vida's lips as she and Jacen took a turn about the gardens. "Perhaps you'll have an heir sooner than expected, and Father and Uncle Deacon can finally stop talking about it."

"Maybe we should focus on your own wedding." Jacen nudged her in the side, revelling in the opportunity to tease her for once. "Meryn Pyralis. That's quite a match, sister. You must be thrilled."

"I will miss Basium," Vida confessed with a dramatic sigh. "Particularly as things are just beginning to get interesting."

"Is that what you call impending war?" Jacen raised his eyebrows.

"It's what I call your impending choice." Vida released her brother's arm, any amusement dropping completely from her voice as she faced him. "I'd urge you to be careful, brother. Carissa might be your wife, but she will never love you as your family does."

Jacen observed her incredulously. Carissa likely wasn't particularly upset about the idea of her people rising against the Morrow family. Was it possible that she actively encouraged it? Surely she would not take such a risk. Maybe Miriam did instead, an old woman with nothing to lose but her own life.

"Carissa is my best friend, but I worry for her." Vida toyed with the hem of her sleeve. "Miriam whispers much in her ear. I fear her grandmother wants retribution, no matter the cost. I fear for Carissa if she is drawn down that path. I know our father would never forgive such a deception."

"What do you think Miriam would convince her to do?" Jacen understood he did not know his wife as well as Vida did, and he hated being forced to rely on his sister's knowledge.

"Miriam acts frail, but she isn't really." Vida shrugged her shoulders. "Everyone knows she's an Imperium. What they don't know is that she's very clever. I think, under her grandmother's influence, Carissa could declare war on Genera."

"She could *what*?" he asked incredulously, alarm coursing through him, shoulders tensing.

War within Basium Jacen understood, and he thought inevitable. But war against Genera? Cobryn was the one who declared the wars, who won the battles. A young woman who'd lost her whole family taking up arms against Cobryn? It could only end in devastation, especially as Carissa had no idea that Cobryn may take Wendell. With two other countries under his control, Basium would be annihilated if they declared war.

"I'm hoping it won't come to that." Vida looked concerned, casting around the gardens to ensure they were alone. "I don't want Carissa getting caught up in her grandmother's push for vengeance."

"We *did* take over her country and kill almost all of her family," Jacen reminded her. Vida had not been present for the Conquest, but he remembered it clearly. "If Carissa was so inclined, I couldn't say that I'd blame her."

"Her anger would certainly be understandable. But war? That's something else entirely, Jacen."

Jacen mulled over his sister's words. He hadn't spent too much time with Miriam, yet he knew how adamantly against his marriage to Carissa she had been. A dangerous word to throw around, war. Could that possibly be what Miriam wanted? She no longer had any power, but Carissa was Basium's Queen, puppet or not.

"Just…be careful." Vida placed a comforting hand on his arm. "I don't want to see you chewed up and spat back out. I know you well enough to realise you care about her, even if you don't love her."

"She's my wife. Shouldn't I care about her?" Jacen exhaled deeply, drawing away from Vida. Everyone in his family disapproved that he and Carissa got on, that while their relationship was based on mutual understanding and lust rather than love, it worked. Cobryn wanted them to work together, didn't he?

"She and Bellona are my closest friends," Vida admitted. "I've come to care about them deeply in the years I've been here, it is true. The stakes are not as high for me. If she had you wrapped around her little finger, Carissa could convince you to do anything she wanted—even go against your own family."

Jacen thought Vida was being dramatic, as his sister was prone to such antics. A friendly and effervescent young woman, there were times when he saw hints of Deacon in her. She may never admit it, but Vida was more like their uncle than she realised.

He got to know Carissa better every day. She wasn't a woman who wanted bloodshed and violence. She wanted to recover from the horrors of the past, not repeat them. Jacen could only hope that ultimately, he was right about Carissa and Vida exaggerated. No matter Miriam's influence, he wanted her to be better than that, to strive for something more.

The inevitability of war was a harsh reality they needed to face. It would strike swiftly as lightning—the only question was *where*. Tensions already rose in Basium. To believe Carissa would turn her back on her protesting people was naïve.

THE REBELLIOUS QUEEN
CARISSA DARNELL

"I have called you here because you must account for your people."

The flames in the hearth licked greedily at the wood as Deacon stared into its depths. Carissa had been astonished that the meeting consisted only of her, Deacon, Vida and Jacen. Even Bellona had not been permitted to attend—which left her irritated to no end, particularly considering Kato's return to Theron.

Vida stood by the doorway, her expression troubled. Jacen lounged in a chair with a languid grace that would have had convinced Carissa he was bored if not for the grimness in his eyes. Deacon was the most agitated—judging by his words, Carissa could hazard a guess as to why. Emlen had not backed down in the least. If anything, reports of rebellion had increased. The leader of the resistance revealed to be a man named Quintin Faustus, allegedly supported by Lord Ambrose.

"I certainly didn't encourage this, if that's what you mean." Carissa planted her hands on her hips, her cool tone indicating her displeasure at the accusation in Deacon's voice.

"Nonetheless it must be dealt with, and swiftly." He spun to face her. "Within the next few days, you will make an announcement condemning this rebellion, and assure the country there will be consequences for those who join— and rewards for those who show loyalty."

Jacen's brow furrowed at Deacon's commands. Carissa merely examined him calmly. He thought he dictated how things went in Basium? Jacen was the King and Carissa was the Queen. Deacon was nothing but the King's uncle and a man who once held power here.

"No."

Carissa knew of the damage that would be done if she did as Deacon instructed. She would turn her people against her forever. They would never trust a Queen who would act as a mouthpiece for the enemy. Basium could not truly be subdued, and it was time the Morrow family learned that for themselves—the hard way, if necessary.

Deacon stepped forward, eyes narrowing. "Excuse me?"

"I said no." Carissa's voice rang through the meeting room as she moved over to stand right in front of Deacon. Once upon a time, she had been the easily intimidated little girl who obeyed his every command. Now, with Jacen by her side, with the knowledge of her power, she found her resolve growing stronger. She tilted her chin up defiantly, daring Deacon to make the next move.

"Your Majesty." Deacon ground the words out, his eyes flashing danger as he tried to pull together the last shreds of his composure. "You must understand how vital this is. Civil war would only tear this country, your country, apart."

"No, I don't think that's it." Carissa smirked in his face. She played a lethal game, but she enjoyed every moment of it, fearless and not thinking of potential consequences. "I believe you are thinking of Genera, not Basium. How unfortunate if you were to lose control, especially of something you've been working on for the past few years. You don't own Basium, Deacon, and you don't own me."

A nerve twitched in his jaw, the only warning before Deacon lost his temper, stepping forward and grabbing her by the throat. Jacen was on his feet in an instant, Vida emitting an audible gasp. Carissa's smugness never faded, having elicited the reaction she anticipated. Deacon remained patient and calm—until he had no control.

"Deacon," Jacen warned.

"Carissa needs to understand the situation." Deacon bared his teeth, voice low and deadly. "She is alive because of our family's good graces. She would be unwise to risk changing her position."

"You need me." Hoarse but strong, the words tumbled from her mouth. "Or else you would have already done away with me."

Deacon snarled, and coldness seeped from his fingers into her neck. Carissa had seen a few small displays of power from Deacon, but he preferred to keep his abilities hidden until he needed them. Now, he would use his gifts in an attempt to force her into accepting his will. Sometimes he might have been manipulative and typically civil, but he had always been a bully. She choked at the chilly sting of the ice against her skin.

Would this be the moment she unleashed her own terrible power? Her nails dug hard into the palms of her hands. All it would take was a single drop of blood, and she could show Deacon a true force to be reckoned with. A tempting prospect, the idea of lashing out against the man who'd oppressed her for years. The darkness beckoned her, and she considered letting it free.

"That's enough." Jacen grabbed Deacon's arm and wrenched him away from Carissa. She stumbled at the sudden loss of contact, tracing the parts of her neck where Deacon started freezing her skin. Deacon looked unimpressed, but Jacen pushed him again, fisting his hands in the fabric of his uncle's shirt. "If you touch her again, you'll answer to me."

"So protective," Deacon sneered.

"I am the King, not you," Jacen reminded him—a fact Deacon seemed all too happy to ignore. "Your time of making the choices is done. Now, you can stay in Basium and aid in putting out the fire you and Cobryn started, or you can return to Genera. Carissa does not have to tell her people what they can and can't do."

Deacon tugged away from him, shooting Carissa a furious look before marching from the room. Vida, who had remained unusually silent throughout the confrontation, walked over to inspect Carissa's neck.

"You shouldn't have baited him."

"Perhaps not," Carissa admitted. Her neck hurt, but Deacon had not iced her deeply enough to cause permanent damage. Some bruising maybe, yet that was all. "But it felt good to put him in his place."

"Don't let power get to your head," Vida warned, spinning on her heel and following her uncle from the meeting room.

Was that what happened? Was Carissa becoming just as obsessed with power and control as people like Cobryn and Deacon? That wasn't what she wanted. She believed in her people having free will, the choice of whether they wanted a Morrow monarch or not. More than that—whether they wanted *her* as a monarch. As much as she wanted to convince them she tried her best, she would not punish them for mocking her or calling her a puppet.

Jacen locked the door behind his sister, the sharp snap making Carissa glance at him as he crossed over to her. With gentle fingers, he swept her dark hair back from her neck to look at the bruises Deacon had left. His fingers were pleasantly warm against her skin. Carissa observed her husband closely. His uncle's magical violence had caused some concern within him.

"Is there a reason you've locked us in here?"

"I didn't want them coming back." Jacen heaved a sigh. "You shouldn't have to make any decrees you don't agree or feel comfortable with."

"Yes, well." Carissa smiled wryly. "Apparently you've missed quite a bit while you've been away."

"It won't be like that anymore," Jacen promised, sweeping a strand of Carissa's hair behind her ear and looking at her with something she could only describe as tenderness. "I am the King of Basium. You are my wife and Queen. Deacon will not harm you."

How little Jacen understood the stakes, the political struggle. If he believed Deacon would surrender control simply because he was not King by name, then he didn't know his uncle. She simply offered him a tight smile.

"I wish I could believe that."

Jacen leaned in and pressed his lips against hers. Once she had responded with hesitation but now Carissa's body betrayed her, and she melted against him. However complicated their relationship might be, this part at least was simple. Her arms slipped around his neck, tugging him closer against her. He might be many things, but right now, he was her protector—and she was grateful for that, no matter Miriam's doubts.

Jacen's lips and hands against her skin made the heat of desire swell within her. He pressed her back against the table, his lips descending down the slender column of her neck—more carefully than usual due to the damage Deacon had done there.

Carissa's breaths quickened as Jacen's fingers yanked at the laces of her dress. It came undone with little effort, baring her corset and the swell of her breasts. Jacen hoisted her up and set on the table, hands snaking up to push her dress up her legs. She caught his wrists, heart hammering in her chest. Whatever she had anticipated happening in the meeting room, it hadn't been *this*.

"On the table?" Carissa raised her eyebrows but a thrill of daring came over her.

"The door's locked," Jacen reminded her, a mischievous gleam in his hazel eyes. He pressed his lips to hers once more, and she laughed against his mouth.

Carissa wrapped her legs around his waist to pull him closer. She wanted him desperately but didn't want to confess to desire making her so weak. Nonetheless, her lust must have burned deep in her eyes.

Jacen ran a hand up her leg as she reached out to undo his pants with fumbling fingers. He positioned himself between her legs, gripping her thighs and pulling her closer. She could feel his hardness pressed against her and she squirmed. By now the heat between her legs was a familiar sensation when it came to Jacen.

It could be easy to forget what they were. To pretend they were just a boy and a girl who craved each other, a normal married couple. Yet Carissa remembered the Conquest every day—while Jacen was good to her, she could not trust him to put her before his family. These early days of marital bliss made Carissa giddy—but she did not forget, and she certainly did not forgive.

Carissa winced as Bellona dabbed at the bruises on her neck with a soothing paste. She insisted she was fine, but Bellona sat her down and started applying the salve regardless. Her friend's touch was not as gentle as Vida's, a livid expression twisting her face.

"I can't believe Uncle Deacon hurt you." Vida stood nearby, wringing her hands and observing the pair of them with apprehensive eyes. After her comment about power, Carissa had been reluctant to speak to her, but Vida appeared apologetic.

Bellona looked up from her task, putting the paste down and glaring across at Vida. Carissa could sense the tension between them.

"Really? You can't believe it, or are you just ignorant?"

Vida blinked a few times. "Excuse me?"

"Your uncle is a monster." Bellona snapped, gesturing to Carissa's bruised neck. "Has it somehow escaped your notice the way he has treated the Queen all these years? Or do you give him leeway to act as such because he's your *beloved* uncle?"

"He has never lashed out at her before now!" Vida exclaimed, indignant.

"So, unless it's physical violence, it's not abuse?" Bellona demanded, her hands balling into fists. It was amusing, the fact that Vida had almost half a foot on Bellona, and yet she was the one on the defensive.

"Bellona," Carissa warned, her tone weary. Soot prowled by her feet, nosing curiously at her ankle. She reached down to scratch behind his ears.

Her friend ignored her. "You do know that your uncle has intimidated Carissa at every opportunity, insinuated he'd like nothing more than to dissolve her marriage to Jacen and force himself on her?"

Vida gasped. "Deacon would never—"

"Yes, he would." Bellona hissed the words, causing Vida to lapse into a stunned silence. Perhaps she had noticed some things here and there, but Carissa knew he would be on his best behaviour around his niece. The truth of Deacon's attitude toward Carissa was difficult for Vida to acknowledge.

"It doesn't matter!" Carissa pushed herself to her feet, her volume making Soot scamper under the bed. She would not see her two best friends pitted against each other over this. She could understand both Vida's disbelief and Bellona's outrage. She glowered between them. "It doesn't matter, because I'm not afraid of Deacon."

Bellona made an exasperated noise. "Carissa—"

"You saw his abilities today," Vida pointed out, eyes wide. "That's just a taste of what he's capable of."

"I have abilities of my own." The uneasy quiet that followed was painful as Carissa awaited the verdict of her best friends. Vida looked stunned, while a knowing smile played about the corners of Bellona's lips.

"Abilities?" Vida repeated, crossing over to her friend with a look of fascinated horror across her face. "You're a Primordial? I mean, what the Basiumites would call Imperium?"

"No." Carissa swallowed hard, ignoring the knot of tension growing in the pit of her stomach. Not knowing how her friends would react made Carissa's skin wash cold, nausea rising into her throat. Miriam was the only person who knew the truth, so she gambled a lot in revealing it. "I am Maleficium."

Taking a deep breath to steady herself, she crossed over to the mantlepiece and picked up the knife she'd left from the previous night's supper. After a moment of hesitation, she sliced across her palm. She winced at the sharp sting. Carissa looked at her watchful, cautious friends. She waited until the stickiness of blood coated her fingers, until the dark magic responded to her call.

Carissa's nightgown rose from where Bellona had placed it on the bed, drifting into the air like an eerie ghost. Bellona pressed her hands over her mouth, while awe sparkled in Vida's eyes as she watched the nightgown ascend toward the chandelier. Before the magic could become volatile, before the magic tempted her to do far worse, Carissa let the nightgown drop back onto the bed.

"You're a blood mage," Bellona whispered, earning a hesitant nod from Carissa. "Who else knows about this?"

"Only Miriam, and you're both sworn to secrecy." Carissa looked firmly between them. "This is a matter of life and death. No one else can know I'm Maleficium, especially not Deacon."

It was liberating to unburden herself to her two best friends, whose opinions she valued most. Bellona was astonished but offered no further commentary. Vida walked over and swept Carissa into a tight embrace. Carissa wrapped her good arm around her friend, not wanting to spill blood on Vida's dress.

"I can't imagine what it's been like to carry that sort of secret." Vida drew back and took Carissa's bloody hand in her clean ones, clasping it tightly. "But you don't have to anymore. You have us."

Carissa's heart swelled with love for them as Bellona approached and placed her hands over Vida's. A pact between them. The support of her friends overwhelmed her. It had been more than she'd hoped for, and it made her realise how lucky she was to have them.

THE TROUBLED KING
JACEN MORROW

Jacen rapped his knuckles against his uncle's door with a sense of purpose. He was done with Deacon's attempts to control Carissa. He had been frustrated about them for some time, but Deacon had gone too far when he used his magic on her. Jacen anticipated having to protect Carissa from his family, yet it was Cobryn that Jacen had been worried about.

"Ah, Nephew." The door opened to Deacon's wry smile, and Jacen fought the urge to punch him in the face.

"I believe the correct form of address is 'Your Majesty' or 'my King.'"

"But you aren't my King." Deacon swung the door open wider, allowing Jacen to stride into the room. "No matter my position here, I am Generan. I answer to Cobryn alone."

"Not when it comes to matters regarding Basium, or my wife." Jacen rounded on Deacon as the door clicked shut. His uncle at least had the decency to look remorseful, his shoulders slumping in defeat.

"I admit that was…not one of my better moments." Deacon strode over to the hearth and indicated the seats and the silver pitcher of wine. "Please, sit."

Jacen did so, pouring himself a glass of wine without asking. Perhaps Deacon had realised the error of his ways. Jacen doubted it, yet it may do some good to have a discussion with his uncle. There had been arguments between them, and the last thing Jacen wanted was to fight family.

"Did your father ever tell you much about our childhood?" Deacon sprawled on the seat beside his nephew, retrieving his half-finished goblet of wine.

Jacen shook his head, not understanding how the topic was relevant.

"No."

"It doesn't surprise me." Deacon took a slow sip from his goblet. "Our father was a different sort of King. He ruled through fear. But our father did not want to expand, did not want to change laws. He was a rigidly traditional man. He was also a brute, not only to Cobryn and I, but to Relda as well."

Jacen shifted in his seat at the mention of his aunt. He had not seen her in many years, as she had been placed in Harith to preside over the newest part of Cobryn's growing empire. She favoured Cobryn more in terms of appearance but was closer to Deacon in age. That was about all he could recall of Relda from the scant childhood memories he had of her.

"I recall the worst incident of all clearly. Your parents had just announced their betrothal, and our father was pushing for Relda to marry. She would have been perhaps fourteen or fifteen. I was ten or eleven, and she convinced me to prank some of her suitors so they wouldn't want anything to do with her."

Jacen wondered why he had never heard this story in the past, yet Cobryn had rarely mentioned his own parents. They had both been dead by the time Jacen had been born, so he hadn't had the opportunity to get to know his grandparents. Judging by the way Deacon spoke about his grandfather, that was for the best.

"I was a little terror, and I delighted in carrying out her request. One of the suitors, a man twice her age, ended up falling into the fishpond. He stalked off, sopping wet, to summon our father—who was enraged. I remember he marched down to the fishpond and dismissed the servants, while Relda and I couldn't stop laughing at how ridiculous her suitor had looked."

"Did he beat you?" Jacen asked. It wouldn't have surprised him. No wonder Cobryn had been known to raise a hand if he became enraged, considering he'd received the same treatment as a child.

"No. Worse." Deacon swilled his wine, looking into the fire. "He grabbed Relda by the hair and held her underwater. He pulled her back up just long enough for her to breathe before shoving her back beneath the water. She was crying and begging him to stop. I was completely frozen. That was when Cobryn came down to the gardens and pushed our father hard enough that he hit his head on the stone ledge of the fishpond. He died immediately. The three of us swore to tell the same story—that he'd slipped and fallen."

"Did everyone believe that?" Jacen asked. In truth, he waited for the part where Deacon explained the relevance of the story. He highly doubted his uncle would divulge such a personal piece of his past—a past Cobryn never talked about—if not for some reason.

"Of course they didn't, but they could never prove otherwise." Deacon set down his goblet with a thud. "I watched as my father almost drowned my sister. After that day, I swore I would never be a bystander or a victim again. I would never stand idly by and allow things I could control slip through my fingers."

"You mean Emlen." Jacen tensed, knowing this discussion had been leading up to the growing resistance. "If this is about forcing Carissa to speak up against what's happening—"

"No. I regret losing my temper with her." Deacon's eyes glinted in the firelight as he observed his nephew. "I want you to be careful around her, Jacen."

Jacen pinched the bridge of his nose. This was the second family member to have said something like this. He wondered if Deacon and Vida had discussed the matter. Why were they so concerned that Carissa would take advantage of him?

"Deacon—"

"I know, you know her better." Deacon raised his hands defensively. "But never forget, to her we are still the enemy. Even you. She might allow you into her bed, that doesn't mean she trusts you. Don't let your lust and a pretty face cloud your judgement."

How would Carissa betray him? They were married. All of their actions reflected on each other. Unless Deacon meant that Carissa would kill him, which Jacen thought absurd. His wife was a great deal of things, but a murderer was not one of them. There were far easier solutions to get him out of her life, including the fact that she could have chosen not to consummate the marriage once Deacon discovered the truth.

"I'm not a fool." Jacen got to his feet. He didn't need to talk about this, not again. He may not have known his wife for as long as Deacon and Vida, but he knew her more intimately.

"No, you are smart." Deacon rose as well. "Yet you are compassionate, more so than most within our family. You pity Carissa for the loss of her family, and it will be your downfall."

"Good night, Deacon," Jacen said firmly. He crossed over to the door and wrenched it open, before glancing over his shoulder at Deacon, who remained by the hearth. "I expect you to apologise to Carissa for your behaviour."

Closing the door behind him, Jacen raked his hand through his hair, his palms clammy. Although he wanted to believe Carissa wouldn't turn on him, what stood in her way? That hint of doubt, created by Deacon and Vida's words, made him question how well he knew his wife—and more importantly, her capabilities.

Only one person knew Carissa far better than anyone else. The woman who hated the Morrow family with her entire being and might convince Carissa that going up against them was inevitable. Miriam could either push Carissa toward war, or she could talk her out of it. Either way, the situation remained the same—Jacen needed to speak with Miriam Darnell.

If people like Deacon used and manipulated Carissa, her grandmother experienced that fate tenfold. According to Deacon, they brought in Miriam often to patch up the injured nobility after tournaments or jousts. As a test, he once forced her to heal wounds he'd sustained during a hunt. How the woman must have hated him, one of the men who'd destroyed her family making her his personal healer.

Jacen stepped into Miriam's rooms, uncertain. He remembered the first time he'd encountered her, when she'd been standing over the butchered body of Carissa's mother Imogen. Jacen might have been a lost boy to her once, but now that he was King, he embodied everything she hated. Nonetheless, she dipped into a stiff but respectful curtsy upon his entry.

"Your Majesty."

"You don't have to call me that." The words were like knives when they came from Miriam. They stabbed and twisted in beneath his skin. "It's just Jacen."

"How can I help you, Jacen?" Miriam clasped her hands together demurely, but her eyes were full of fire. "Does someone need an herbal remedy, or a wound healed? Or would they like to know their future?"

"None of those." Jacen leaned against the wall, folding his arms over his chest. Miriam had been turned into a laughingstock, her granddaughter into Genera's pawn. Miriam loved Carissa fiercely and would do anything to protect her. "I've come to talk to you about Carissa."

"My granddaughter?" Miriam brow creased. "What is it you wish to discuss?"

"My family thinks I should be wary of her." Jacen cast his gaze around before deciding he didn't feel comfortable enough to take a seat. "I wanted your opinion on that."

Miriam burst out laughing, and Jacen's cheeks flared with heat. He had been wrong to come here, wrong to speak to Miriam about Carissa. What had he expected, that she would divulge everything she knew about her granddaughter? No, Miriam was too used to men like Deacon—men who sniffed around for any sign of weakness and then exploited it.

"Carissa has survived the deaths of almost her entire family. She has survived being forced into becoming Queen at fourteen years old. She has survived your predatory uncle and his manipulations. Of course you should be wary of her."

"You've seen something." Jacen had been told that Miriam caught glimpses of the future—that she'd warned her husband Patrick about the Conquest. By the way Miriam's laughter died, he knew he was right. "What have you seen?"

"Your conflict," Miriam said, her voice lacking amusement. "You don't know whether to choose her, or your family. Indecision is weakness, Jacen, especially for a King. Playing both sides will only work for so long before the decision is thrust upon you."

A deep sense of unease overcame Jacen at how much Miriam knew about him. He shifted his feet, uncertain how to respond. She was right—he was not doing a good job as King. He hadn't even attended one proper council meeting. He usually left that to Carissa. Perhaps it would be better if they were both present. He had wanted them to work together, after all.

If Carissa decided to wage war on Genera, where would that leave Jacen? He was her husband and the King of Basium. Cobryn thought it wise to install his only son in a foreign seat of power, yet Jacen thought that might have been a mistake. The more he got to know Carissa, the more time he spent with the Basiumite court, the more he began to think of it as home.

"You want your future?" Miriam gestured to an empty chair beside the bed. "Take a seat and give me your hand."

"M-my hand?" Jacen stammered as he sank into the chair. He'd believed that Miriam could see the future regardless. He watched with dread as the woman crossed over to him, despite the fact he had almost a foot on her.

"Yes. It helps pinpoint my visions to the individual that I have contact with."

Jacen hesitated before holding out his hand. Miriam took it in hers, closing her eyes and concentrating. Jacen waited impatiently for her verdict. He was not magical himself, and Deacon's magic differed from Miriam's. The woman gasped and lurched away from him, eyes snapping open.

"What?" Jacen's heart thundered in his chest as he took in her shock. "What did you see?"

"A bloody sword in your hand." Miriam wrung her trembling hands. "You were standing in the courtyard. There is war and violence in your future, Jacen, mark my words."

"The future is always changing," Jacen argued. He didn't want to believe that. He didn't want to think that some day he might not be any better than Cobryn.

Miriam gave him a grim smile. "My husband thought the same. He was brutally murdered in the same way I'd foreseen. Yes, the future changes. But to dismiss such visions as though they would not happen is foolish."

Carissa had the cat on the bed and stroked his fur when Jacen entered the room. Soot leapt off the blankets and onto the floor while Carissa got to her feet and approached her husband. Once she had simply turned on her side and ignored him, but she didn't seem to mind interacting with him a little more. Jacen's gaze raked over her, garbed only in her thin nightgown, dark hair falling in waves around her face. *What a beautiful woman.*

"You look shaken," she remarked, leaning in to kiss him.

Jacen drew back, shaking his head. "I just want to lie down."

Since their consummation, Carissa had been quick to offer up her body. How much did he really know about her? He wanted his wife to be more than just a trophy, more than just a means for children and someone to warm his bed at night. Carissa had slipped into the role of doting wife for her own survival.

Carissa tilted her head to the side curiously but offered no comment as Jacen crossed over to flop down on the bed. Miriam's vision of his future had admittedly shaken him. All this time he'd strived to prove himself a better man than Cobryn or Deacon, but what if he was just as bad? What if he turned out to be worse?

Carissa approached the bed cautiously, sitting down beside Jacen and crossing her legs. For a few moments, silence stretched between them. Could she be Imperium, as Deacon suspected? If she was and hadn't told him, it indicated that she didn't trust him, and she could fear how her magic would be used if it was revealed.

"You don't want to talk?" Accusation edged her tone.

"What is there to discuss? Emlen? The fact that it feels everyone in this damn court is hiding things from me?" Frustration coloured Jacen's tone despite his best efforts. "It's not worth discussing."

"You can't expect the court or the council to have blind faith," Carissa chastised, reaching out to caress his hair. "The council doesn't even trust me, as we've plainly seen. There will always be those who dissent. They're allowed to."

"Especially if their Queen allows it." Jacen caught her wrist before she could touch him. Carissa had worn a mask during his masquerade ball, but the real mask was the one she hadn't taken off around him since—the façade of being the good and obedient wife.

Carissa frowned. "What are you talking about?"

"You seem to be very good at doing nothing." Jacen rolled her onto her back, pinning her wrists either side of her head. "You haven't supported Emlen, yet you won't condemn them. Where do you really stand, Carissa? The only enthusiasm you've shown is in bed, and I wonder if even that is an act."

Carissa squirmed angrily against him. He knew he was being unfair, though for some reason he couldn't bring himself to care. He had been quite open with Carissa, but she stayed closed off to him. She divulged parts of herself here and there, yet otherwise remained an enigma.

"I didn't realise Deacon whispering poisonous words in your ear would have you believing anything he said."

"Who said I'd been talking to Deacon?" Jacen's temper flared because she was right in suspecting his uncle. She kept up her attempts to evade him. He held her pinned to the bed. "I'm not naïve enough to believe everything my family tells me. You seem to need Miriam to tell you every step to take."

"I assumed Deacon because right now, you're acting just like him," Carissa spat.

She's right. Shame flooded his cheeks and Jacen released her, sitting back. His uncle had lashed out in frustration at Carissa, and he had proven himself little better. No wonder she couldn't trust him when, instead of speaking to her about his suspicions, he made blatant accusations and insulted her. He rested a hand on her shoulder as she sat up, ridden with guilt.

"Carissa—"

"Don't touch me." She jerked away from him, as she had every right to. Regardless of her indecisions, of what her stance truly was, Jacen had no need to mistreat her. The jab about being like Deacon was a cruel barb, but a brutal truth. "I don't need to justify my decisions, or lack thereof, to a man who can barely call himself King. You were given a wife and a country. I had everything taken from me."

Jacen couldn't object to that. He had forgotten how much Carissa had lost, forgotten how she'd come to be Queen in the first place as a girl of fourteen. He had placed his frustrations and indecisions on her shoulders when she had more than enough to bear. He wanted to offer an apology. She wouldn't accept it. How could he atone for what had been done to her?

Something had to be done about Emlen, one way or another. Sitting in Marinel and deliberating it caused tension. He had promised Cobryn he would prevent things getting out of hand. Perhaps it was time to call a council meeting and decide on their best course of action.

"I declare a royal tour." Carissa clambered off the bed and planted her hands on her hips, glaring down at him. "We will visit the major cities, as is generally custom for new monarchs after their coronation. Which, as you can imagine, did not occur after mine."

She may as well have hit him across the face—the words struck him hard. Jacen had been too busy thinking about himself, what might happen to him, that he hadn't considered how much Carissa had missed. It seemed that Basiumite traditions had already been butchered, even if Jacen strived to preserve them.

"Considering Emlen—"

"Our presence will be most important there." Carissa picked up a cloak and draped it around her shoulders. "Now, if you'll excuse me."

She swept from the room before Jacen could say anything else, leaving him with a heaviness in the pit of his stomach. This was his fault. Just when he and Carissa had started to form a sort of relationship, he had to go and ruin everything. Jacen lay back against the pillows. Hours dragged by before his mind quieted enough for sleep to take him.

THE VOYAGER QUEEN
CARISSA DARNELL

Preparations for the impending royal tour were underway, and Carissa's stomach tied itself into knots. She and Jacen had been at odds since their argument about her indecisiveness, and she didn't believe their tension would be a good thing during the tour. It was stubborn to refuse him forgiveness, but Jacen had to earn it first.

It also troubled Carissa that Miriam would not accompany them on the tour. She had been pleased to learn Bellona and Vida had both accepted her invitation, yet Miriam had stated her preference for staying in Marinel. The evening before their departure, Carissa went to visit her grandmother, aware it would be at least a month before she saw Miriam again.

"I wish you would come with us, Grandmother." Carissa placed Soot down and watched the cat scamper over to Miriam. She couldn't bring him with her on the tour, and she had made Miriam aware the cat would need attention during her absence. "I could use your guidance."

"You are a grown woman now." Miriam reached down to stroke the cat's dark fur. "Besides, you will have company. One day, I won't be here to offer advice anymore. You will have to learn to do things without coming to me."

"Don't talk like that." Carissa shook her head slowly. Although her grandmother spoke the truth, it would be a dark day indeed when she finally lost Miriam. Her grandmother had been a fundamental part of her life, her reign. She could never have gotten this far without Miriam.

"Do you love him?" Miriam eased herself up from where she pet the cat to fix Carissa with a serious look. They both knew precisely who she referred to, the matter even being in question made Carissa uneasy. She shook her head vigorously.

"No. I care about him, but love is something else entirely. I don't know if I ever could love him."

Jacen's family, and the fact his father was the Warmonger, would always overshadow everything else. Carissa remembered the first time she'd seen Jacen, when she'd been on her knees in the gardens, watching her family members being slaughtered one by one. He'd appeared sickened by the violence, but he'd never done a thing to stop it. Perhaps that would always be too much to expect—for Jacen to be anything more than a bystander in his father's crimes.

"You need to be careful during this tour." Miriam took Carissa's hands in her own. "If you give the people any reason to suspect you're simply doing the bidding of the Morrows…"

"I know." Carissa snatched her hands back. This conversation exhausted her. It was always 'be careful'. If Miriam wanted her to figure things out for herself, she needed to be more than cautious. She would give the people something dangerous, something they needed: hope.

It had taken Carissa some time to come to terms with how she wanted to approach the resistance. It had been Jacen's mockery on her indecision that made the cogs of her mind turn. Although she feared what her husband might think, her loyalty to her people came first.

She was not the only one who had suffered during and after the Conquest. Deacon may act as though he had done them favours, but Carissa knew of how hard things had hit her people. Many of them had been enslaved, forced to come to Marinel to rebuild the broken city and to work in the Generan mountain mines.

Others suspected to be loyal to the Darnell family had been cast out, displaced to make room for Generan spies. The people had reasons to hate the Morrow family that had nothing to do with the slaughter of their former King.

"I'm going to take back Basium," Carissa said, soft but strong. "With or without Jacen's help."

Miriam's expression brightened as she inspected her granddaughter. Was this what she had wanted? It didn't matter, because Carissa knew she had made the right choice. The choice would lead to hardship and struggles, but being a Queen was not meant to be easy.

"It will be difficult. There will be a fight and if that doesn't simmer down, possibly even a war."

"I'm aware." Carissa felt invigorated. It had been a nerve-wracking thought just months before, but how long was she expected to play the dutiful wife before she got tired of that game? She had been the passive monarch long enough. She had let Deacon dictate matters and intimidate her, but no longer.

"Make allies during the tour." Miriam stepped forward and kissed her granddaughter's cheek. "I know you will make your parents proud. You are stronger than you give yourself credit for."

Miriam's words made her swell with confidence. The Morrow family underestimated her. They saw a broken girl, a Queen they shaped with no say in how her own country was run. Carissa would prove she was more than that. Like the Darnell monarchs who had come before her, she would fight for what she believed in.

Carissa stood vigilant in front of her tent and observed the lights of Marinel in the distance. It had been many years since she had left the capital, and under very different circumstances. They had ventured to Theron to celebrate the coming of age of Theodore, Carissa's oldest brother. She must have been around eleven at the time. It seemed a lifetime ago, although Carissa vividly remembered some parts of the journey.

Theodore basking in all of the attention despite teasing from his younger siblings. Peregrine getting drunk after convincing Theodore to sneak him some ale. Sebastian accidentally setting one of Theodore's best shirts on fire. Carissa vaguely recalled other antics, not precisely what had happened, but that they'd caused her to laugh so hard her stomach hurt. Her brothers had always been able to elicit that sort of amusement from her.

The thought of it pained her, the knowledge that this journey was hers alone. It should have been Theodore here with the swan crown upon his head. He'd have a wife and a child by now. Instead Deacon had cut off his head and tossed it dismissively to the ground in front of his family in an act of sheer cruelty.

Peregrine and Bellona would have been married by now. They'd have greeted Theodore in Theron, the two brothers embracing and ruffling each other's hair with ridiculous grins spreading across their faces. Bellona would have looked at Carissa knowingly and rolled her eyes, but she would have been smiling too.

Sebastian…little Sebastian. He would be fifteen now, with his birthday coming up in under a month. He would listen to their father's spiel about getting married in the near future, pulling faces behind Frederick's back while Carissa tried to stifle her giggles.

The idea of what could have been agonised her. Carissa pressed a hand over her mouth to hold back a sob, tears streaming down her cheeks. The distant lights of Marinel blurred as Carissa reached up to wipe her eyes. She once saw tears as a weakness, before Miriam had taught her she could weaponise them.

Her vengeance would not just be for her family. It would also be for her people. If this was just about her, she might be able to live a happy little lie with Jacen, but it wasn't. The people of Basium deserved to be free of oppression, and Carissa planned to give them that.

"Carissa?" Jacen's concerned voice drew her from her reverie, but she made no attempt to disguise her tears as she spun to face him. She would save her false smiles for the noble families and the court. Around her husband, she could afford to show weakness—for now at least.

"It brings back memories," Carissa murmured.

Jacen frowned. "Bad memories?"

"Worse, good ones." Carissa let him put his arms around her, let him hold her close. She buried her face in the front of his shirt. Warmth radiated from his chest, soothing her. How he would hate her if he knew what she truly planned.

How could she explain such extreme loss to someone who had never experienced it? She dismissed waking herself up in the night, crying out, as nightmares. She was certain that while Jacen may attempt to comfort her, he would never understand what she had been through, what she still went through.

Bellona did. When she wanted to talk about the traumas of the past, it was Bellona she went to. Bellona's mother had been raped and murdered by Generan soldiers. Bellona rarely spoke of it, though it was obvious the event haunted her.

This tour would change everything. Carissa would, after four years, be able to connect with the people who had suffered under Morrow rule. She would be able to get an understanding of how they felt about Deacon and Jacen, not to mention Cobryn. Unfortunately, it would mean getting to know how they felt about her—and not every response would be positive.

She feared going to Emlen the most and she was filled with small amount of anxiety associated with the fact that it was the last on their list. House Ambrose had permitted their visit, but Carissa didn't think they would go beyond civility. She wondered what cause Lord Ambrose had to hate her and resolved to ask him when she reached Emlen.

"You should come inside." Jacen took her hand and led her into their tent. "It's beginning to get cold."

Carissa took a deep breath as she slipped into bed. It was her first time away from Miriam since the loss of their family. While she wanted to believe herself capable, knowing she had no security net left her vulnerable. What would happen if she lost control of her magic? Her grandmother would not be there to save the day. The thought terrified her.

"Do you know much about Lord Benedict?" Jacen asked as he slipped into bed beside her. He referred to the Lord of Fortua, the first city they would visit.

"A little." Carissa barely recalled Tiago Benedict, although Miriam disapproved of the man. He had been to court a scarce few times since her coronation, yet his dealings had mainly been with Deacon. She did not know if he could be trusted, but she intended to find out.

She allowed Jacen to drape his arm loosely around her waist. At first, she had not permitted him to touch her when they went to sleep, but she had grown comfortable around him since. Some part of her craved the intimacy that her relationship with Jacen provided, although she felt guilty at times. How could she want a man whose family had destroyed her? How could she enjoy having sex with him, and eventually bear the grandchild of the Warmonger?

How could she expect things to be easy between them, given the history of their families? Closing her eyes, she allowed herself a faint smile at his fingers softly brushing her hair back in a rhythmic motion. This marriage would never be simple, but that didn't mean every part of it had to be difficult.

When the men grew restless, Deacon proposed a hunt. Bellona wanted to accompany them, but Carissa—fearing some 'accident' could befall her best friend by Deacon's hand—forbade it. Bellona was not impressed but agreed to stay at the camp with those who did not wish to hunt.

Hunting in the Gracewood—the woods between Marinel and Fortua—was said to bring ill luck. Even the royal hunting parties had ranged north in the past, unwilling to risk the superstitions being correct. Of course, Carissa did not mention this to Deacon. She thought she would like it if her husband's uncle met a bad fate.

By the time the men returned, Deacon seemed to be fairly drunk, staggering as he slipped off his horse. He requested more ale as he crossed over to the fire where Carissa sat warming her hands. How she wished she could somehow take advantage of his inebriated state—poison him, push him into the flames. Unfortunately, everything she did would endanger not only her, but Miriam.

Carissa watched in silence as some of the men set to work skinning the deer they'd managed to shoot. The sound of the wood crackling in the fire broke when Deacon decided to speak.

"I must say, you seem uncomfortable with this journey." Leaning back, he arched his eyebrows. "Could it be that travel does not agree with you, Majesty?"

"It could be the company," Carissa replied coolly, aware of Vida's fingers encircling and tightening around her wrist in a wordless warning. Yet where once she had feared speaking up against Deacon, she had grown bolder. She was not a frightened child in a powerful man's shadow. She was Queen of Basium, and Deacon clung to power by a thread.

"You know, we have a custom in Genera." Deacon's eyes glittered with malice as he stared across the fire at Carissa. "Related to the bedding ceremony after a wedding."

"Oh, Deacon, don't," Vida protested.

Carissa cast around for Jacen, who usually would have spoken up against his uncle by this point. Her husband was nowhere to be found. She wondered if he had gone to change into clean clothes.

"The consummation of the wedding is witnessed in Genera." Deacon eased himself to his feet, gazing down upon the fuming Queen. "It's traditional, to ensure the marriage is legal. Quite useful, don't you think?"

Carissa clenched her jaw, the urge to lash out at him rising. She wasn't certain who among the party would catch onto the implications, but she despised him for hinting at the fact that she and Jacen had not consummated their marriage on their wedding night. Shrugging Vida off, she pushed herself up and marched over to her smirking nemesis, planting her hands on her hips.

"I don't like your tone, Lord Morrow. You will apologise for it."

Deacon's smugness immediately vanished, replaced by confusion. Carissa had never been overly proud, so the sudden demand for an apology must have come as a shock. She was tired of being stepped on, tired of people thinking she was a pawn or a doormat for the Morrow family to move around as they pleased. Vida and Bellona whispered quietly across the fire, alarm on their faces.

"It was merely a joke, Your Majesty." Deacon's smile returned, but it was icy this time. "Perhaps we simply do not share the same sense of humour."

A ghost of an apology, but if she pushed, then people would think her bossy and domineering. If she backed down, she would be seen as weak and submissive. Why could Carissa never win? As she stood there deliberating, Deacon raised his hands over the flames. Water swirled to him and plummeted down, dousing the small blaze in an instant.

Carissa recognised the threat. She could remember the feeling of Deacon's chilly fingers around her throat. The memory made her swallow hard. Deacon's lips curved into a triumphant smile as Carissa turned away from him to look for her husband once more.

"Where is Jacen?"

"Last I saw, your husband was still in the depths of the Gracewood." Deacon tilted his head to the side. "With Sir Bryce Ambrose."

Sudden dread seized Carissa as she marched for the thick canopy of trees that made up the Gracewood. She did not trust her husband alone around Lord Ambrose's younger brother. With darkness falling quickly, Jacen needed to be found—and quickly. She turned to glance behind her at Bellona, who was already on her feet.

"My Queen?"

"Come with me, quickly. Bring your bow."

Bellona's freckled face paled, but she nodded. "With pleasure."

THE ENDANGERED KING
JACEN MORROW

Bryce Ambrose insisted he'd seen wolf tracks, and the idea of having a pelt to gift to Carissa thrilled Jacen too much to relinquish. Jacen had hunted a lot in his lifetime—it was one of his first bonding excursions with Cobryn as a boy. As he grew older, he learned to track down and kill more advanced prey. The pride Cobryn showed in him when he brought home his first wolf pelt was a memory he would cling to forever, although his father had never been anything but cold to him in some time.

However, it occurred to Jacen that remaining in the Gracewood with the brother of a man who despised his family was not the cleverest idea. It was too late to turn back or show fear. He and Bryce had meandered some distance from the campsite, leaving Jacen uncertain of his intentions. He should have asked for some of the others to remain with him, but he'd been sure of his own prowess and unquestioning of Bryce...until now.

Dusk began to fall over the Gracewood, hues of pink and orange settling over the sky. If they lingered too much longer, their chances of finding the supposed wolf would disappear. Although he had seen no such tracks, he had trusted Bryce's claim—perhaps foolishly. Raking his hair back, he cast around for any sign of this wolf or its tracks.

"It's getting late. Perhaps we should return to camp."

"When we are almost upon the wolf?" Bryce turned to look at Jacen, his expression incredulous.

"Are we?" Jacen asked, suspicious, and something changed in Bryce's expression once he realised the King was no longer comfortable with the situation. His hand moved to the hilt of his sword. A subtle movement, but Jacen had spent three years fighting in the Island Wars—he knew the look of a man preparing to attack.

"We are certainly hunting, King." A sneer crossed Bryce's face, and metal grated as he drew his sword from its sheath. With no option left, Jacen pulled out his own sword, immediately sinking into a fighting stance.

Bryce lunged with frightening speed, and Jacen raised his sword to block the blow. Cobryn taught him to avoid defensive forms, so Jacen shifted into the mode of the aggressor. As Bryce struck again, Jacen brought his sword up hard to meet his, the sound of clashing steel ringing through the trees.

The man staggered at the force behind the block and Jacen took advantage of his stumble. He may not have aimed to kill, but he needed to disarm his opponent at the first opportunity. Jacen feinted for his neck, shifting his grip at the last moment so the edge of his blade grazed Bryce's arm. The man hissed as the fabric of his shirt tore, angry scarlet seeping through.

As Bryce swung his sword toward Jacen, his movements controlled by fury instead of precision. He fought like a man used to winning, and now that he edged on losing, his slashes became sloppy. For all his tourneys and jousts, Bryce had never been in the field of battle, and it showed. Jacen tilted his sword to block the blow, grimacing as Bryce's sword nicked his leg as it ricocheted back.

A dull thump made the knight stagger and yell out in pain. As he twisted around, Jacen spotted an arrow protruding from his back.

Two familiar figures stood over Bryce's shoulder, and Jacen nearly stumbled in shock. Bellona lowered her bow, her expression troubled. Carissa stood beside her, hands balled into determined fists.

"You would choose him?" Bryce spat the words, staggering toward the young women despite his injury. "You would choose the Generan over me?"

"I would choose neither at all," Carissa said imperiously, eyes flashing as Bellona nocked another arrow, levelling this one with Bryce's chest. "Yet you would invite war with a single stroke of your sword. Killing my husband will do nothing but spill the blood of one who didn't initiate the Conquest. If you seek the enemy, Sir Bryce, it is not here."

"I seek retribution!" Bryce exclaimed, fingers curling tighter around the hilt of his sword. He turned to face Jacen, teeth bared and sword raised. "As you would, were you not too spellbound by this *boy*."

"I beg of you, don't do this." Carissa stepped forward, ignoring Bellona's terrified whisper of her name as she watched her Queen walk toward a dangerous and agitated man. "You could be the better man, Bryce. Killing Jacen won't avenge anyone. Focus your rage on the ones truly responsible."

Nothing Carissa could say, nothing she might promise, would be good enough. Bellona's second arrow whizzed across the space between them and struck Bryce in the back of the neck. The knight swayed momentarily before hitting the ground hard with a crunch that made Bellona wince.

Jacen swore softly. She had chosen him over Bryce. She risked war with Emlen in killing Lord Ambrose's brother. Regardless if Bryce had been in the wrong, it would be just the excuse needed to declare war. If it had been Deacon in the Gracewood, Carissa would have let him die. So why had she let him live over her countryman?

Bellona leaned forward and retched, vomiting all over the dead leaves and dirt. It was likely the first time the poor young woman had killed someone. He remembered that sensation, the way that coldness crept up his spine as his knees had trembled and his palms had gone clammy. It was a horror that would stay with him for the rest of his life. He did not envy Bellona now, but when he crossed to her side, she held up her hand, glaring up at him.

"Make no mistake, I didn't do this for you."

Carissa stood beside her friend, rubbing Bellona's back as she continued to retch. Only once Bellona had stopped vomiting did she lift her gaze to Jacen. Where he might have expected tenderness, he saw cold determination. There had been a shift in her, and he wondered how he had been too blind to see it before.

"Why did you do it?"

He had to know the answer. He didn't think he could endure this tour, arrive in Emlen and look Lord Ambrose in the eye without knowing why the Queen had authorised the death of the man's younger brother.

"Because it was right." Though she dismissed him, Jacen knew she had a reason. As Carissa turned to walk back towards camp, he caught her by the arm. Bellona's hand moved to her bow once again, but Carissa shook her head.

"Go on ahead. We'll catch up."

Bellona looked between them, her eyes narrowed as they landed on Jacen. Nonetheless, she did as Carissa instructed. There was true loyalty, Jacen thought admiringly as he watched Bellona stalk off through the Gracewood. A woman who killed for her Queen even if she didn't like the man she protected.

"What do you think would have happened, had I let Bryce kill you?" Carissa moved in front of him, folding her arms over her chest. "We both know how that situation plays out, and it involves far more death and destruction for Basium. Cobryn losing his eldest son to a brutal murder? There is no mercy to be found there."

"You think there is from Emlen?" Jacen gestured to Bryce's body. "We both know that regardless of the circumstances, Lord Ambrose will take this as a personal affront. His brother killed attempting to murder a Generan? There will be blood for that, Carissa."

"Then we lie."

Silence fell over them as they both took in the seriousness of what Carissa suggested. There had only been four of them in the Gracewood. Bryce was dead and Bellona would listen to what her Queen said. The truth could be whatever Carissa and Jacen made it to be. The idea made him uncomfortable; however, it could be what saved them from the looming threat of war.

"What would we say?"

Carissa took a deep breath. "That it was me Bryce tried to kill."

Smart. Whilst Lord Ambrose didn't care at this point whether Carissa lived or died, the rest of Basium had their own opinions. Bryce attempting to murder Jacen would be brushed off. An attempt on the Queen, a young woman who had experienced so much hardship… It would cause issues.

Jacen examined his wife, wonder growing within him. Resilient, intelligent, compassionate—there was so much to love about Carissa. Every little thing he got to know about her deepened his feelings for her. He cared for her, and in this act, she had proved that she cared about him in return.

They returned to camp in silence, both of them deep in thought about what Carissa suggested. There would be questions asked, particularly in regards to Bryce's absence. Jacen thought it prudent to let Carissa answer them, as she knew the way she wanted the story to go.

"You return without Sir Bryce." Deacon observed them both with a mixture of confusion and suspicion.

"You can find his body in the Gracewood." Carissa sank onto one of the large logs surrounding the fire, staring into the depths of the flames. Her words caused some of them to look at each other apprehensively.

"Your Majesty, what happened?" A young knight regarded the Queen with some concern.

"Sir Bryce made an attempt on my life." Carissa tore her gaze away from the fire, tears welling in her eyes. "If not for Jacen and Bellona, I would be dead."

Concerned muttering filled the camp. When Jacen looked to Deacon, his uncle did not look astonished. He regarded Carissa with a displeased expression. He knew she lied, but what could he do about it? The only person who could say otherwise was dead. Carissa reached up to wipe her eyes. Jacen suspected the tears were real.

"Why would he do such a thing?" Sir Perron asked.

"I don't know." Carissa shook her head slowly. "All we can do is have his body sent ahead to his brother and question Lord Ambrose on the matter when we are in Emlen. I suspect Bryce did not act alone."

"You accuse Lord Ambrose?" an older knight demanded.

"I accuse no one." Carissa looked up sharply, her brows knitting together. "I simply seek a solution to a puzzling situation. I do not know if Bryce acted on behalf of his brother, or someone else entirely. But rest assured, I intend to find out."

Carissa got up and moved away from the fire in a swirl of skirts, marching toward her tent. After a moment's hesitation, Jacen followed. He would either be the last person she wanted to see right now, or the thing she needed. When he peered hesitantly through the flap, he saw Carissa curled on the furs with her face pressed into her hands, sobbing openly.

Closing the tent behind him, Jacen cautiously approached and knelt down before her on the furs. Carissa removed her hands from her face. Her cheeks were tear-stained, and her expression confused. Jacen gently took her hands in his own as Carissa sniffed.

"This isn't the sort of Queen I wanted to be," she murmured softly.

"No, but it's the sort of Queen you have to be." Jacen wished that things were easier for her, but he had never imagined their reign would be without conflict. "You were crowned Queen of a country that lost a vicious and bloody battle. How many years has it been since Basium saw a Queen who was not a consort?"

"I…I don't know," Carissa admitted, taking a moment to consider the question. "Over a hundred years at least. It's rare."

"Precisely. There was always bound to be controversy." Jacen leaned forward to kiss the top of her head. "You are doing the best you can under the circumstances you've been pushed into. I'm honestly surprised you haven't had Deacon killed, considering what a snake he is."

The words elicited a small smile from Carissa, which was all he wanted. However hard things were for him, it was a lot worse for his wife. There had never been any chance of Cobryn sparing her brothers, but he wondered what sort of reception any of them would have had as King. According to the court, Theodore and Peregrine were admired and respected throughout the country, while Sebastian had always been the darling of the people.

"Do you think Bellona will go along with it?" To Jacen, she was the riskiest factor. If she decided she didn't agree with what Jacen and Carissa were doing, then she could expose the truth about what had happened in the Gracewood and doom both of them.

"Of course I do." Carissa spoke with fierce conviction. "She's been my best friend since we were children. She knows why I have to lie, and what it would mean to tell the truth. We can count on Bellona."

If it was up to her, she would have convinced Bryce in the Gracewood, talked him into lowering his sword. Jacen agreed with what she'd said by the fire—Bryce was not doing this for his own benefit. Someone had convinced him that murdering Jacen and bringing about war would be the best thing for Basium. If Lord Ambrose had answers, Jacen planned to get them out of him—one way or another. The thought brought back dark memories of the torture he had inflicted during the Island Wars, but he shook them off.

I was just doing what I had to. As I will again, if I must.

The Devious Queen
Carissa Darnell

The biggest struggle was speaking with Bellona about the lie Carissa and Jacen had agreed to tell. She knew how her best friend felt about her husband. Shooting down Bryce could not have been easy for her—to Carissa's knowledge, she had never killed before. Carissa approached Bellona cautiously the night after the incident in the Gracewood. It had not escaped her attention that Bellona had been distant and withdrawn.

"May I enter?"

Bellona looked up from the knife she'd been sharpening. "You are the Queen. You can do whatever you wish."

Carissa sighed. "Bellona, please. Do you want me here, or not?"

After a moment's hesitation, her friend nodded, patting the spot beside her. Carissa crossed over and sat beside Bellona, observing her closely. Killing was a traumatising act, or so she had heard. She had wanted to save Jacen, but that meant Bellona carrying out a swift execution. How she wished she'd never had to place that burden upon her friend's shoulders.

"I'm sorry for what you're going through. For the fact that Sir Bryce's death haunts you."

"Yes, well." Bellona's eyes welled with tears, but they were fierce as she fixed them on Carissa. "I would do anything for my Queen, even if it means killing a fellow noble to protect her husband."

"It's about more than just Jacen," Carissa assured her, putting an arm around Bellona's shoulders. "One day, we will truly have Basium back. But Jacen's death would have resulted in an angry and vengeful Warmonger. We couldn't have faced that. Not yet, not until we are united."

Bellona's brow furrowed. "You plan to rebel?"

Carissa nodded. She could not divulge the entirety of her plan, for in truth she did not have one. But visiting the cities was the beginning. She needed Emlen, another reason why she had to ask Bellona to lie for her. Her friend did not deserve to bear it, but Carissa had no other option.

"That's why we cannot tell the truth about what happened in the Gracewood."

Bellona looked alarmed. "Goddess above, Carissa. What are you saying happened?"

"That it was me Sir Bryce tried to murder." The words lingered in the air between them, the taste of them foul on Carissa's lips. She was aware that no matter the circumstances, Bellona would hate such a lie. Her friend set down the knife she'd been sharpening, staring at the Queen incredulously.

"Why would you say such a thing?" Her voice was barely above a whisper.

"If the truth is known that I chose my husband over my countryman—"

"Which you did," Bellona reminded her sharply.

"If Lord Ambrose knew, he'd want war. We need unity, not division. We need to be fighting the Generans, not each other."

"How can you claim that?" Bellona pushed herself to her feet, freckled face contorting in accusation. "You were the one who chose a Generan. You may be my Queen, Carissa, but I don't have to agree with or condone your actions."

Carissa pinched the bridge of her nose. "I need you to imagine for a moment that we'd done things the way you wanted to. That we chose to let Sir Bryce murder Jacen in the Gracewood. I want you to think beyond that to what would happen next."

Bellona sighed dramatically. "I don't know, but I'm sure you're about to tell me."

"You remember the Conquest." Carissa rose as well, straightening her skirts. "That was Cobryn's response to my grandfather refusing to make him a deal that would let him have access to Emlen. Can you imagine how he would respond to his only son and heir being killed by Basiumites?"

Bellona nodded slowly, taking in what Carissa said. There would have been more blood and violence, until Basium burned to the ground. Sir Bryce's death, though regrettable, was the only way that Carissa could begin to pave a path to freedom—and, in some time, perhaps peace.

"I understand, but I still hate it."

"As you have every right to." Carissa gently caught Bellona's arm. "But please, I need your help on this one, Bell."

The childhood nickname softened her friend. "Fine. I just need you to promise me you won't come to me if Jacen turns out as bad as the rest of them."

"He isn't." Carissa shook her head fervently. She may not trust Jacen, but she believed in his potential. "He wants to be better than Cobryn."

"Even monsters believe they're acting in their loved ones' best interests." Bellona's expression turned grave as she clasped the hand that Carissa had on her arm. "I urge you, as both your best friend and your subject, to be careful. You've been hurt enough already."

Carissa squeezed her hand. "Bellona…"

"I will kill for you; you know that now." Bellona drew her hand away, and the pain of Sir Bryce's murder burned in her eyes. "But don't ask me to kill for him again."

Fortua was an ugly city. It was some miles out from the Gracewood, with only sparse vegetation. Situated on a large hill, the city had no decoration aside from the flag of House Benedict—a raven on a red background—flying from its tallest turret. The heat of the sun bore down upon them, with few trees to shelter them. Carissa fanned herself often, which did nothing to stop her clothes sticking to her skin.

Despite having the second smallest population of the core five, the city bustled. The houses all had flat roofs and brick walls, a few painted in neutral colours. The cobblestones were worn and in need of repair. The streets wound around in tiers, built higher and higher until they stretched to the castle, perched above it all.

Tiago Benedict awaited the Queen's entourage inside the city gates. He was a man in his late thirties, with a young wife and two small children. Lord Benedict bowed stiffly from the waist as Carissa dismounted her horse and crossed over, hoisting her most charming smile across her features.

The swan crown sat heavy on her head. Miriam had insisted she bring it along with her and wear it to at least her first meeting with the nobles upon arrival in their cities. It made Carissa uncomfortable to flaunt a crown she was never meant to wear, but Miriam deemed it necessary.

"Lord Benedict. A pleasure to see you."

"Your Majesty." He rose to place a kiss on the back of her hand. "It's been some time. Last time I saw you, you were barely above my waist. Now you're all grown up, and Queen no less."

With the pleasant greetings done, Carissa found herself at a loss for what to say. She had never been particularly good at small talk, but considering Deacon had been in control and known precisely what to say, she'd never needed to be. Now she didn't have a man to dictate her words and actions, for Jacen was happy to follow her lead in the proceedings.

"I am looking forward to exploring Fortua."

"Indeed, you and the ladies could see the local markets we have here, whilst your husband and I discuss some business."

The statement made Carissa blink, unpleasantly surprised. Jacen and Lord Benedict involved in discussion without her? She didn't think that likely. The idea that she could be so easily dismissed was an affront, though she beamed and tried again, hoping Lord Benedict would realise he had misspoken.

"On the contrary, Lord Benedict. I would like to be involved in any political business as well—as I'm certain you are aware from your cousin's reports on council meetings in the capital."

"When your husband was not present, yes. But now that he has returned…"

Carissa fought back the wave of irritation that accompanied his words. She had met several nobles who were under the impression that a man would be a stronger and more capable ruler than a woman. It seemed Lord Benedict also carried that belief, and it disappointed her that one of the core five houses could be so sexist.

"Now that he has returned, nothing has changed. I am still Queen of Basium, and I intend to sit in on meetings regardless of if my husband is present or not. I would appreciate it if you respected my choice, Lord Benedict."

Lord Benedict opened his mouth to say something, and Carissa braced herself for an objection. However, Lady Benedict nudged her husband in the side, and they shared a look. Lord Benedict's shoulders slumped in defeat and he sighed.

"Very well, Your Majesty."

"I will show you to your room." Lady Benedict stepped forward. She couldn't be much older than Jacen, with warm eyes and a dimpled smile. "I'm sure it's been a long journey."

Carissa linked her arm through Lady Benedict's and allowed the woman to lead her into the castle and through the corridors. Even inside, there was little in terms of decoration. It was practical, not pretty. Carissa thought she knew which of the Benedicts had decided that.

The bedroom Lady Benedict showed her to was simple, with none of the books or candles that Carissa would have kept in her room back in Marinel. Lady Benedict released her arm and immediately went to sweep open the curtains, flooding the room with light. It smelled of sage and something woody.

"I apologise for my husband's behaviour. He doesn't seem to know what to do with a woman in power."

"I do hope he'll adjust." Carissa smiled tightly. This promised to be a very tedious week in Fortua if Lord Benedict insisted on excluding her because of her gender. "He does not seem to dislike my husband."

"The King is young and strong." Lady Benedict crossed over to Carissa. "Tiago believes Deacon and Jacen are both decisive men, and he respects that, regardless of where they're from and who they are."

Carissa could not help but feel insulted that Lord Benedict had more respect for Deacon than for her. Despite her frustration, there was nothing she could do about it that wouldn't serve to rile Lord Benedict and further cement his opinion of her. Weariness crept in, and she sighed heavily and collapsed onto the bed. The mattress squeaked under her weight, and she could feel a spring digging into her back.

"Your Majesty?" Lady Benedict's tone was uncertain. She stood over the Queen, wringing her hands. "If I might ask, where is Sir Bryce? I noticed he was not with your entourage, and he is a childhood friend of my husband's, so I merely wondered…"

Carissa took a deep breath and braced herself to disclose the lie she and Jacen had created. She had known this time would come, when Bryce's absence would be questioned, but she had not assumed it would be as early as in Fortua.

"Sir Bryce is dead."

The mood at the dinner table was solemn, and Carissa knew her confession of Bryce's execution following an attempt on her life had brought about such grimness. It was difficult to know what Lord Benedict thought. Could he be wishing that Bryce's attempt had succeeded? The thought sent chills down Carissa's spine as she picked at her marinated lamb.

Whilst Carissa had not expected festivities for her arrival, disappointment crept over her that nothing more colourful occurred to take her mind off Bryce's execution. The silence was painful as she sipped her wine and glanced across at Jacen, who busied himself with his food. Carissa had wanted Bellona present, but her best friend had wanted dinner in her room.

The dining hall in Fortua was smaller and more dimly-lit than the one at home in Marinel. The table was shorter too, allowing for fewer guests. Carissa suspected it was mostly Lord and Lady Benedict who dined at the table.

"I find it difficult to believe that Sir Bryce would attempt to kill you." Lord Benedict surveyed Carissa. "That does not seem like him at all. He is proudly loyal to his country and his Queen."

"Perhaps he thought me a puppet for the Generans." Carissa set her goblet down, meeting the nobleman's hard look. "There are many who do. Believe me, Lord Benedict, the attempt was as surprising to me as it is to you."

"I personally believe the Generans have done a great deal of good here." Lord Benedict leaned back in his chair. "The Darnell family never deserved what happened to them, but old King Patrick—may the Goddess keep him—was not a reformist. He was a stickler for traditions when what we needed was change."

"I believe my husband has had too much to drink." Lady Benedict laughed lightly, but fear widened her eyes. Was she worried her husband might insult Carissa with how carelessly he spoke, or was there something else she feared?

"What sort of change, Lord Benedict?" Jacen asked sharply, reaching across to grasp Carissa's hand. Her fingers trembled in his. Whatever she had anticipated from Lord Benedict, it hadn't been for him to commend the Generans while speaking ill of her deceased family. Across the table, Deacon's eyes glittered with triumph.

"The laws on dark magic, for a start." Lord Benedict set his knife and fork down. "It was utterly ridiculous and superstitious to have Maleficium living in such fear of themselves and their abilities, simply because someone banned them from practising their craft."

"Tiago," Lady Benedict hissed.

"You have a strong opinion on the topic," Carissa said, taking care to keep her tone even. "Are you perhaps personally affiliated with a Maleficium or two, Lord Benedict?"

"Of course." Lord Benedict gestured to his wife. "My Vanessa is a shadow mage."

The entire table lapsed into silence. Lady Benedict's nostrils flared, upset and embarrassed at the fact her husband had outed her as a Maleficium. Carissa had to admit she was more curious than anything else. She had briefly met a handful of Maleficium, but none of them had been amongst the nobility. She felt a sudden kinship toward Lady Benedict.

"Please excuse me. I suddenly feel ill." Lady Benedict threw her napkin onto her plate, her chair scraping back against the stone tiles. "I believe you have said enough for one night, Tiago."

"Lady Benedict, please," Carissa implored gently. "There is nothing for you to be afraid of. In fact, if you feel up to it, I would like to see what you can do."

She knew her interest lay in the realm of personal curiosity, but she couldn't help it. It thrilled her to know there was another high-status Maleficium in her midst. It was too dangerous for Carissa to confess the truth and display her gifts. She hoped that Lady Benedict doing so would give her the courage she needed to eventually demonstrate her own dark magic.

Lady Benedict looked to her husband, desperation shining in her eyes. When her Lord Benedict nodded, she took a deep breath and closed her eyes. The candles in the middle of the dining table flickered and died out, and slowly but surely the room filled with shadow, so dark Carissa could barely see a foot in front of her. She had to marvel at Lady Benedict's ability, even if she felt completely smothered by the darkness. After a few moments, the shadows receded.

"That was spectacular, Lady Benedict." Deacon smiled brightly, which gave Carissa cause to be suspicious. Anything that made him so happy was certainly a reason for concern. "I am glad the change in law means that you are able to demonstrate and use your powers without fear of consequences."

"I am sure my grandfather had his own reasons for implementing the ban," Carissa stated, her mind drifting to what Miriam had told her about Jameson Burnett. A law created through fear, certainly, but one Patrick had no doubt believed would protect his people from harm.

"Perhaps, but the time for baseless laws and fear-mongering is over." Deacon waved a dismissive hand. "You were one of the most ardent supporters of the legality of dark magic, Your Majesty."

Carissa bristled. "I have not forgotten, Lord Morrow."

The conversation became increasingly uncomfortable. While she understood Lady Benedict now felt confident in using her abilities, she did not like how pro-Morrow Lord Benedict was. King Patrick had his flaws, like any ruler. But he was not the villain Cobryn was. He had not murdered senselessly.

Carissa wondered how many ugly truths about her family might come out during this tour, things she had not known as a carefree teenager before her coronation. As much as Carissa wanted to remain under the belief that her family had been good… What if they weren't?

The Morrow family had caused their share of hardship and disaster, but the more Carissa heard about her grandfather's rule, the more she wondered if he had been doing the same in his own way.

Carissa woke to an empty pillow beside her and power thrumming in her veins. Jacen typically woke earlier than her, but where had he gone? Paranoia seeped into her like a disease, and she knew it was associated with Bryce's death. Would Jacen and Bellona stick to the lie, as she desperately hoped?

Raking her fingers through her tangled black hair, Carissa tugged back the sheets to realise her monthly bleeding came. She paused at the disappointing crimson stain, a reminder of her failure to beget an heir. Miriam had struggled throughout her childbearing years, and Carissa's father Frederick had been her only child to reach adulthood.

On the other hand, Carissa's mother Imogen had borne four healthy children— though her three sons had been snatched away by something more brutal and horrifying than illness or deformity.

It was clear from the start that Cobryn intended to have his bloodline rule Basium, and his impatience for a grandchild of Darnell blood was no secret. Carissa's body rebelled against this wish. While she lacked a baby growing within her, the dark magic dwelling inside her was more prominent than ever when she bled. She could not decide which of the two ideas frightened her more.

With no family aside from Miriam, it was imperative that Carissa have an heir, or risk Basium falling into uncertain hands should anything happen to her. It was a pressure that rested on her shoulders since she was only fourteen, but since Jacen's return, it became critical.

Carissa knew nothing about being a mother. Only Sebastian had been younger than her, and by a scant two years. She had not interacted with enough babies to form a solid opinion on maternity, though having a child wasn't about that. No one cared whether Carissa loved or hated children. They cared about her fertility and whether she could provide the union of Morrow and Darnell bloodlines that Jacen's family craved.

She fumed with the indignity and unfairness of it all. Before the Conquest, Carissa was considered a handsome marriage prospect. She had her pick of suitors. Now she had been reduced to nothing more than a broodmare, tasked with carrying and birthing the future heir to the thrones of both Basium and Genera.

Kicking the sheets aside with more force than necessary, Carissa stalked over to the door and summoned the servants. They replaced the sheets timidly, never looking her in the eye. Her failure was apparent even to them, judging by the way they scurried out with the bloodied sheets. She tried not to think of what Lord Benedict and Deacon might think. Their triumph made the darkness in her swell, eager to break things, to cause damage.

Carissa took several deep breaths to compose herself. She had always been prone to stress and anxiety, but it had hit with more force since she became Queen. She closed her eyes and focused, just as Miriam had taught her. She'd be damned if she would let panic drown her. She was more than just a young woman pushed to become a mother—she was a dark mage, an impending storm. She was Maleficium, even if none of the others knew it.

THE BURDENED KING
JACEN MORROW

The week in Fortua went by in a colourless blur. Jacen had not been certain what to make of Lord Benedict's fervent belief in the decisions Deacon had made during his time as regent. Oddly, Carissa's spirits had been lifted by the realisation Lady Benedict was a Maleficium.

Could it be that there was magic in Carissa's blood too, as Deacon claimed? Possible, since strong magic passed down the female line in her family. The idea concerned Jacen. The thought Carissa would hide something so important from him niggled away at him.

Carissa spent a good deal of time with Lady Benedict and her two children—both girls, perhaps two and five. It had been interesting for him to watch her interaction with the children. Carissa was patient and kind with the girls, and it made him think she would be a good mother when the time came.

It had been almost six months since Jacen had returned to Basium and at least a few since they'd consummated the marriage. He didn't know how long it took a woman to become pregnant, but he hoped it would be sooner rather than later. Having an heir was of great importance—particularly considering the recent attempt on his life.

Lord Benedict's attitude toward Carissa had not changed, something that frustrated Jacen. He had hoped that seeing how positively Carissa interacted with Lady Benedict would have helped the man see the sort of Queen she was. Unfortunately, it seemed that Lord Benedict's sexism prevailed—he spoke more with Jacen and Deacon than Carissa.

Nonetheless, the week in Fortua proved useful. Jacen knew what Carissa planned, why this tour had been so important in the first place—she wanted to get to know her people. She wanted to see how the core five worked, what made them tick, who their allegiance was to. So far, Lord Benedict's loyalty was in question, especially considering how he raved about Deacon.

A bloodcurdling scream woke Jacen abruptly. Carissa tossed about in the sheets beside him, struggling into a sitting position. He stirred and rolled over onto his side as she raked her hands through her hair, her breathing rapid. He knew she got nightmares from time to time, but it never usually progressed to audible screams of horror.

"What is it?" Jacen reached out to tentatively rest his hand on her shoulder. "What's wrong?"

"It's nothing," Carissa insisted, but her voice quavered. She tugged her knees to her chest, wrapping her arms around herself. The movement made her seem small and vulnerable, making Jacen want to embrace her, though doing so wouldn't help the matter.

"If it disturbs you so, it isn't nothing." Jacen hesitantly shifted closer. When Carissa remained silent, he persisted. "Won't you tell me?"

"I remember that night." Carissa's voice was soft but steady. They both knew precisely to which night she referred. She closed her eyes, tears spilling down her cheeks. It struck Jacen that although she had spoken about the Conquest with him before, she had never openly grieved in front of him.

"Of course you do. You lost everything."

"My little brother..." Carissa swiped at her tears, anger replacing her anguish as her violet-blue eyes burned. "They only ever found fucking pieces of him."

Jacen could never forgive Cobryn for some things, but it was not his place to withhold forgiveness for the Conquest. He couldn't begin to imagine how much Sebastian's fate pained Carissa. The idea that someone could do that to a child horrified him. The idea of anything of the sort befalling his little sister Ayesha made him feel physically ill.

He wanted to relate to his wife, yet at the same time he understood that he didn't, and never could. Carissa's trauma was not his to understand. He could only be there for her, a complicated scenario considering the fact it had been his family to cause her so much hurt. When she looked at him, did she see Cobryn staring back?

What could he say to her? He had been there during the Conquest. He had done nothing as her father and her brother were executed right in front of her. The idea of stepping in and playing the hero then was foolish, almost as foolish as trying to comfort her. The Conquest would always be the divide between them, the thing that separated him and Carissa no matter how hard they tried to be united.

"You mentioned to Bryce that they should suffer for it."

Carissa glowered at him. "Perhaps that was unwise with a member of the Morrow family present."

"I don't believe people who commit crimes should go unpunished." Jacen didn't know what he was trying to say. He did not want his father dead, partially because he was not ready to be King of Genera as well as Basium. Deacon was another matter—the longer Jacen remained in power, the more his uncle seemed to resent it.

"If I were to punish them, I doubt you'd agree with my methods." Carissa rolled back onto her side, tugging the blankets around her slender form.

"What methods?" Jacen asked.

Carissa stayed quiet for a long time. He thought she may have gone back to sleep before she let out a huff and rolled over to face him. Darkness shadowed her eyes, unexpected and astonishing.

"I would give them what they gave me. I would rent open a wound that never heals and keep letting it bleed."

Jacen swallowed hard at the venom in her tone. He had never believed Carissa pure of heart—how could she be, considering what she had been through? After Bryce's death and her dark words, he began to wonder how deep that hatred ran. Was this Miriam's doing, or had Cobryn caused this all on his own?

It was a relief to be riding away from Fortua and toward Theron. Carissa seemed happier as they departed, chatting animatedly to Bellona. The redhead had been reserved for some time following Bryce's execution, yet she started to come out of her shell. Jacen was pleased to be away from the overbearing Lord Benedict, his Maleficium wife, and his conflicted loyalties.

Theron was a safe haven for Carissa, as Bellona's father, Kato, ruled it. From what Jacen understood, the man was a father figure to Carissa, considering he had been close friends with Frederick. Carissa did not have to stress about whether Kato was faithful—or did she? Loyalties were ever-changing in times of turmoil, and those that were once dearly beloved and trusted could become traitors.

"Your wife appears less gloomy today." Deacon spurred his horse beside Jacen's. "It seems that each day, Sir Bryce's death weighs less on her conscience. Murder becomes easier over time, after all."

"It wasn't murder," Jacen contradicted. "It was an execution. Bellona shot him down because he would have killed Carissa otherwise."

"Really?" Deacon arched his eyebrows. "It was *Carissa* that Lord Ambrose's brother took issue with?"

Jacen understood his uncle's implications, and he despised them. Of course, Deacon was too observant to believe Bryce had made an attempt on Carissa's life. He hated that his uncle knew him so well. He gripped the reins tighter in his hands until his knuckles turned white.

"What business is it of yours?"

"My nephew's safety is my business." Deacon's expression became serious. "I told you that I don't let things slip through my fingers. Your health and wellbeing are paramount."

Jacen didn't believe that for a moment. Deacon would get rid of him the first chance he got. Jacen had no male heir—if anything was to happen to him, Deacon would not only achieve his goal of marrying Carissa and laying claim to Basium, but should Cobryn die before him, he would inherit Genera also.

"Enough, Deacon. Save your gilded lies for those who believe them."

His uncle was not the only member of his family to approach him, for as soon as Deacon had given up, Vida drew her horse up beside her brother's. She had always been excellent on horseback and he found himself unsurprised she did not ride in the carriage along with Carissa and Bellona. He had not interacted much with Vida in Fortua—she had been too busy exploring the city, her curiosity insatiable.

"How are you feeling about Theron?"

Jacen shrugged. "As apprehensive as I felt about Fortua, and as I feel about visiting any of the core five cities. Why?"

"Well, because it's Bellona's father that rules there." Vida tossed her blonde braid over her shoulder.

Her comment only served to remind him that his sister was more familiar with members of the court. It caused him no small amount of frustration, that he was forced to go to those more knowledgeable for guidance on his own people.

"What is Lord Lenore like?"

"He dotes on Bellona." Vida looked to the carriage where her friends rode together. "He is, of course, a strong supporter of the Queen's. His wife suffered an…unsavoury fate during the Conquest."

"Killed?" Jacen asked.

"Raped and murdered." Vida shuddered, and the words sent made Jacen's entire body tense. Such things happened in war, but it still disgusted him. He remembered his own men partaking in such vile activities during the Island Wars, and he had put a stop to it whenever he noticed. Unfortunately, he couldn't protect everyone.

"I imagine Lord Lenore is protective of his daughter."

"He is, but he knows that Bellona is a force to be reckoned with on her own."

After having seen Bellona in action, Jacen did not doubt that for a moment. He supposed he should be grateful it was Bryce she'd put her arrows in, and not him. The young woman clearly harboured intense dislike for him. Jacen hoped to change that. Somehow.

"I'm surprised you joined us, sister, considering your impending marriage."

Vida rolled her eyes. "Precisely the reason I want to see as much of Basium as I can before I'm shipped off to Severino."

Despite her dramatic tone, Jacen knew Vida did not mind—she had been aware her whole life that Cobryn would one day use her for a political match, and it would strengthen their still rocky relationship with the Generan islands. Jacen dreaded when his little sister Ayesha would be old enough for a match to be made for her.

He wondered what the people of Genera thought of him. The only son of a tyrant King, who'd fought against the Generan islands and helped force them back into submission. What about when Cobryn died, and a stranger came back to Genera to claim his father's throne? Jacen didn't think it would go well.

Where did he belong, Basium or Genera? It was getting more difficult to decide which he regarded as home. Why did he bother meeting the core five families if they weren't supposed to matter to him? Cobryn might have been dismissive, but they needed the support of the nobility, or else they'd crash and burn.

Jacen enjoyed camping. The smell that lingered on the air after it rained, the sound of the fire crackling in the fading light of dusk, the merry chatter as people called to each other across the clearing. He had spent a lot of time in his youth out in the Generan wilderness with his friends. It hadn't been about the hunting—it had been relishing the freedom. In the forest, he had no responsibilities.

Laughter rang through trees, along with the clash of steel. Sir Perron and Bellona were embroiled in a mock duel. The young woman was small of stature, but she had an indomitable will as she hit at Perron again and again. She was not the best swordswoman, though she had clearly trained, but her ferocity made up for her lack of size. Perron grinned while Bellona concentrated, her expression intense.

Summer had arrived in excellent form. It had always been Jacen's favourite season. He inhaled the smell of pine, knowing that things would be different once they reached Theron. No fresh scent of nature, no freedoms.

Jacen's gaze cast across the campsite to where Carissa and Vida talked animatedly. As the young Queen laughed at something her friend had said, Jacen's stomach did a somersault.

The light atmosphere of the camp broke when a messenger clad in House Ambrose livery—a roaring bear with a dark blue background—rode into camp. Carissa was promptly summoned from where she socialised with Vida. She insisted Jacen accompany her, to which he made no objection.

"Your Majesty." The messenger bowed deeply before her, straightening up again with a troubled expression on his face. His eyes cast to the ground as he twisted the parchment in his hands. "I bring word from Lord Ambrose regarding the death of his brother, Bryce."

Carissa straightened up, lifting her chin. She looked every inch a Queen with her proud demeanour, despite Jacen knowing her stiffness was the result of tension rather than elegance. He noted that the messenger had not acknowledged his presence, but he should have anticipated that from someone who represented House Ambrose.

"Yes?"

The messenger broke the seal of the parchment and handed it to Carissa, who scanned over it. Jacen leaned over her shoulder, but she brushed him away.

Whatever Lord Ambrose's words, they were for Carissa only. Her lips moved as she read silently over the letter, perhaps twice, before she thrust it back into the messenger's hands.

"What does it say?" Jacen asked.

"Lord Ambrose requests that once we arrive at Emlen, we meet with him immediately to discuss Bryce's execution and the circumstances. He also requests the presence of Bellona during this meeting, knowing she was the only other person present and that she was the one who carried out the execution on behalf of the crown."

That made Jacen nervous. What was to say that Bellona would not change her story in front of her fellow nobility, tell the truth and admit it was Jacen that Bryce had attempted to murder? Carissa might trust Bellona, but Jacen didn't. She was loyal to her Queen—not to him. Carissa's sharp tone also indicated there was more to the letter she hadn't shared.

"Anything else?"

Carissa took a deep breath. "You are the only Morrow permitted within the city walls. Deacon and Vida will come to no harm, but Lord Ambrose would have them camp outside of Emlen. He will not welcome them into his city, and certainly not into his halls."

Jacen's blood boiled. "If he thinks he can—"

"It's his city, Jacen." Carissa scowled as she spun to face him in a swirl of skirts. "These are his terms, and we should be glad they are bloodless. I will ensure some of my men remain at the camp as well. I will not force Lord Ambrose to accept anyone's presence, least of all Deacon's."

"Deacon I can understand, but *Vida*?"

"Thank you for riding so far to bring me this letter." Carissa turned her attention back on the messenger, her smile strained. "Please, feel free to rest and regain your strength for your journey back to Emlen."

"Thank you, Majesty." The messenger dipped his head before walking briskly off through the camp.

"Are you out of your mind?" Jacen demanded once the messenger was out of earshot, taking care to keep his voice low as he towered over his wife. "You would cave to the demands of Lord Ambrose? You are his Queen, his superior. You have every right to tell him that you will bring whoever you want in your entourage."

"Have a care in how you speak to me." Carissa's eyes narrowed, chin tilted defiantly upwards. "I am not a fool, and I am not weak. Just because I do not push my position like a tyrant, does not mean I have forgotten who I am. We need allies, and what you suggest would only serve to alienate Lord Ambrose."

Jacen shook his head slowly. "This could well be a test to see if you push back. He could be thinking along the same lines as Lord Benedict, that women are weak. In essentially rolling over and showing your belly—"

"How fucking *dare* you," Carissa hissed, her tone vicious. A storm brewed in her eyes, and he realised he'd touched a nerve. "How dare you come here, back to Basium after years at war, and tell me I am showing weakness. You have no idea how strong I had to be to survive."

"Carissa, I only meant—"

"I know what you *meant*," Carissa spat, her hands balling into fists. A strong wind swept through the camp, picking up the leaves and tossing them about. "Men who have been given their dues wouldn't understand. If you want to understand strength in submission, you should talk to your stepmother, Lilith. For there is a woman who has seen hell and I admire her courage. If I were her, I don't know how I'd have stopped myself from smothering Cobryn in his sleep."

The wind batted leaves across Jacen's face, through his hair. Carissa stood steadfast in the midst of it, shaking with fury. Whatever he had tried to say, Jacen realised he had insulted and demeaned her. Apology would not be enough in this instance—Carissa would take time to simmer down from the rage his words had elicited. Though not a fiery-tempered woman, when angry she could certainly hold a grudge.

"We are doing this my way." Carissa's firm tone broached no argument. "If you want to go against Lord Ambrose, you do so alone. We are walking on a tightrope, Jacen. I suggest you don't go cutting us down."

Jacen let her turn and walk away, the breeze carrying through the camp dying down as she marched off. The suddenness of the gust, and how quickly it had dissipated, made him certain she had been the cause of it. In her wrath, Carissa had alerted Jacen to what he had come to suspect: there was magic in her. What she could do was unclear, but she could do something.

He could not tell Deacon. Whatever happened, his uncle could not be made aware of a potential threat and rival. Miriam's magic was seen as harmless, yet they didn't know what Carissa could do. If Deacon knew the truth, he would utilise her as a weapon—against her own people, most likely.

Whatever she was, it was beautiful and terrible all at once. Carissa had spoken of Bellona as being a force of nature—perhaps not realising she was too.

What are you, Carissa?

THE EMBATTLED QUEEN
CARISSA DARNELL

Theron was a far lovelier city than Fortua. The castle sat on the edge of a shimmering lake. Bellona had grown more animated as they approached the city, and Carissa could not blame her—the young woman was eager to be reunited with her father. As much as Bellona did her duty as one of the Queen's ladies, she would always miss Kato.

As the portcullis opened to allow them passage, Carissa looked over the lake and thought of happier times. How wonderful it would be to dive into those waters and forget who she was, the weight that rested upon her shoulders. It couldn't be done, but a swim was not out of the equation. Carissa fondly remembered swimming excursions with Bellona and her brothers when they had been young.

Kato waited for them in the courtyard with his household as they reached the castle, and he dropped to one knee as Carissa stepped out of the carriage. She wondered if he would be so loyal if he knew the truth of the Gracewood, and the secret she had forced his daughter to keep. Nonetheless, Carissa smiled, and her heart swelled with happiness at the sight of her father's old friend.

"Please rise, my lord. You have known me since I was a baby, such formality is not necessary."

"It is always a pleasure to see you, Carissa." Kato walked over and swept Carissa into an embrace. She closed her eyes for a moment and let herself be enveloped in his warmth. It was almost like having a father. When she drew back, she noticed Kato's calculating gaze landed on Jacen.

"This is my husband, Jacen."

"Your Majesty." Kato's greeting for Jacen was far stiffer as he inclined his head. Although not as overtly hostile as Bellona, he had no love for Jacen. If her husband had been anticipating a greeting like Lord Benedict's, he must have been sorely disappointed.

Jacen returned the curt nod. "Lord Lenore."

"I was wondering if we could perhaps speak before the feast." Kato offered an arm each to Carissa and Bellona, leading them towards the castle and away from their entourage. The glass spires and colourful flags caught the light and held Carissa spellbound for a few moments.

"A feast?" Bellona grinned and tossed back her hair. "For my return home? Father, you shouldn't have."

"I must speak with the Queen alone, Bell."

Bellona nodded and released her father's arm as they entered the castle, ever the loyal daughter and subject. Part of Carissa felt bad for leaving Jacen alone with people he barely knew, but part of her didn't care. He had Deacon and Vida with him, at least. After his awful remarks to her at camp, Carissa did not feel too kindly toward her husband.

Comfortable silence lingered between Kato and Carissa as he led her through the halls. She remembered them vaguely from when she was a child, but it felt so different now that she was grown. The halls did not seem as open and wide, the tapestries more aged and the stone more worn than she recalled.

She recalled listening outside the meeting room as Kato and Frederick talked, and being scolded by Imogen when she happened upon Carissa and Bellona eavesdropping. The recollection made her smile as they entered the meeting room.

"Last time you were here, I think it was under very different circumstances." Kato sat down in one of the chairs, gesturing for Carissa to do the same. She remained standing, gripping the wooden back of the chair in front of her.

"Yes. Peregrine and Bellona's betrothal."

"I never imagined such a future for you." Kato's brown eyes filled with pity—pity Carissa wanted none of. She had seen enough of that when her family had been murdered, and she needed none of it now. "Your parents would be proud of the strong woman you've become, Carissa."

"Thank you, Kato." She did not know what else to say.

"I must ask, do you trust your husband?" Kato clasped his hands together, leaning forward over the table. The question caught Carissa off-guard. There were certain matters where she thought she could use Jacen's opinion, that she might involve him in, but trust? She shook her head.

"No."

"Has he done something to you?" Kato was immediately full of paternal concern, but Carissa quickly placated him.

"Of course not. As you can imagine, after the Conquest, it's just…it's hard to put your faith in people. Especially when that person is the Warmonger's son. Jacen is a good husband for the most part. I do not trust him, because I do not think he would necessarily put me and Basium first."

Kato nodded slowly, yet the fact he had wanted to have this discussion so abruptly made Carissa concerned. Had something else happened, something further to the letter she had received from Lord Ambrose regarding their visit to Emlen? Shifting to fold her arms over her chest, Carissa sought to get to the crux of the matter.

"What is this about?"

"You must understand, Carissa, I have known Lord Ambrose many years. He is not an unreasonable man. He does not want to watch war ravage Basium any more than the rest of us."

Carissa frowned. Why did Kato defend Lord Ambrose? Why did he treat the matter with delicacy, as if she may lash out at any moment over it? She remained silent, pressing her lips into a firm line as she waited for Kato to explain further.

"It's not you that Lord Ambrose has issues with, but this situation as a whole. Surely you can understand why there are many who are concerned, who think you may have been corrupted by the Morrow family—"

"Is that what you think?" Carissa asked softly. His opinion mattered more to her than most, so she wanted to hear the truth from Kato's own mouth. Did he think she might have been turned to Cobryn's agenda, that she was a tool through which the Morrow family could implement their will in Basium?

"Of course not." Kato shook his head fervently. "But I believe that you would be wise to set about conceiving an heir as soon as possible. If anything were to happen to you, the throne would fall into the hands of your husband's family, and that I could not abide by."

Carissa bit her lip. It certainly wasn't as though she hadn't tried. Yet some months after her birthday and the consummation of their marriage, Carissa had not conceived. She had her moon's blood in Fortua and wondered why she found herself so bitterly disappointed at an occurrence that had become common to her. Could it be that she wanted an heir too?

"What has Lord Ambrose got to do with any of this?"

"Not long ago, he approached me about his cause. About ridding Basium of the Morrow family, for good."

Carissa was not entirely stunned that Lord Ambrose had done such a thing, but more that Kato seriously considered it. The idea troubled her deeply. Whilst Kato claimed he was not against her, what would happen if Lord Ambrose managed to make him believe he should be?

"Oh, Kato."

"Please, Carissa." Kato eased himself up from his seat, walking over to clasp his hands in hers. "I urge you to talk to Lord Ambrose yourself when you reach Emlen. He doesn't hate you. On the contrary, he wants to help the Darnell line flourish once more. I would never agree with anything that might cause you harm."

"Agree with…" Horror enveloped Carissa at the realisation that Kato had in fact come to some kind of arrangement with Lord Ambrose. What had Lord Ambrose promised Kato? Worse, what had Kato promised Lord Ambrose?

"Enjoy the festivities tonight." Kato pressed a kiss to the top of her head. "We will speak on this matter further after you have spoken with Lord Ambrose. I have pledged nothing but my support should the Morrow family lash out at Emlen."

Carissa nodded mutely, unable to fight back the feeling of trepidation that matters quickly spiralled out of her control. She had chosen a side—chosen her people. But what if her people were not unified? If her people were scattered and divided, what would she do then?

The festivities were a spectacle to behold. Carissa had forgotten that despite his often-serious demeanour, Kato did host some of the most incredible celebrations. In this instance, she attempted to put aside her apprehension regarding her earlier conversation with Kato and enjoy them. With lively music and a moderately drunk Bellona, it was easier than she'd anticipated.

Bellona and Vida had convinced her to wear one of her loveliest—and most daring—gowns for the evening. It was a deep purple dress that shimmered with silver sparkles and showed more cleavage than she generally had on display. Carissa felt self-conscious about the low V dip of the neckline, but she was not in the capital with prying eyes. She liked to believe that Theron was safer than Marinel, although Kato's confession left that to be decided.

"Your Majesty." It was Deacon who approached her, offering a hand and dampening her predominantly positive mood. "May I have a dance?"

Although Carissa wished nothing more than to refuse, she found herself nodding in acceptance. She was exhausted from debate and had no wish to argue with Deacon, as he would no doubt paint her as overdramatic for declining his offer. She allowed her husband's uncle to lead her in the centre of the hall. Her eyes caught Jacen's where he stood at the edge of the room, his expression hardening as he noted Deacon beside her.

"I must say, you are looking radiant." Deacon slipped one arm around her waist, eyes raking over her figure. Carissa forced herself to ignore the way he leered at her.

"Thank you, Lord Morrow."

"Your friend has certainly recovered from her role as executioner." Deacon's gaze drifted to Bellona as he twirled Carissa. When she spun back to face him, he smirked. "One would be shaken at the attempted murder of their best friend, no doubt. Not to mention having to execute the would-be killer—certainly not an easy task."

"She handled it well." Carissa's cool tone indicated her displeasure with the topic of conversation, but Deacon persisted.

"Was it you that Bryce intended on killing? It seems unlikely to me, considering his brother's desire to preserve the Darnell line instead of eliminating it entirely. Which leads me to the conclusion that it was Jacen who was the intended target."

"You're entitled to believe whatever you like." Carissa made her scorn evident. Deacon pulled her close enough so that she could feel his hot breath on her neck.

"I know it was Jacen." The whisper chilled her to the bone. She tugged away from Deacon, observing him with horror. How could he possibly know? Was Deacon remarkably perceptive—or had he a role in the attempted assassination?

Carissa had thought the celebrations would make her put her at ease, yet panic rose inside her. She hurried from the hall without a backward glance or an explanation to anyone. Knowing the castle well was a blessing—it was easy enough to make her way out of the hall and onto one of the balconies overlooking the lake. Dark water glimmered in the moonlight, calm beneath the slight breeze.

Carissa eased herself up onto the ledge, letting her feet hang off the side as she'd been chastised for doing as a child. The summer air was warm on her skin and she closed her eyes, listening to the trees as they whispered among themselves. She wished she could be alone like this more often, but there were always those who gravitated toward her like she was the sun and they needed her warmth.

"Carissa?"

The familiar voice made her sigh impatiently. "Go back inside, Jacen."

"What did Deacon do?"

The question made Carissa twist to face him. "It wasn't what he did, but what he said. But you'd know all about that."

Jacen flinched at the venom in her words, and she realised she had been unfair. He had been trying to make amends after what he'd said at camp—after she'd almost lost control of her dark magic and caused the wind to rise and the leaves to billow about. She'd seen it in his eyes as he'd looked at her. He may not know the whole truth, but the suspicion in his expression indicated he knew something was amiss.

Carissa patted the ledge beside her. She expected Jacen to turn around and go back inside, but instead he hoisted himself up onto the ledge to sit beside her. For a moment they sat there in silence, the young King and Queen overlooking Theron's lake, their quiet eclipsed by the inner turmoil Carissa felt.

"Deacon knows that it wasn't me Bryce tried to kill."

"What's he going to do about it?" Jacen scoffed. "Deacon wasn't there. His word holds no power. He wants to scare you into making a wrong move, Carissa. Don't listen to a thing he says."

It reassured her to hear Jacen dismiss Deacon so easily. Tentatively, she reached out her hand until her fingers brushed against his. Jacen took her hand in his. He squeezed lightly, and she glanced over to him.

"What I said at the camp…"

Carissa shook her head. "Forget about it."

"No, I don't want to forget about it." Jacen insisted. "I was wrong. About you, about the situation. I came up with my own idea about how I thought it should be handled, and I pushed that onto you. I never meant to say you were weak. You are one of the strongest women I know."

A humourless smile crossed Carissa's lips. It was kind of him to say so, but she was a survivor, not someone to be placed on a pedestal. She knew Jacen began to suspect some of the truths about her. Once he realised what she was and what she stood for, she doubted he would be showering her with praise.

"Then you agree to Deacon and Vida staying outside of Emlen?"

"I don't like it, but yes."

Carissa knew that having a child would need to be discussed, yet she felt too awkward doing it now. Nature would just have to take its course. Making the matter more embarrassing would do nothing for either of them. Neither of them had control over the fact that she wasn't pregnant yet.

Being a mother had never been something she had needed to think about until the Conquest. It had always been assumed that one of her brothers would be the first to have a child—in fact, she'd teased Bellona incessantly, reminding her friend that she would be an aunt to her child. How things had changed since then. Now Carissa would be the one to have a baby first.

What if it wasn't an heir? What if Carissa bore a girl? She understood girls could inherit if there were no surviving male family members—it was, after all, how she had come to gain her crown. Jacen's family would be considered surviving family members, though, and would take the title away from any daughter that Carissa and Jacen might have. A potential daughter displaced, cast out. The thought terrified Carissa.

"I am going to bed." Carissa shifted back, slipping off the ledge and disentangling her fingers from Jacen's. "This journey and its events have drained me, as has Deacon tonight. I need sleep."

She was relieved that Jacen said nothing in response and did not offer to accompany her. Sometimes she needed to be on her own, and tonight was certainly one of those nights. The idea of shutting herself away in her room and sleeping off all the worries the day had added was a welcome one.

THE TRUSTING KING
JACEN MORROW

Lord Lenore had kept a close eye on Jacen throughout the festivities. When he returned to the hall without Carissa, the Lord of Theron beckoned and then departed. Jacen ignored his trepidation as he slipped away from the music and light and laughter and followed. Lord Lenore had not been welcoming, however he was more civil about his dislike than his daughter, Bellona.

Their footsteps echoed off the stone walls as Jacen followed Lord Lenore down the corridor and into the meeting room. Had this been where he and Carissa had disappeared to upon arrival? Lord Lenore's silence was perhaps the most fear-inducing part of the entire situation, and Jacen folded his arms over his chest as Lord Lenore closed the door softly behind them.

"I wanted to speak with you about Carissa."

Jacen had assumed as much, but he did not think it wise to provide a sarcastic response, so he nodded instead.

"I have known Carissa since she was a small child. I know her better than most of those who keep close company with her today, with the exception of Miriam and Bellona. She sees the worst in situations, and the best in people."

"You want to know if I'm worthy of her."

He desperately wanted to be. The more he watched Carissa with her people, the more she laughed and smiled, the more he fell for her. There had been girls before her who Jacen had shared flirtations with, but nothing like this. He had never fallen this hard and this fast. He wanted to protect Carissa from anyone that would harm her. He wanted to make this marriage between them work.

"Oh, I know you aren't." No malice darkened Lord Lenore's voice, just the shadow of confidence possessed by a man who knew he was right. "Carissa

131

deserved better than to be married against her will just so her husband's family could gain power over Basium. Unfortunately, we cannot change the past."

"Is it the future you want us to change?" Jacen raised his eyebrows. Lord Lenore behaved with the grace expected of his station, yet he could see it in the older man's eyes—if permitted, he'd strike Jacen down for the crimes the Morrow family had committed, the wrongs they had inflicted upon Carissa.

"I want to believe that you will never hurt your wife."

Jacen's brow creased into a frown, and then he remembered the man this came from. Lord Lenore, whose wife had been raped and murdered during the Conquest. Of course he didn't wish such unspeakable violence to befall a girl he considered to be like a daughter figure to him.

"I'd never raise a hand to her."

"I am not just talking about physical violence." Lord Lenore looked old in the light of the fire. His ginger hair receded and lines etched around his eyes. Jacen suspected he was not much older than Cobryn. "She has faced enough without having to worry if her husband would betray her to satisfy his family."

"Do you want to know the truth, Lord Lenore?" Jacen took an awful risk with what he was about to say. This man cared deeply for Carissa—and that gave Jacen hope that by turning the tables and putting Lord Lenore into a position where he could betray the Queen, the man would be as good as his word. "It wasn't Carissa that Bryce attempted to kill in the Gracewood. It was me."

"You lie." The words were hasty, but the way that apprehension dawned in Lord Lenore's eyes indicated that he suspected Jacen told the truth. "What reason would Carissa and my own daughter have to twist the story?"

"Because Carissa believed sparing my life over Bryce's would lead to war."

Lord Lenore raked his hands through his hair, and Jacen hoped that his gamble had been worth it. Carissa would be infuriated when she learned what he'd done, but she trusted Lord Lenore…didn't she?

"Who else knows?"

"Only myself, Carissa, and Bellona." Jacen moved toward the hearth. "Carissa thought if her people suspected she favoured a Generan over one of her own, they would turn on her. So, tell me, Lord Lenore, was she right?"

"Bryce's attempt was ill advised." The older man sucked in a deep breath. "I would never endanger Carissa. If that means keeping this a secret, I will do so. Was it you, Majesty, who dealt the killing blow?"

"No." Jacen wished he could lie but found himself unable. "It was Bellona."

Lord Lenore sank into a chair by the hearth, burying his face in his hands. No man wanted to hear that their child had to become an executioner because they had been forced into a dire situation. Jacen wondered if he had gone too far, divulged too much. If there was an indication that Lord Lenore might turn on Carissa, might expose information that could have Basium turn on its Queen, Jacen was prepared to deal with that problem.

"Killing me would only have brought retribution from Cobryn, and Carissa knew that. She made the best choice she could have, given the circumstances."

"Bellona would have let you die," Lord Lenore said quietly. He looked up at Jacen. "It was because of Carissa that she brought Bryce down."

"Yes." Jacen swallowed the sudden lump in his throat. "Carissa tried to talk him down, assure him that it wasn't the way...but he didn't want to listen. Even when she spoke of revenge, which I would suspect involves my father and Deacon."

"Do you believe she meant that?" Lord Lenore asked.

"Revenge?" Jacen paused, but only for a moment. "Yes. I do."

There was silence between the two men for a few moments. Lord Lenore had information that could cause problems for Carissa if exposed to the general public. Either he would betray her, or he would keep his troubled mind to himself and keep her secret. It had been a selfish position for Jacen to put him in. He wanted to ensure those closest to Carissa truly had her best intentions at heart.

"Have you heard of the Jackals?" Lord Lenore's question caught Jacen off-guard, and he frowned at the older man, trying to decide whether he had heard correctly. He had the feeling that Lord Lenore was not referring to animals.

"The Jackals?"

"They are...a group." Lord Lenore pushed himself to his feet. "Once you reach Emlen, you will find out about them soon enough. Suffice to say that Lord Ambrose is a powerful mouthpiece to be certain, but his morals come from a different place."

Jacen wondered why the Lord of Theron told him this, but perhaps it was an exchange—one secret for another. Jacen had entrusted Lord Lenore with the truth of Bryce's death, and so Lord Lenore gave him the name of a group in Emlen. A group that did what, exactly? The mention of the name troubled Lord

Lenore, making Jacen wary.

"I see your conflict." A wry smile crossed Lord Lenore's lips. "The question is not whether you are loyal to Basium or Genera. You are loyal to the idea that we can have peace in Basium, even after the Conquest."

"It's a nice idea," Jacen admitted, shrugging his shoulders. "But I know war is coming. I don't know where or when. I just know that Basium has been under my father's boot for long enough."

"Goddess help you if Basium rises up." Lord Lenore opened the door and stepped back, his gaze piercing Jacen's soul. "Because even Elethea herself wouldn't be able to help you if Carissa chooses her people over you."

It had become no secret that Carissa's favourite place in Theron was the maze out in the gardens. Apparently, it had been a place where she and her siblings, along with Bellona, had played games as children. Jacen had not yet explored the maze but on their final day in Theron when he could not find his wife, he had the distinct feeling he would find her within.

Making his way into the heart of the maze took some time. Although he personally did not enjoy the wretched place so much, he supposed not only did it hold childhood memories, but many plants grew in the nooks and corners throughout. Perfect for someone like her.

Carissa sat on the ageing stone bench in the centre of the maze in peaceful contemplation. Jacen approached hesitantly, uncertain of how welcome he would be. When Carissa caught his eye and smiled, he took that as an invitation to join her on the bench. It was easier to sit in silence with her, for he found the quiet that stretched between them grew comfortable.

"You aren't ready to leave."

"No." Carissa heaved a sigh, clasping her hands in her lap. "I have not visited Theron in many years, but there is a sense of home about it. Something I can't find in Marinel anymore."

The idea that she did not find peace in the capital did not surprise to Jacen, but it made him pity her. He wished he could do something to make her feel secure in a space that had once been her beloved home and had turned into a gilded prison.

"There is something I have to tell you." Jacen cleared his throat. He knew the moment he told Lord Lenore the truth that he would need to inform Carissa.

"I told Lord Lenore what really happened that day in the Gracewood."

"What?" Carissa was on her feet in an instant, violet-blue eyes burning with indignation. "Why would you do that?"

"You don't trust him?" Jacen asked, wondering if he had made a terrible mistake and misjudged how much faith Carissa had in him.

"Of course I do. That doesn't mean you get to make decisions about this yourself. It's something we're both involved in, something we agreed on what story we were going to tell."

Carissa paced back and forth, agitation in every line of her body. How could he explain why he told Lord Lenore? He didn't think she would agree with him putting Lord Lenore's loyalty to a test.

"I thought it wise that he knew. He is Bellona's father, and one of your fiercest supporters. I wanted to indicate that we trusted him to know something only the ones involved in the situation were privy to."

Carissa ceased pacing and looked at him with an expression Jacen couldn't quite place. A tight smile spread across her lips, easing the knots that had formed in his stomach. He did not enjoy fighting with Carissa, especially when he began to suspect she was an Imperium. She could have powers he didn't, abilities he could not comprehend.

"I suppose you're right."

Whatever words Jacen had been expecting from his wife, it hadn't been for her to concede defeat. One of Carissa's weaknesses was her fervent belief in the justice of things she did. Everyone could be wrong at times, and he was glad that Carissa could acknowledge she had overreacted. She gathered her skirts and sat back down beside him, eyes roaming the well-trimmed hedges of the maze.

"Don't tell me you want to plant a maze in Marinel next."

"Of course not." Carissa shook her head, but the jest brought a smile back to her lips. "There's certainly not room. I would definitely like to plant more when summer is over, though."

Deacon had sneered at such a hobby, deeming it unladylike and unbecoming of a Queen. Jacen believed that planting and gardening suited Carissa. Everyone needed an outlet, and at least hers was a healthy one.

Rising to his feet, Jacen offered her his hand. Carissa did not want to leave, but the next few stops on their tour were important—particularly the last. The safety and security of Theron and Lord Lenore's hospitality would be missed, but they could not stay forever.

"What do you say? Shall we find our way out of this maze and prepare for our journey to Seneca?"

Jacen tentatively approached Bellona as the redhead sat by the fire, warming her hands. She had grown glum since they had left Theron, no doubt due to leaving her father behind. He had only interacted with the young woman in Vida or Carissa's presence, and was now determined to get to know her better. It wouldn't do to be on bad terms with someone so close to his wife.

Bellona glanced at him sharply as he sank down beside her, stretching his hands out as well.

"The Queen is with Vida trying on dresses in which she may greet Lady Renatus."

"I don't want to speak to Carissa, I wanted to talk to you." Jacen sighed at Bellona's tense posture. "I do not wish us to be enemies, Bellona. You have known my wife a long time, and I wish us to be friends."

"Friends?" Bellona repeated the word with no small amount of scorn. "Let me be plain with you, Your Majesty. I tolerate you because you do not mistreat the Queen, and because she seems to be fond of you. There is absolutely no need for us to be friends."

"So, you will forever hate me due to the crimes my family committed?" Jacen's shoulder slumped, his brow creasing in frustration at her response.

"What of your own crimes?" Bellona drew her hands away from the flames, raising her eyebrows. "I could forgive you standing idly by during the Conquest. But forcing your own people back into submission because they defy Cobryn? Making no attempt to rectify things here now that you have returned?"

"That's precisely what I'm doing." Jacen frowned. "This tour will help me better get to know the people, their problems, their concerns."

"You know who has the real power here." Bellona's voice cast low, green eyes glimmering in the firelight. "You know that it isn't Carissa. You play both sides, Jacen. That is why I don't like you."

Bellona got to her feet and marched off before Jacen could protest. Her words, however harsh, were not inaccurate. Perhaps he lived in a world of fantasy where things could move forward, where they could go on without reflecting on the past. Such an idea was foolish. How could he ask the Basiumites to simply forget about the Conquest and its aftermath?

It would have been easy to let Bellona go, and maybe it was dangerous to follow her, but Jacen did so anyway. He had the distinct impression catching her by the arm would lead to being punched in the face regardless of his station, so instead he called to her.

"Bellona!"

"Yes?" She spun on her heel to face him, hands planted on her hips and eyes narrowed in accusation.

"I am trying." Jacen licked his dry lips. "Trying to be a worthy husband to Carissa, to be a good King. But things here are…different to home. I'm still learning."

"Deacon said something about consummation in Genera…" Bellona hesitated. "Was that true?"

"That it's witnessed? Yes." Jacen raked a hand through his hair. How merciful it had been that Carissa hadn't experienced such a humiliating ordeal. He had argued against it, reminding his father that the Basiumites would not take it well.

"I'm glad it was you and not Deacon." Bellona's words came out unusually soft, but her eyes were fierce. "He would have hurt her, and I would have tried to kill him for it. No woman should ever suffer such a fate."

"Your mother…" Jacen approached the topic apprehensively, giving Bellona the chance to knock it back if it wasn't something she wished to discuss. Instead, she looked at her hands and took a deep breath.

"She was raped and murdered by a Generan soldier." Bellona's eyes shone with unshed tears when she looked up. "I witnessed the whole thing from the cupboard my mother convinced me to hide in."

Jacen reeled back. He'd known about the incident, but not that Bellona had seen it firsthand. He knew the young woman would not want to be pitied. He began to realise how much people in this country had suffered, how much trauma they carried with them. What was he to say to that? How could he offer comfort when he didn't understand? He had only experienced the horror of war as a victor, not a victim.

"I…I didn't know."

"Not many people do." Bellona angrily wiped at her eyes. "But you see why I would do anything to protect Carissa. I stood by helplessly while unspeakable violence was committed against my mother. I won't do so again."

Jacen could see Bellona only wanted what was best for Carissa—from her perspective, Jacen could easily turn into the aggressor. He wished he could say something to prove he would never harm Carissa, yet his words were like dust.

There was no promise he could make that these people would believe. So instead of words, he would have to hope that action—investing himself in the wellbeing of Basium—would be good enough.

THE ELUSIVE QUEEN
CARISSA DARNELL

Carissa hoped to find a kindred spirit in Celestine Renatus. Seneca was the only one of the core five houses governed by a woman, so Carissa expected less sexism here than in Fortua. A lush forest surrounded the city, reminding Carissa of the Gracewood. She shuddered at the memory of a place now tainted, tarnished with Bryce's blood.

The dress she wore upon her arrival to Seneca was her most resplendent yet, red and complete with beading that glittered in the sunlight. This time, she chose not to wear her crown upon arrival. It was something she considered donning during the welcome feast that Celestine would have set out, but she had no need to remind the woman of her status.

Seneca glimmered brightly in the morning sun, wind chimes tinkling gently through the city upon the arrival of the royal entourage. The streets were wide to allow passage of carts and carriage, the cobblestones gleaming as though they had been polished. At the top of the gentle slope of the main street, a beautiful blonde woman waited with her hands patiently clasped.

"Your Majesty." Celestine sauntered forth with an inimitable grace, bending into a curtsy before kissing both of Carissa's cheeks. "It is a pleasure to welcome you here to Seneca."

"As it is to be received by you." Carissa reached a hand behind her, and Jacen took it without being prompted. "My husband, Jacen."

"Majesty." Celestine curtsied before him as well. After Lord Benedict's blatant sexism toward Carissa and Kato's evident disdain for Jacen, it was refreshing to have a happy medium. "I believe we met several times in the capital, yet this is our first official meeting. How are you enjoying your tour so far?"

"It has been…interesting," Jacen said, shifting between his feet. It struck Carissa throughout the duration of the tour that she had done most of the talking. Jacen lacked Deacon's silver tongue—his discomfort in courtly small talk came from Cobryn.

"I have a dress and some lovely jewellery I would be honoured to lend you for tonight's feast." Celestine turned her attention to Carissa, offering an arm. "Would you like to see?"

"Of course." Carissa slipped her arm through Celestine's, allowing the older woman to lead her into the castle. It was beautifully decorated, with intricate paintings, tinkling windchimes, and bold tapestries covering the walls— brighter and more inviting than the gloomy corridors of Fortua or the minimalist practicality of Theron. She had the feeling Celestine wished to talk about more than pretty trinkets, however she was subtler about her intentions than Kato had been.

"This will be the room you share with Jacen." Celestine opened the door, and Carissa had to marvel at just how beautifully the room had been decorated. The windows overlooked the forest outside, a fine mist having settled over the tops of the trees. The room was decorated in various shades of green, the primary colour on House Renatus's proud panther-adorned sigil.

"Is this the dress?" Carissa examined the gown that had been laid out on the bed. It was a dark emerald green, paired with paler green accessories, a stark contrast to the ivory white blanket it lay upon. She had to appreciate Celestine's eye for detail. She ran her fingers over the dress, the fabric soft to the touch.

"It is indeed." Celestine lifted her chin, smiling at the wonder in Carissa's eyes. "I hope you don't mind that I picked it out for you."

"Of course not, it's lovely."

"I thought we could discuss other matters." Celestine's light-hearted tone became more serious, causing Carissa to tear her gaze away from the dress. "Matters regarding your marriage."

"Ah." Carissa smiled wryly, bracing herself for more disdainful opinions. "I take it you dislike my husband also."

"Unlike Lord Ambrose, I have nothing against Jacen personally." Celestine's eyes glimmered with mischief. "He is a handsome young man, isn't he?"

"I…I don't understand what my husband's looks have to do with anything." Carissa's cheeks burned with heat. She found Jacen attractive, but attraction was not something to base a relationship off.

"I see the way he looks at you." Celestine seated herself on the bed. "Deacon too, for that matter."

Carissa did not know what to say. She wasn't a fool—Jacen had made it obvious he found her beautiful, though she thought Deacon's interest had less to do with beauty and more to do with a lust for power. If he obtained Carissa, he legally obtained the throne of Basium—which he coveted more than he should.

"I don't think it's quite like that."

"I've known men for a long time." Celestine ran her fingers through her silky blonde hair. "All men are different, it's true. There can be no denying that there is a certain power women can wield over men, should they choose to."

Carissa knew precisely what sort of power Celestine was talking about. It wasn't a weapon she wanted to use. She was more than just her sexuality, and she had other avenues of getting what she wanted. The idea that she would use feminine wiles on Jacen—and, goddess forbid, on *Deacon*—made her skin crawl.

"That's not my chosen power."

"It is an option." Celestine tossed her hair back. "Deacon may not be fooled, but your husband is young. Boys that age think of few things, but sex is certainly one of them. Men want to dominate women, yet they don't ever think perhaps they're behaving exactly how a woman might want. In surrendering your body, you can gain control over them."

"Jacen knows he couldn't rule Basium without me." Carissa folded her arms over her chest. "I don't need to wield anything over him."

She understood what Celestine meant, and saw the wisdom in it, but the thought of such a method left her uncomfortable. She had her own ways of gaining information. She and Jacen had sex because they wanted to, because they hoped to have an heir—not because she used her body as a weapon.

"Of course not." Celestine smiled gently, but her eyes steely. "It must have been a long journey. I will let you rest and recover before the feast tonight. It has been some time since there was anything to celebrate in Seneca."

"Celestine. Do they ever accept it? Having a woman ruling them instead of a man? Do those who were opposed to it ever come around?"

The words were out of Carissa's mouth before she registered that she exposed her vulnerabilities.

"Some do, and some don't." Celestine turned to face the Queen as she rested her hand on the brass door handle. "Your Majesty, if I may give you some advice? Do what's right, not what's popular. There will always be those there to fight you, to use your gender as a slight. Don't let them win. Hold your head high and make your choices regardless of what they say."

Celestine certainly knew how to host a celebration. As Carissa entered the hall with Bellona's arm linked tightly through hers, she noted how the music was louder than Theron, the alcohol flowing more freely, the people in more joyful spirits. Theron was troubled, plagued by the knowledge that Lord Ambrose had come knocking. Seneca was carefree—or was this simply a masquerade?

One of the musicians appeared to either be a vibrant sort or had consumed a fair few wines already. The woman with the fiddle beamed with pearly white teeth as she cast around the hall, playing her instrument with reckless abandon. Jacen stood nearby with a fascinated expression on his face. When Carissa examined him, she realised that he wasn't staring at the woman, but rather the fiddle she played. Grinning, she slipped her arm from Bellona's and approached her husband.

"Do they not have fiddles in Genera?"

"They certainly do." Jacen tore his eyes away from the instrument to glance at his wife. His gaze raked over her appreciatively, and Carissa was pleased at his attention. She would need to thank Celestine again later for letting her borrow the dress. "You look lovely."

"We were discussing the fiddle."

"Oh, yes." Jacen reached up to scratch the back of his head, embarrassed. "You see, I enjoyed playing the fiddle. Vida was the one taught music, but I had a love for the fiddle that she never did. Father quickly put his foot down and said it was a feminine hobby and I should not indulge in it."

That did sound like the sort of thing Cobryn would say, and Carissa despised the man even more. Jacen averted his eyes even discussing the fact that he'd taken up the fiddle. Learning music was for everyone, not just women. Tilting her chin up boldly, Carissa took matters into her own hands.

"Well, that's not how I see it, and certainly not how anyone else in Basium does, either. If you want to give the fiddle a try, you should."

"I don't know about that." Jacen's brow furrowed, yet his hazel eyes kept flicking over to the instrument. Carissa would not force him to do something he was uncomfortable with, though she could tell he itched to give it a try.

"If it's something you enjoy, why not?"

Apparently, the words convinced him. A smile spread across Jacen's features, and he took a step toward the musician. The woman raised her eyebrows but recognised him as the King and sank into a curtsy.

"Your Majesty."

"I was wondering if…if I might have a turn?" Jacen indicated the instrument, and Carissa's spirits lifted further when the musician handed him the fiddle. Her husband's eyes shone as he raised the fiddle and the bow with uncertain hands.

In moments, a merry tune belted out across the feast hall, sounding like a sea shanty rather than a song of the court. Although Carissa did not recognise the tune, she found herself tapping her foot along. Some of the guests appeared startled by the King playing the fiddle, yet they soon went back to dancing along.

Vida caught Bellona's hands and spun her in circles. Carissa clapped her hands along to the beat, unable to help the ridiculous grin that crossed her face. She couldn't remember a time when she had felt so giddy with delight, so perfectly content with where she was and the people she was with. Seeing how much it thrilled her husband, watching him play the fiddle with no hesitation—it brought her genuine satisfaction.

Then she caught Deacon watching from other side of the hall, his arms folded over his chest, and the smile froze on her lips. Something dark haunted his expression, something that gave her chills about the way he didn't join in the dancing and music with the rest of them. His eyes weren't set on her, but rather Jacen. His lips twisted down and she realised then what she saw. *Jealousy.* When Deacon looked at Jacen, he felt envy.

The idea seemed laughable. Deacon had power, he had everything that he could ever want. Seeing all eyes on Jacen, seeing the people of Basium enjoying his nephew's presence, seemed to be what turned Deacon cold. Perhaps underneath it all, Deacon wanted to be loved and respected. The idea that he may not be a heartless monster was one that vehemently disagreed with Carissa.

Deacon's eyes locked onto hers, and Carissa turned away, her attention moving back to Jacen. He laughed and tapped his foot as he continued to play the fiddle like he was born to it. When the song ended, he handed the instrument back to the musician to cheers and applause. Carissa was the first at her husband's side, pushing aside all thoughts of Deacon.

"That was brilliant!"

"You seem surprised," he teased, hazel eyes glittering.

"Perhaps that her husband considered taking up such a ridiculous hobby." Deacon approached with a disdainful look on his face. "Really, Jacen? The fiddle is better suited to Vida."

"Jacen's music brings light and laughter to this hall." Carissa spun to face him before Jacen could feel ashamed of his actions. "Your presence does not."

Deacon tilted his head to the side, observing her curiously. She felt uncomfortable under his close scrutiny, although she attempted not to show it. She rested a hand on Jacen's arm when he moved forward, silently urging him not to speak as his malevolent uncle smiled darkly.

"It's interesting that you speak for your people, Carissa. Can they not speak for themselves?"

The implication that her people didn't have a voice did not sit well with Carissa in the slightest, but she could not find a way to express her anger in a way that wouldn't result in repercussions. The best response was to ignore Deacon, to act as though he hadn't gotten under her skin. Taking Jacen's arm more firmly, she steered him away, although she could feel Deacon's eyes on them.

"Are you alright?" Jacen asked quietly, and Carissa loosened her fingers around his arm.

"Deacon has a habit of trying to bring out the worst in me." Her smile was tight. "I don't want to think about it. He is nothing more than vindictive. You were right, I was surprised at how good you were playing that fiddle."

Knowing that she would one day have to defeat Deacon frightened Carissa. There were those among her nobles, such as Lord Benedict, who believed in some of the things he'd done. As much as she wanted to throw off Basium's oppressors, she constantly worked uphill. She could only hope that once they arrived in Emlen, this tour would be worth it.

A cold chill of realisation ran up Carissa's spine as she acknowledged perhaps this was what it had been about all along—finding out whether the rebellion was something worth investing in. The day would come when Jacen would see that too, see right through the pretence of bonding with the core five families and the subjects.

Carissa did want to learn more about her country and make it a better place—only in a different way than Jacen likely imagined.

Spending a week with Celestine had been more productive than Carissa could have hoped. She had shadowed the older woman, feeling like she learned what it meant to be a woman in power in a country that favoured men. With her mother dead and her grandmother a powerless relic of a past age, there were few women that Carissa could learn command from.

The people of Seneca respected Celestine, but many of them watched Carissa with cautious or disapproving eyes. It made her disheartened, although she strived to push past the feeling, smiling and interacting with her subjects. It tired her more than she'd imagined, and she found herself grateful when Celestine suggested they return to the castle.

She had deliberately excluded Jacen from many of these outings. Whilst his presence had been a welcome one at the feast, after the attempt on his life in the Gracewood, Carissa found she had recurring nightmares about something similar happening. She also didn't want Jacen to overhear any potentially dangerous discussion of rebellion, especially when Carissa began to suspect that Celestine knew more about Emlen than she let on.

"They don't seem to think much of me." Bitterness crept into Carissa's voice as they made their way back up to the castle. She knew she couldn't win everyone's heart, but at the moment it felt as though she wasn't winning any. Then there were the whispers that circulated throughout Seneca—*goddess cursed.*

"This is what it means to be in bed with the enemy." Celestine's fingers tightened on Carissa's arm. "They won't stop judging you for it, no matter how much Jacen tries to be a respectable figure."

"I will just have to work on proving my worth to them." Carissa met Celestine's gaze. "I don't suppose you have heard word from Lord Ambrose?"

"He mourns his brother's death, of course." Celestine released the Queen's arm as they stepped into the shade. "He is puzzled as to why Bryce would make an attempt on your life."

Celestine's quiet gave Carissa room to answer, but she avoided doing so. Too many people already knew the truth of the matter. She liked Celestine, yet she wasn't certain that she could trust her with the truth of Bryce's execution.

"It's a mystery to us all." Carissa gave a light shrug of her shoulders.

"Forgive me, Your Majesty, but you don't seem too perturbed for a woman who experienced an assassination attempt."

The words pricked at Carissa, like needles under her skin. Nonetheless, nothing good could come from making Celestine an enemy—particularly when Carissa did so want her as an ally.

"I watched my father and brother being violently murdered right in front of me, Lady Renatus. There is little that perturbs me after that."

Celestine flinched. "My apologies, my Queen. It wasn't my place to question you. You're right—people react to different situations in different ways."

Carissa's feet ached like lead as she traipsed back into the castle. She could only hope that one day, all of these secrets and lies would be worth it. One day, Basium would see the sort of Queen she really was—not merely the Morrow family's puppet. Such a goal required patience and persistence.

THE APPREHENSIVE KING
JACEN MORROW

Jacen watched Carissa stand at the helm of the ship as it glided across the shimmering sapphire sea, eyes closed and expression peaceful as her black hair whipped around her face.

The city of Isadore was located on the only island in Basium, Ardelis. It was not unlike the Generan islands in terms of the landscape. Ardelis had more raised terrain than Jacen had anticipated, sloping up towards one end of the island. The city of Isadore stood atop a cliff, yellow flag flying proudly in the breeze. He couldn't see the sigil at this distance.

Carissa had told him that she had never visited Isadore before, although she had met Lord Tamarice a handful of times. It unnerved Jacen that this would be their final stop before Emlen. The idea of meeting Lord Ambrose, a man who despised him, terrified him.

As the ship approached the docks of Ardelis, Jacen spotted a tall man with steel-grey hair in fine robes waiting for them, along with several others of similar garb who must be members of his family. Carissa made her way down the ship as the crew prepared to dock.

The assembled group all sank to one knee as Carissa and Jacen disembarked. The wooden slats of the dock shone as though they had recently been oiled. No other boat docked could compare to the splendour of the royal ship. Scattered around the dock were dinghies and fishing boats, bobbing up and down in the water, tiny in comparison. Jacen took his time examining his surroundings while Carissa immediately approached the grey-haired man. He eased himself to his feet, pressing a kiss to the back of the Queen's hand.

"It's a delight to see you, Majesty."

"Thank you for welcoming us to your home, Lord Tamarice." Carissa's smile was gracious. She had learned to greet and be greeted like a true monarch. She stood straight, chin up, and though her smile reached her eyes, Jacen knew her intimately enough to see that she simply went through the motions. She found little joy in the pleasantries of court.

Lord Tamarice nodded. "I must say, it's an unexpected surprise to have another of my kind here."

Carissa's smile stayed plastered across her face, but her brows furrowed. "One of what kind, Lord Tamarice?"

"An Imperium, of course!" Lord Tamarice chuckled. "Aside from your grandmother Miriam and a select few others, there are too few of us amongst the nobility."

A tense silence followed, the only sound the waves lapping against the dock and the murmurs of Lord Tamarice's company. Carissa's eyes widened in alarm. Jacen examined his wife in shock. He had suspected the magic in her blood, of course, but hearing it confirmed...

Deacon's hazel eyes shone, and a victorious smile crossed his lips. The idea Carissa had powers that could rival his intrigued him—which terrified Jacen. The last thing he wanted was for Deacon to establish Carissa as a threat.

Lord Tamarice's smile faded as he took in the astonishment in their faces, the stunned silence his remark left. He immediately looked to Carissa for clarification.

"My apologies, your Majesty, did you not know?"

"I...I did," Carissa admitted, clasping her hands in front of her and staring at the wooden panelling of the docks. "But the others did not."

Jacen glanced over at Bellona and Vida, expecting to see shock and perhaps betrayal on their faces. Instead, their expressions were grim. Some, it seemed, had known of Carissa's secret. The Queen turned to face the others with a tight smile.

"Lord Tamarice is an Imperium who can sense others of his kind. An unusual gift, to be sure."

The man's cheeks reddened with embarrassment at the fact he had exposed Carissa as an Imperium before the others, and hastily attempted to amend his mistake by changing the subject completely.

"Come, Your Majesty. We are having pheasant for dinner. I've a grand feast prepared in your honour."

Carissa offered a pretty false smile and took Lord Tamarice's outstretched arm, casting a glance over her shoulder at Jacen. Her secret exposed, Carissa's eyes filled with blatant fear.

Isadore was the least populated of the five major cities that made up Basium's core nobility. The height of the castle on the cliff was impressive—Jacen had to crane his neck back to look up at the turrets. Apparently, they had a thriving fishing trade, and their men made up a third of Basium's navy.

Lord Tamarice's halls streamed with ribbons of colour from the stained-glass windows lining the corridors. The distant boom of waves crashing against the foot of the cliff was audible even inside, but Jacen suspected the castle was far too high for the sea to be any real threat.

Their sigil, as it turned out, was a rat. Voice light with amusement, Lord Tamarice described its origins. Apparently, his ancestors had been notorious pirates prowling the Razmaran coast and had earned themselves the derisive nickname of 'sea rats'. When House Tamarice came to power, they had made it a private joke.

The feast was a lively occasion. Carissa ate and drank her fill but smiled politely when offered dessert and claimed the journey on the ship had upset her stomach. When she left the hall, Jacen partook in dessert but departed before a final round of mead. In truth, Jacen wanted answers from Carissa. She had not outright lied to him, but nor had she trusted him with the truth.

Indeed, when Jacen entered the room, Carissa sat by the hearth in her nightdress, a crystal glass of red wine in her hand as she stared into the flames. She glanced over her shoulder, heaving a sigh. Carissa made no move to leave the chair. She didn't speak a word. She took another deep sip from the glass.

"Why didn't you tell me?" Jacen asked, folding his arms and observing his wife. When she looked across at him again, he noticed her red-rimmed eyes. She had been crying, and he wondered why the revelation of her power distressed her so. Did she suspect, as he did, that Deacon would use this to his advantage?

"Because I didn't trust you." Her blunted words stung but at least they were honest.

"You trusted Bellona and Vida." He tried and failed to keep the accusation out of his tone. The knowledge that his sister had known Carissa's secret while he had not hurt him.

"They are my best friends." Carissa set her glass down, getting to her feet. "Even they discovered the truth recently. Now everyone knows. *Deacon* knows. Can you imagine what will happen once word reaches your father, once he considers me a threat and that he would have been better off killing me?"

Cobryn would not have killed Carissa, for he would have had no claim to the Basiumite throne. Jacen decided not to point this out, instead moving across and placing his hands lightly on her shoulders. Carissa watched him apprehensively, as though worried he may lash out.

"If we are really trying to rule together, we need to trust each other, Carissa. Forget about Deacon and my father. This is you and me. What is it that you can do?"

"I'm an empath." Carissa swallowed hard, casting her gaze back toward the fire. "I can feel the emotions of others. Influence them to an extent."

That didn't add up with the fury Jacen had witnessed at their camp, how the leaves had blown around them with such wildness, but he said nothing. Perhaps it had been related to Carissa's strong emotions at the time. He didn't know exactly how her magic worked, so he wasn't one to question it. He used his thumbs to rub small circles on Carissa's arms, and she relaxed under his touch.

"What is it you're so frightened of?" he asked.

"Deacon." Her violet-blue eyes flew wide as they flicked up to meet his. "You know what he's like, Jacen. He will use my abilities for his own gain if he knows what they are. He can know I'm an Imperium, but he doesn't need to be aware of what I can do."

Jacen pressed a kiss to her forehead, holding her close as she trembled against him. He took her distress regarding Deacon seriously, especially as he knew just how manipulative his uncle could be. Carissa had already been a puppet on strings pulled by Deacon. He wouldn't let it happen again, not when he was now King of Basium.

"I won't let him use you," he promised.

"Jacen," she said softly, her smile gentle as she drew back to rest her hand lightly against his cheek. "You may not get a choice."

Jacen went to confront Vida. Although he could understand Carissa keeping such a secret from him, the fact that his own sister kept this from him hurt. He found his sister in the hall, flirting openly with Lord Tamarice's younger brother, Claudio. Jacen frowned, crossing over to catch Vida's arm and forcing a smile.

"I was hoping we could speak in private, Vida."

"Of course, brother." Flashing Claudio a charming smile, she accompanied Jacen out to the balcony. Leaning on the railing, Jacen could see the ocean glittering below—something he had not seen in any other part of Basium. The island was not large, with Isadore the only major city, but several smaller towns sprawled across the edges. He could see some of the lights from Isadore, the highest point on Ardelis.

"Claudio? Really?"

Vida shrugged, tossing her blonde hair over her shoulder. "What of it?"

"You're to be married," Jacen reminded her, wondering what Meryn would think of how close his betrothed was to a Basiumite lordling.

"I'm not married yet." Vida frowned, her tone becoming defensive. "Nothing would come of Claudio and I. Why do you insist on spoiling my fun?"

"You never mentioned Carissa's abilities."

"It wasn't my place." Vida's eyes narrowed when Jacen opened his mouth to retort. "Nor is it my fault your wife doesn't trust you enough to talk about them."

Jacen refrained from asking whether Carissa trusted anyone. Had she told Vida about what happened in the Gracewood? He had his doubts. He thought Carissa shared different pieces of herself with different people, and few knew everything about her. Miriam and Bellona, if Jacen had to guess.

"She's concerned about Deacon."

"Jacen." Vida turned from the magnificent view to survey her brother, hazel eyes flashing with impatience. "I am just as aware as you that our uncle is not always a good man. However, he is not pure evil, and you'd do well to stop seeing him as such."

The statement did not surprise Jacen, nor did Vida defending Deacon's character. Their uncle possessed a soft spot for her. Jacen wondered if she reminded him of Relda. He didn't believe Deacon was evil, but he was corrupt and would use whatever means necessary to maintain control over Basium. In name, Jacen may be the country's King, but Deacon was unwilling to relinquish the power he'd held over the nation in his nephew's absence.

"He's not evil, but he'd stop at nothing to control Carissa and use her against her own people."

"Sometimes, I wonder if you wanted this or not." Vida gave a wry smile but a storm gathered in those hazel eyes. "A marriage to Carissa. You could have said no at any time."

"Do you really think that's the truth?" Jacen asked, disbelieving. Could Vida know so little about what Cobryn was like, or did she choose to turn a blind eye? "Of the two of us, I would safely say that you're the one who's been given more freedom."

"What would you know?" Vida demanded, whirling back to face him with her hands balled into fists. "You've been given everything. Always Father's favourite. A country, a crown…and what do I have? An impending marriage to some upstart heir with no power and no influence, but the ability to turn on Father at any moment. I am a gift, a guarantee of the Generan islands being taken seriously."

Jacen was stunned into silence at Vida's words—no, at the bitterness that came with them. She was not Cobryn's only daughter, but she was the eldest. As she and Jacen had grown up, they had become pawns in the widespread game that Cobryn played. They both had their shackles, and he'd been a fool to assume Vida's carefree years in Basium would not come at a cost.

"You're right, Vida." Jacen reached forward to grip one of his sister's hands in his own. "I'm sorry. I know you probably wanted a better match."

"I had some silly ideas." Vida's smile lacked its usual sincerity. "I thought that because you'd formed such a powerful political match that I might have a choice in my husband. But marriages are contracts and it was stupid to think mine could have been anything more."

"You aren't married yet," Jacen reminded her, sensing Vida's apprehension regarding her upcoming wedding. "I don't know Meryn very well, but there's every chance he could care for you. He's a lucky man and he should know that. Married to the King's oldest daughter—he's married above his station."

Even as children, Vida had been the more tempestuous of the siblings, prone to tantrums and tears. Jacen would do anything in his power to make his little sister happy, pulling faces or coming up with silly jokes until he could coax a smile out of her. That hadn't changed as they became adults—Vida cracked a small smile, and his spirits lifted.

"I'll do what's expected." Vida squeezed Jacen's hand tightly. "As we've always done."

The words made Jacen realise that even in rulership of Basium, he was not free. He never would be, not until Cobryn was gone. He would always be his father's creature, operating on the Warmonger's will. He might have his own country to rule, yet Cobryn and Deacon expected that it would be ruled a certain way.

With tension brewing in Emlen, an assassination attempt on his life and the revelation that Carissa was Imperium, Jacen doubted things were going the way his father had planned. Basium would not be silenced and suppressed. Carissa had been enigmatic about how she felt—which made Jacen certain she may well be considering aiding the resistance.

I've seen enough war, Jacen thought, though the Generan islands had only been the beginning. If Basium went to war against Genera, the stakes would be magnified tenfold—a fight that would eventually engulf the continent of Razmara.

The pieces were beginning to move. Jacen needed to decide if he was content in playing Cobryn's pawn.

The Saviour Queen
Carissa Darnell

The fortress city of Emlen loomed overhead, cold and unwelcoming. Carissa wanted to shrink in on herself like she had as a child whenever she'd gotten shy, when she had her brothers to speak for her. There was no one to talk on Carissa's behalf, to represent her. Not even Miriam was with her. The prospect made the closed-off city and its rebellious lord all the more intimidating.

Carissa knew that was precisely what they wanted. A timid Queen shaking at the thought of confrontation would confirm Lord Ambrose's theories on her being a Morrow puppet. She had to appear strong and confident, even if she didn't feel it. A masquerade, like on Jacen's birthday.

She stared up at the huge city walls as they approached the gate. Deacon, Vida, and the others would be camping just outside these walls, and while she was privately glad for Deacon's absence, she could understand how forcing such a measure would lead to more tension. She had decided upon a small entourage, knowing that bringing too many people with her could be mistaken for flexing Marinel's might.

The portcullis opened with loud squeaks and groans, and Carissa found her stomach tying itself in knots as she rode through into the city beyond. Jacen and Bellona trotted at her back. Despite their close proximity, knowing so much weighed on her conversation with Lord Ambrose went left her isolated.

They followed the winding path up to the castle. Carissa twisted in her saddle and glanced at Bellona, who gave her best friend a firm nod. With that silent assurance, Carissa continued onward, anxious but determined. Once they reached the courtyard, a cry came from one of the Ambrose guardsmen.

"Her Majesty, the Queen!"

Excruciating silence followed. Carissa spotted Lord Ambrose and his wife immediately, their expressions stern and guarded. Swinging a leg over her saddle, she dismounted her horse, shoes clicking across the cobblestones as she walked toward the noble family. The assembly should have bent the knee, but Lord Ambrose stood straight and proud. Carissa's legs shook and her hands grew damp, yet she approached with her head held high. The noble family stood by a large stone statue of a man Carissa knew from her history lessons to be the Lord Farran Ambrose, founder of Emlen.

"Lord Ambrose." She didn't follow up with the traditional 'it's a pleasure'. He was in his early forties, with tired yet watchful grey eyes. He inclined his head stiffly, although his gaze flicked to Jacen, who approached tentatively a few steps behind Carissa.

"Your Majesty. I take it that Lord Morrow and the King's sister are outside our city walls as requested?"

"Of course." Carissa's smile strained as Bellona appeared by her side. "I would not want you or your people to feel uncomfortable."

She mentioned nothing of Deacon and Vida's comfort, for Deacon's did not matter to her and she doubted Vida's mattered to Lord Ambrose. No matter what, House Morrow was the enemy. He had not acknowledged Jacen's presence.

"I believe there is much to be discussed." Lord Ambrose raised his eyebrows, turning to head into the castle. "Should we start with the death of my younger brother?"

Deep unease came over Carissa. She had known that this moment would come, yet it didn't make it any easier. She opened her mouth to reply as they followed Lord Ambrose to the castle before a movement in the corner of her eye made her glance over her shoulder.

The boy in the jackal mask. She could tell from the nearly lavender blue of his eyes that it was the same one who'd danced with her at the masquerade. Her stomach twisted into knots. He must have seen her looking, for he tilted his head to the side and stepped forward.

She cast around for Jacen. He walked ahead, as though determined to enter the castle and escape the presence of House Ambrose as swiftly as possible. Lord Ambrose spoke with Bellona, both of them apparently oblivious to the boy in the jackal mask.

"Jacen," Carissa called desperately. She brushed past some of the others, freezing in horror when the bright glint of steel in the boy's hand caught the sunlight. The boy in the jackal mask moved quickly, stepping in front of Jacen and stabbing him in the stomach.

Someone screamed. Jacen staggered back. The boy in the jackal mask ripped the knife free, his wiry body tense. Carissa hurried to her husband's side as his white shirt bloomed crimson. When she pressed a hand to the wound, he cried out, and her fingers came away stained red. The boy had not retreated, and there was no doubt in Carissa's mind that he meant to strike again, to finish the job.

Carissa cast around wildly, before thrusting her blood-covered fingers in the direction of Farran's statue. She concentrated on the magic inside herself, called it forth with startling ease. The darkness came to her, eager and willing. She unleashed it in mere moments, letting the magic take hold of her.

The stone at the base of the statue gave way with a loud cracking, and Farran's likeness came tumbling down toward the boy in the jackal mask. His eyes widened and he rolled, the statue crashing to the ground where he'd stood mere moments before. The mask skidded away. As he rose, Carissa saw the horrified face of someone strangely familiar.

It can't be, he's dead.

The boy recovered his composure, his expression hardening. Before Carissa could get a second look at him, he'd darted off, retrieving his mask and disappearing through the panicking crowd.

Carissa immediately turned her attention to her injured husband. Jacen struggled to stay on his feet, and she wrapped a firm arm around his waist to hold him upright. Bellona came to her side in an instant, green eyes wide as she took in the King's wound.

"Did you see who it was?"

Carissa shook her head. *Your mind is playing tricks on you, it's just a coincidence.* "He needs urgent help."

"Come on." Bellona moved to Jacen's other side, heaving a sigh. "We'll get him into the castle."

Furious didn't begin to cover how Carissa felt. Her blood boiled, especially when she considered the convenient timing of the assassination attempt. Their group had just arrived when the boy in the jackal mask had attacked. Lord Ambrose insisted they had much to discuss, and Carissa certainly agreed. While Jacen slept and recovered, she demanded a meeting with Emlen's ruler.

The would-be assassin haunted Carissa as she entered the castle's meeting room, closely flanked by Bellona. She doubted her best friend would be letting her out of sight anytime soon. The shade of the boy's eyes, the familiarity of his features…it sent shivers down her spine. *He's dead. You know he's dead.*

"Your Majesty." Lord Ambrose pushed himself abruptly out of his seat, bowing his head. He displayed a humility that he hadn't upon her arrival. Lady Ambrose remained seated and silent beside him. "I am deeply apologetic about what happened to your husband."

"Are you?" Carissa would usually not have voiced her thoughts so boldly, yet her anger exceeded her caution. "Or are you simply sorry the assassin didn't succeed? It seems strange to me, Lord Ambrose, that this should happen so soon after our arrival. Not to mention, this is not the first time I have seen this boy. *Emlen never forgets.* That was what he said to me at my husband's masquerade."

"Are you certain it was the same person, and not just another wearing the same mask?"

Carissa's eyes narrowed. "Do not insult my intelligence, Lord Ambrose. I want to know if this boy came to kill Jacen at your bidding."

"No, of course not." Lord Ambrose's brow furrowed. "If I wanted to murder your husband, do you think I would have done it so obviously? It was a messy attempt at best. Whoever the boy was, he acted of his own accord—or perhaps at the behest of another."

Carissa took a deep breath, forcing herself to remain calm. Getting riled would do nothing but make Lord Ambrose an enemy. She had come to see if she could salvage the crown's relationship with Emlen, not distance it entirely. Lord Ambrose was cleverer than today's attempt—if he wanted to kill Jacen, and she suspected he did, he would have made it far subtler. The boy in the jackal mask did not serve House Ambrose, but someone else.

"You wanted to discuss Bryce?" Carissa braced herself for how this conversation would go. Now she would learn the truth of the matter. Had Bryce acted alone, or for his brother? Pain clouded Lord Ambrose's eyes at the mention of his deceased brother, and Carissa wished that the confrontation in the Gracewood hadn't ended in death.

"He was executed." Lord Ambrose's eyes flicked to Bellona, who stared at her feet. "I was informed it was because he made an attempt on your life, Majesty. I do not understand. My brother has always been loyal to the crown. He has never been an ambitious man, nor one of strong political beliefs."

"That was not what we witnessed in the Gracewood." Bellona spoke softly, her eyes sharp. "We saw a man corrupted by hatred. Hatred of what this country has become under Morrow rule. Something he saw fit to blame Carissa for."

Lord Ambrose shook his head fervently. "I cannot believe Bryce would try and kill the Queen. We share certain views on House Morrow, but…"

"Is there something you wish to tell us, Lord Ambrose?" Carissa asked, her voice quiet but deadly. She would be damned if she was the first to speak the truth.

"Very well." Lord Ambrose heaved a weary sigh, his grey eyes fierce. "It was I who ordered Bryce to murder Jacen."

Beside him, Lady Ambrose pressed a hand over her mouth and turned away. Carissa wondered if she hadn't known, or if her husband choosing to speak the truth shocked her. Carissa found her astonishment of Lord Ambrose's confession mirrored in Bellona. He realised this too, looking between them with a frown.

"You knew."

"We suspected." Carissa folded her arms over her chest. "We lied because we knew that, despite the circumstances, your brother's death instead of Jacen's would be used as a pretext for war. A civil war within my own country is something I want to prevent at all costs. You had your reasons for your deception, as I did with mine."

"Why?" Lord Ambrose examined Carissa with genuine confusion. "Why would you save a son of Cobryn Morrow? This could have been our chance for vengeance, and you took it from us."

"Haven't enough of our people died?" Carissa threw her arms up, exasperated. "You would have your brief victory, but Cobryn would rain hell down upon us at the murder of his son and heir. I did what I had to do to spare Basium from more violence and bloodshed, and if that costs your fealty, so be it."

Bellona gasped at her final words. Clearly, she hadn't anticipated that Carissa would openly condemn Lord Ambrose. Carissa hoped it would not be the case, yet she continued to observe Lord Ambrose, awaiting his response.

"You have a good heart, Majesty. I believe that. But you must realise why there are many among us who are concerned. You have been trapped in Marinel for four years now, first with Lord Morrow and now with King Jacen. There have been Morrow men influencing you since the Conquest. How can you expect us to loyally serve?"

"I do not *expect*." Carissa prickled with irritation. "I hope you will see that despite the enemies surrounding me, I am a Darnell."

Nothing more she could say to convince Lord Ambrose she was no Morrow puppet, so she turned and departed, Bellona close on her heels. Only once the door closed behind them and they were alone did Bellona catch Carissa's arm and tug her into the shadows of an alcove.

"People are talking about Farran's statue." Bellona's green eyes blazed, her expression expectant. "There are many who say it was the goddess's will. That she did not want your husband to die."

Carissa raised her eyebrows as her heart thundered in her chest. "What do you believe?"

"I believe what I saw." Bellona folded her arms over her chest. "Which was you reaching for that statue with Jacen's blood on your fingers. You brought it down, didn't you?"

A shiver ran down Carissa's spine. How many others had seen what Bellona had? How many others realised she was Maleficium? She had the feeling the lie she'd told about being empathic, about being Imperium, would soon be exposed. She fought back a wave of panic as she nodded slowly.

"Carissa…" Bellona appeared at a loss for what to say, eyes widening with alarm. "You need to be more careful. I know you showed Vida and I what you can do, but if Deacon finds out—"

"I know." Carissa swallowed hard. "That's why I lied and told Jacen I was Imperium. If anyone else discovered the truth, I fear they'd turn on me. If Lord Ambrose knew, he'd have another reason to question me."

"What about Jacen?" Bellona spoke quietly. "What if he realises what you did to save his life? He's clever, Carissa. The statue falling on its own might seem convenient to some, but he knows better."

"Did he see what I did?" Carissa didn't know if she could look him in the eye if he had. How could she explain that she had lied about putting her trust in him as well?

"I…I don't know." Bellona's apprehension worried Carissa. It disturbed her to realise how rattled Bellona was. Her friend could usually take anything in her stride. The only thing to have perturbed her so far was Bryce's execution.

Was it the attempt on Jacen's life that frightened Bellona, or the power Carissa had displayed in the courtyard? There was a reason the use of dark magic had been banned in her grandfather's time, although she could acknowledge he had been paranoid.

"What of the boy?" Anger surged through Carissa at the thought of the boy in the jackal mask.

"They're still looking for him." Bellona's troubled expression didn't fade. "He is dangerous. You need to be careful in case he decides to come after you next."

Carissa didn't mention that the boy in the jackal mask had every opportunity to kill her at the masquerade. She wasn't the one he wanted dead. He had, however, made his disdain toward her clear. *I could destroy him.* The darkness in her brought such a thought to the forefront of her mind. She allowed her blood magic to take hold in her desperation to save Jacen's life. What if next time, it consumed her?

"Have Deacon and Vida been informed about what happened to Jacen?"

Bellona shook her head. "I'm to leave as soon as possible to let them know."

Carissa bit her lip. Would Deacon take this as an excuse to crush Emlen once and for all? If he didn't, what would Cobryn do when he found out? This was precisely what she had been attempting to avoid when she'd lied about the first attempt on Jacen's life in the Gracewood.

Was Carissa truly goddess cursed, as the people often whispered? It had been some time since Carissa had spoken to the goddess. She needed Elethea's guidance more than ever. Her prayers had never been answered before and she felt forgotten, left alone with the goddess's back turned to her. Despite knowing that she, and not divine intervention, was responsible for Jacen's survival, it had been a while since Carissa had put herself in the goddess's hands.

How could such a being care so little about the massacre of her family? That thought led to Carissa's visits to the chapel becoming less frequent. Yet Jacen living through both attempts on his life had Carissa wondering if, after she'd forsaken the goddess for so long, perhaps the goddess watched over her. Perhaps she was not goddess cursed after all.

From the walls of Emlen, the Morrow campsite looked small. As Carissa headed out to the camp early in the morning, she found that the walls loomed ominously, disappearing into the cool mist. She would have found it wondrous, if the city and its occupants didn't fill her with dread.

Vida appeared in minutes, just as she had promised she would. Carissa knew announcing a visit to the camp would mean bearing Deacon's presence when she only wanted to speak with Vida away from prying eyes. Dark circles pressed under her friend's eyes as though she hadn't slept. Vida's hands wrung at her dress. The news about what had happened in Emlen had taken a toll.

"How is he?" Vida asked softly.

"He's recovering well." Carissa raked her fingers through her dark hair, damp with mist that settled over it. The knot in the pit of her stomach refused to go away, tightening like a noose. She thought she might explode from the stress, but she could only keep going. She could not afford to break down.

"I should have been there." Vida shook her head slowly, tears brimming in her hazel eyes. She raised a hand to wipe them away, and Carissa enveloped her in a hug. This couldn't have been easy for Vida, either. She had committed no crimes against Basium. Nonetheless, Lord Ambrose insisted on her being out of sight.

"He's strong."

"How did your discussion with Lord Ambrose go?" Vida extricated herself from Carissa's arm, tilting her head to the side.

Carissa bit her lip. There was so much she hadn't told Vida. Her best friend might know about the nature of Carissa's magic, but she didn't think now was the time to disclose the truth regarding Bryce Ambrose. Vida would be grateful that Carissa had chosen Jacen, but who might she tell? It was best to keep the secret as close as possible, between only those it affected.

"He doesn't respect me. I don't know if I'll be able to win him over."

"I wish I could be there, with both you and Jacen." Vida's normally cheerful demeanour had vanished, replaced by a misery etched across her pale face. Carissa couldn't think of a single thing she could say that might soothe her.

"Lord Ambrose doesn't trust you." Carissa rubbed her arms, a chill raising the hairs on her skin. "It's ridiculous, but I don't want to give him another

161

reason to condemn me."

Vida smiled tightly. "At least you trust me."

Guilt squirmed deep in Carissa's stomach. She didn't, not completely. She might have involved Vida in the truth of her magic, though there were many things she hadn't told her best friend. Once all this was over, once she knew who her true friends were, it would change. For now, she had to keep her cards close to her chest.

"Yes," Carissa lied, because she had to sacrifice the truth for keeping the peace. "Of course I trust you."

THE WOUNDED KING

JACEN MORROW

The bandages covering the stab wound itched, and Jacen longed to rip them off and scratch until satisfied. When sitting up brought a grimace of pain, he knew he shouldn't touch the bandages, and that his wound was far from healed.

The room he'd been placed in was smaller than any he and Carissa had stayed in previously, but large enough that he recognised they'd been allocated a decent guest room. From the bed, he could see the courtyard below. Servants still gathered pieces of the statues, and Jacen became nauseous as he realised that some of the servants cleaned blood off the cobblestones. *His* blood.

"I swear to the goddess, if you reopen that cut…"

The familiar voice made Jacen look to the doorway, where Carissa leaned in the frame with her arms folded over her chest and her eyebrows raised. His memories blurred after he'd been stabbed, probably because of the blood loss he'd suffered, but he did recall that it had been Carissa who had caught a hold of him. She had been the one who'd kept him out of harm's way when the statue collapsed.

"Carissa." He cleared his throat to try and shake the hoarseness.

She crossed over and perched herself on the edge of the bed, gazing out into the courtyard. He couldn't begin to imagine how difficult it had been to come here, despite the fact her every instinct must have urged her to run. She was not a confrontational person, so facing the people who openly questioned her reign was not an easy choice.

"You spoke to Lord Ambrose." Jacen sat up a little straighter. "What did he say? Does he refuse to acknowledge you?"

"I don't know yet," Carissa admitted, her voice soft and uncertain. "Lord Ambrose is still considering his options. I can only hope I convinced him I am not his enemy."

If Lord Ambrose had made up his mind about the Queen, nothing she said or did would get through to him. Jacen hoped Lord Ambrose might realise the true enemy was the one who had taken down Basium in the first place, not the young woman who had been forced to ascend as its Queen.

What would he do if Lord Ambrose decided to declare war on Cobryn? Cobryn deserved retribution from the countries he'd subdued, but Jacen doubted he would enjoy it. Cobryn was a great many things, but among them was the man who had raised Jacen.

"What did Deacon say when you told him?" Jacen said, sure his uncle would have put on a show of fury just as an excuse to lash out at Emlen. He dreaded what the city might face if Deacon had his way.

"I assured him the attempt was not carried out on behalf of Lord Ambrose."

Jacen leaned back against the pillows. "Is that true?"

Carissa gave a light shrug. "I don't know yet. He insists he didn't know, and I want to believe him, but—"

"You don't know who you can trust," Jacen said quietly. He had known that about her for some time. It was clever of her, but he couldn't imagine how lonely it must be. Carissa constantly had to watch her own back because she didn't think anyone else would. Reaching forward, Jacen clasped her hand in his. Carissa glanced at him, lips parted as if she wanted to say something—yet she didn't.

"I love you." Jacen blurted the words out with such ease despite the weight of them. Carissa's violet-blue eyes widened.

It was true, and he had known it for a while, although he had been scared to put a name to what he felt for her. It had been evident from the beginning that he'd cared for Carissa, but this was more. This was a willingness to put her before members of his own family, to ensure her safety and her wellbeing above anyone else's. Carissa had always been his wife, but until recently, their marriage had been one of convenience. There was nothing convenient about falling in love with her.

"I..." Carissa stared down at their interlinked fingers, and his stomach sank as he realised she wasn't going to reciprocate the statement. She had built a fortress around herself—it had been too much to ask her to love him too. He gave her hand a light squeeze.

"You don't have to say it because I did. It's alright not to feel the same."

"I don't know what I feel," Carissa whispered, her eyes downcast. "I haven't really had the chance to think about it. I've been too focused on everything happening during the tour."

Jacen leaned forward to kiss the top of her head. His wound stung in protest, but it was worth it for the smile that crossed her lips. His confession had made his wife hesitant, nonetheless he wouldn't wish it unsaid. He didn't want her to feel a pressure to return the sentiment. He preferred she hadn't, rather than hearing her echo his words emptily.

"I'm probably going to be in bed for the majority of our stay in Emlen."

Carissa crossed over to the window, casting a glance at Jacen. "I fear for your life while we're here. Once this business is sorted with Lord Ambrose, I want to return to Marinel."

"Don't let him get to you," Jacen insisted. If Lord Ambrose believed Carissa weak, it would be another reason for him to insist the Morrow family controlled her. "You said we were going to spend a week in each of the cities, Emlen should be no exception."

Carissa pressed her fingers against the glass windowpane, staring down into the courtyard. For a few moments she remained silent, lost in her own thoughts. Something haunted her eyes, something she didn't want to share. Pushing her would result in nothing but an argument. He couldn't pressure his wife into trusting him. He had to hope that the trust would come in time.

"You're right." Carissa smiled tightly, her eyes glimmering. "Let them see their Queen is strong."

It took days of rest before Jacen could leave his room, let alone to visit his family. He made his way out of Emlen's gates and to the camp nonetheless. He went without Carissa—she had too many matters in the city that needed attending to. Besides, he knew Deacon would speak treachery, and it would rile her.

Vida came to her brother's side in an instant with an excited cry, throwing her arms around him despite his attempts to bat her away. She examined him with concern, taking in the way he winced as he moved.

"Bellona told us what happened. I can't believe you stayed in that city rather than—"

"Vida." Jacen gripped his sister's shoulders. He understood her indignation. He also needed her to realise that despite the attempt on his life, there were more important things at stake. "I couldn't just leave, not when Carissa is yet to determine whether Lord Ambrose is loyal."

She scoffed. "What if he isn't? Carissa shouldn't have to beg for his approval. If he's disloyal, then he should suffer the consequences."

Jacen released her, shocked at her words. He wondered what sort of things Deacon had whispered in her ear in the days they had camped outside the city walls.

"The same fate as the Islands, you mean?" Jacen asked, making no effort to hide his disapproval. Brushing past Vida, he headed deeper into the campsite. Deacon swept over to his nephew and tugged him into a tight embrace that made Jacen grimace.

"I was shocked to hear of the attempt on your life." Deacon stepped back, looking over his nephew with a critical eye. Jacen schooled his features into a neutral expression. "Although I must admit, it was lucky the statue fell when and where it did. The gods must truly be smiling upon you."

"Perhaps." Had it been the will of the gods, or a force more sinister—like magic?

"It would be a difficult city to take." Deacon's eyes raked over the thick walls, the stone fortress that Emlen had become to defend itself against the wrath of its enemies. His expression turned calculating, his eyes oddly hungry. "But it wouldn't be impossible."

"Deacon, we are not tearing Emlen down," Jacen said firmly. "I believe Lord Ambrose knew nothing of this attempt on me. I won't punish him for the actions of one of his citizens."

Maybe that wasn't entirely true, but he did believe in Carissa. If she thought that keeping Lord Ambrose's name clear was in their best interests, he would conform to that statement. Deacon arched an eyebrow in disbelief, though he remained silent—for a few moments at least.

"Indeed. You should probably return to Emlen and your wife, especially considering your injuries. It's unwise for you to be exerting yourself."

Jacen bit back a retort at the implication. He glanced across at Vida, who tended to her horse with gentleness. She'd always had a way with animals, and he recalled how many times she had pleaded with Cobryn to allow them another pet. He made his way across to his sister, taking care not to wince or show any other sign that his wound pained him.

"Another thing." Jacen turned back to face Deacon, boots swivelling in the soil, boldness coursing through him. "I was wondering if you would escort Vida back to Genera for her wedding. After all, it seems there is little for you to do now in Basium."

A nerve twitched in Deacon's jaw, causing Jacen's lips to curve into a smile. His uncle's days in power had been done from the moment Jacen had returned to Basium. Of course, Deacon did not like to relinquish control. Jacen hoped this excursion through the major cities reminded his uncle of how little power he had.

Or did he? Their first stop had proved some in Basium welcomed Deacon's ruthlessness, the way he had ruled with an iron fist. Despite the bloodshed Cobryn had caused, some nobles thought it had paved the way for change. The idea disturbed him. Deacon in power frightened Jacen, particularly when his uncle wasn't King. With Cobryn focusing on taking Wendell in the near future, he believed his uncle's presence would be more beneficial back in Genera.

"I'd be delighted to see my eldest niece wed." Deacon spoke pleasantly, but his eyes were cold.

Vicious satisfaction surged through Jacen. Deacon was a danger to everyone who did not serve Generan interest. Perhaps that only mattered to him now that he cared about his wife more than his ambitious uncle. Having toured the country and acknowledged the views of the nobility, Jacen had the horrible suspicion that bringing Deacon along might have done more harm than good.

Once Jacen had recovered from his wound, Lord Ambrose invited him to dine with him. The invitation had been extended to him several times, and he could no longer politely decline. He didn't grimace when he took too heavy a step or sat down too hard. Jacen could not ignore the inevitable—he would meet with Lord Ambrose.

He entered the hall to find he was not alone, which eased the knot in his stomach and released the tension in his shoulders. Lord Ambrose sat at the table beside a brunette woman Jacen recognised as his wife.

A trio Jacen suspected to be Lord Ambrose's children sat along the side of the table closest to the hearth. Bellona and Carissa sat across from them, with a spare space beside Carissa. Jacen immediately made for the space, easing himself into the seat. Everyone stopped talking to stare at him, and his cheeks flamed with heat at the intense observation.

"It's nice that you could finally join us, Jacen." Lord Ambrose's cool tone and lack of using Jacen's proper title told him the lord found it anything but nice. "May I introduce my wife, Livia, and our children—Sidonia, Jarl, and Meliora."

"Pleasure," the eldest girl, Sidonia, murmured. She was of an age with Jacen. The younger two remained silent. Jarl was maybe Carissa's age, and he didn't look up from his meal to greet the King. Meliora, the youngest, was fifteen or sixteen. She offered Jacen a fleeting smile before turning her attention back to her plate.

Jacen supposed expecting a warm welcome would have been too optimistic. These people did not know him. They looked at him and they saw the Warmonger's son. The Conquest blinded them to anything but the pain it had caused. The thought made Jacen lose what little appetite he had.

"I was wondering if you'd made any progress in finding the boy who tried to kill Jacen."

Carissa looked to Lord Ambrose expectantly. Jacen didn't know whether his wife had been deliberately waiting until he was present to ask the question, but he had his own theories on the young would-be assassin.

"The Jackals," he muttered, remembering what he'd been told in Theron.

"Pardon?" Meliora's head jerked up, dark blue eyes full of alarm. *She knows something*, Jacen realised. Although her parents and older siblings had expressions of curiosity and mild surprise, young Meliora appeared shocked by what he'd uttered.

"I was told about them by Lord Lenore." Jacen's gaze shifted to Lord Ambrose, seeking a reaction. "The Jackals. They're rebels here in Emlen, and they wear jackal masks, the sigil of House Morrow."

"I am aware of the Jackals." Lord Ambrose neatly sliced up his vegetables. "Yes, there are a group of malcontents within my city. I've no doubt the boy is one of theirs. But you must understand, the fact they wear masks makes it difficult to point the finger."

"Excuse me," Meliora murmured. She pushed her chair back from the table and left the room without another word, leaving Jacen intrigued and suspicious. The girl refrained from saying something, and he wanted to know what that was. Unfortunately, the likelihood of him speaking with Lord Ambrose's youngest daughter alone was low.

Jacen's eyes flicked to Carissa. She gave him a meaningful look before returning to her meal. Perhaps it didn't have to be Jacen who spoke to Meliora. Lord Ambrose may not give Carissa the respect she was entitled to, but he trusted her a great deal more than he did a member of House Morrow.

Jacen remembered the boy in the jackal mask, remembered the undisguised hatred in his eyes when he'd plunged his knife into Jacen's stomach. Whoever these Jackals were, whatever horrors they'd endured because of the Conquest, they would not see logic or reason. Lord Ambrose might be willing to think of diplomatic solutions, but to the Jackals, there was only one end they would be satisfied with: Jacen's death.

THE MERCIFUL QUEEN
CARISSA DARNELL

Carissa was adamant on speaking to Meliora Ambrose before they left Emlen. After the way the girl had reacted during their dinner with Jacen, how agitated she had become when they mentioned the Jackals—she was involved somehow. Meliora would talk, even if the rest of her family wouldn't.

Approaching the girl was not difficult. She indulged in the same hobbies as Sidonia, the same hobbies that Carissa had once enjoyed before she'd been forced to become Queen of Basium. Ladylike activities, as Miriam would call them. Sewing, embroidery, playing with each other's hair.

Meliora's head jerked up like a frightened rabbit's when the Queen entered her room. Easy to spook, quick to take flight. Meliora placed her embroidery down with fumbling hands, scrambling to her feet to curtsy before Carissa. She recognised the flustered civility, the desperate need to show obedience in the presence of someone who could crush you. She despised the impact she had on Meliora.

"Your Majesty," the girl murmured, keeping her eyes averted.

"Meliora." Carissa forced a smile. "I was hoping that I could talk with you. About the Jackals."

"What do you mean, my Queen?" Meliora rose from her curtsy, brow furrowing despite the wideness of her eyes.

"I think you know more about the Jackals, more than the other members of your family." Carissa gazed around the room at where Meliora's embroidery decorated the walls. The girl had a talented, steady hand. Carissa remembered pricking her fingers constantly. Embroidery had not been for her, especially when she had discovered her love of the garden.

"You think my father is their leader." Meliora shook her head fervently. "He isn't. My father is a good man, Your Majesty."

Carissa held up a placating hand. "I don't believe he is the leader. I want to know if you know who some of them are. Their leader and the boy who tried to kill the King. I feel like you've seen one of them unmasked, haven't you?"

Meliora pressed her lips into a thin line and nodded. Realising that Carissa sought a verbal answer, she exhaled deeply and went back to looking at her feet.

"I know, but that doesn't mean I can tell you."

Alarm coursed through Carissa. "Is your family in danger if you say?"

"No, nothing like that." Meliora's eyes welled with tears as she finally looked right at Carissa. "I can't say because I love him."

Whatever answer Carissa had anticipated, it had not been that. Lord Ambrose's youngest daughter and the boy in the jackal mask, star-crossed lovers. Hiding her astonishment, Carissa took a steadying breath. She wanted to appear stern, but she was not Deacon—Carissa would not threaten or manipulate to get her own way. As much as she wanted answers, she would not torment Meliora in order to gain them.

"The boy you love attempted to murder the King. Do you really want to protect such a creature of chaos?"

"The King has killed too, Your Majesty." Meliora spoke quietly, steely eyes fixed upon Carissa's.

"Things are different in war," Carissa said, nausea coiling through her stomach at the notion that she sounded like she defended Jacen's actions.

"What if there's a war coming?" Meliora asked, tilting her head to the side. "Would my love's actions be just then?"

"So, you won't give me a name." Carissa paused, letting the words sink in as the younger girl squirmed uncomfortably under her gaze. "You're denying a request from the Queen."

"It's a request." Meliora chewed thoughtfully at her lip. "Doesn't that give me the right to refuse?"

She was sharp despite her demure nature, Carissa would give her that.

"You realise that, had he succeeded, you'd be an accomplice to murder."

"We all have our secrets, Your Majesty." Meliora sat down again, smoothing out her skirts and plucking up her embroidery. She didn't look at Carissa, but her tone and demeanour indicated she was done with the conversation.

One of Meliora's pieces caught Carissa's eye. Someone—she could not tell if it was a man or a woman—standing in front of a throne. The monarch had the head of a swan, and in their hand they dangled the head of a jackal. Nausea came over Carissa, bile rising in her throat. She did not know what the embroidery meant, and part of her did not want to.

Turning on her heel with a murmured goodbye, Carissa swept from the room in haste. Lord Ambrose had been her greatest concern when she had first arrived in Emlen, but she suspected Meliora was someone she should be more careful of. The girl was timid, yet she had secrets she struggled to conceal. What would Meliora do to conceal the boy's identity? How far would she go?

Carissa wasn't certain she wanted to know the answer. People driven to something by passion or strong emotion—love, hate, anger, sadness—could do dangerous things. Carissa would know. She had seen hatred burn half of Marinel to the ground.

"I feel as though I have accomplished nothing."

Carissa's voice was small as she sat cross-legged on the furs, avoiding looking at Jacen. It was the first night of their journey back to Marinel. All of the plans she'd had regarding Emlen, the things she had hoped to achieve—nothing had come of it.

When she had asked Lord Ambrose for his fealty, he had smiled sadly. It cut like a knife to know she could not have it. Lord Ambrose said nothing of his plans for Emlen—a city now cut off from the rest of Basium until he decided to bend the knee.

The weapons being mass produced had been nowhere in sight, though the blacksmiths had worked tirelessly day and night. Carissa had seen the fires of their forges in the dark. Her stomach sank as she realised the weapons would likely be turned on them. She was drowning, and no one would reach a hand to save her.

They had no faith in her, in her ability to rule. She could not condemn them, not unless they moved against her. Bryce's execution had ruled out any chance of peace with Lord Ambrose. No matter how she tried to explain it, he could never understand why she would spare Jacen's life.

"That is not true." Jacen sat beside her, and she looked up from the furs to meet his fierce gaze. "You have spoken to Lord Ambrose and offered up the truth. You gained perspective into how your people think. That's progress in itself."

"None of them want me." Carissa's vision blurred as tears spilled down her cheeks. Her voice cracked and she hated how vulnerable she seemed, how broken she sounded. "They wanted someone stronger. A man. One of my brothers."

"Maybe they did," Jacen admitted, reaching forward to gently wipe away her tears with his thumbs. "But instead they got a woman with more sense and practicality than any of them. They got *you*."

Carissa welcomed the idea that she could be fierce and determined, instead of meek and malleable. Even if his words were designed to lift her spirits, it worked. With a smile, Carissa leaned forward and pressed her lips to his.

The kiss quickly became something more passionate, more intoxicating. Carissa took Jacen's face in her hands, peppering kisses across his jawline as his breath became more ragged. His hot hands traversed her curves, and she gave a sharp gasp as he caressed her breasts. She knew what he wanted—because she wanted it too. This time it had nothing to do with duty or what they were supposed to be doing, and everything to do with desire.

She found herself near consumed with lust for him. Jacen's lips moved to her neck as he unlaced the front of her dress, and Carissa made quick work of shrugging the garment down to her waist. This tour might have been many things, but it had ended with a husband who loved her—and who she had conflicted feelings for in return. Was it love? Was it almost? Or did she just want him?

Jacen gripped Carissa by the hips and easily moved her into his lap. When she raised her eyebrows, a devious grin spread across his face.

"You're running things. Tonight, you're in control."

Giddy triumph and delight surged through Carissa, and she laughed out loud as she pushed him back against the pillows.

Summer reached its end as Carissa and Jacen arrived back in Marinel. The first thing she did was seek out Miriam—it had been a long few weeks without her grandmother. After a fierce embrace, she informed Miriam exactly what happened in the Gracewood, her lies about her magical abilities, the assassination attempt on Jacen in Emlen, and the secrets that Meliora kept.

"You should have investigated further." Miriam's brow creased as she examined her granddaughter, who had settled in a chair with Soot in her lap. The cat was thrilled at his mistress's return, purring loudly and rubbing against her legs, but quickly grew bored, dozing with his head rested on Carissa's dress.

"I don't want to be that sort of ruler." Carissa stroked the cat's sleek dark coat rhythmically. He had grown a lot in the past few weeks, likely chasing mice through the castle in her absence.

"Sometimes, you have to be ruthless." Miriam sat in the chair opposite her. "There are some choices you make that will have you struggling to sleep at night, but they are made for the good of the country. That is what it means to be Queen, Carissa."

"I am not my grandfather," Carissa said firmly, irritation creeping into her tone. She had been fourteen when the Generans murdered Patrick—too young to remember his politics, the way it had impacted the people. It hadn't been something she had focused on. There were those who remembered his reign all too well, and none too fondly.

"I trust you have heard some stories on your journey." Miriam raked a hand through her hair. "I will not lie—your grandfather made mistakes. All monarchs do. I thought you wanted a resolution to what was happening in Emlen, particularly with Lord Ambrose unwilling to swear fealty."

"That is on Lord Ambrose." Carissa scooped Soot up and set him on the floor. "Not his daughter. Whatever romance she has going on with this would-be assassin, it isn't my place to question or judge. She wouldn't give him up for anything."

"Will Bryce be replaced on the council?" Miriam asked.

It was something Lord Ambrose and Carissa had discussed, although not at length. He had made it clear he wanted a representative on the council despite his refusal to accept her—but he implied that based on what came of the council meetings, he may change his mind about Carissa and Jacen.

"Yes, Sidonia will sit in his place." She would be the second woman to have a place on the council, with Bellona being the first. Carissa thought it would be healthy to have more women voicing the opinions of their families, of the people.

Miriam gave a light shrug of her slim shoulders. "If it should come to war, at least you will have a hostage."

Carissa threw her grandmother a horrified look. Her grandmother spoke of taking Sidonia prisoner as casually as if they discussed the weather. Hearing the word 'war' from Miriam's own mouth made it seem like a real prospect.

"I don't want it to come to that. It won't come to that. Deacon is slowly being driven out of power; Vida is returning to Genera for her wedding soon. The only Morrow they will have to contend with will be Jacen."

"Have you not heard the word about Wendell?" Miriam's brown eyes were sad. "Carissa, Cobryn has marched on Canute and Dyre. If Wendell falls, he will have another country to add to his list of conquests. This isn't just about whether Lord Ambrose likes you. It's about the fact that if he doesn't fall into line, Cobryn could destroy him."

Carissa had not considered that. She had been too busy trying to ensure her people liked and respected her as a monarch. The danger lay in Cobryn seeing rebellion against a King he'd put on Basium's throne. It had never taken much for Cobryn to crush resistance, as with the Island Wars.

One false move—not from her, but from any of her nobles, anyone who held any power in Basium—and they would be decimated.

THE FALTERING KING
JACEN MORROW

It was dark in the gardens, the pale moon and distant stars the only light offered. Two women waited in the darkness, silent—Carissa and Bellona. His wife had requested he meet them to discuss everything that had happened during the tour. Whilst Jacen and Carissa had talked about the attempts on his life and the nobles they had met, the Queen wanted to converse with both him and Bellona at once. Glancing around to make sure no one followed, Jacen crossed over to them.

"This is an interesting place to meet."

"We wanted somewhere private." Carissa ran her fingers through her black hair. "Lord Ambrose knows, of course, that it was you Bryce attempted to kill. We can't know when he will go public with the information that I chose your life over a Basiumite subject's, but we have to be prepared for the idea that he might."

"What does Miriam think?" Bellona asked, as if the former Queen's word was law. It had not escaped Jacen's notice how serious Carissa had become since their return to Marinel. Was it the burden of Emlen, of all she had learned in their journey, or had Miriam said something to her?

Carissa shook her head slowly. "She doesn't know what to do, since it would mean Lord Ambrose would implicate himself in the attempt too."

"He could implicate himself in both attempts," Bellona grumbled, folding her arms over her chest. "First Bryce in the Gracewood and then the boy in Emlen."

"I suppose it's lucky the statue fell when it did." Jacen smiled mirthlessly.

Carissa and Bellona exchanged a grim look. Carissa looked down at her clasped hands, while Bellona's lips pressed into a firm line. Something passed unsaid between them, something Jacen could not fathom. Carissa and Bellona were hiding something from him.

"Deacon is returning to Genera with Vida soon," Bellona reminded them, tossing her ginger braid over her shoulder. "That should ease things a bit, since there are quite a few people who despise him."

"There are also some who think he's done a lot of good." Carissa sounded troubled. "He *did* legalise dark magic. It's brought more Imperium and Maleficium into the court. I can hate him all I want, but there's no denying some people agree with his methods."

"Lord Ambrose certainly doesn't agree," Bellona scoffed.

"Lord Ambrose needs to be careful, or he's going to get himself killed." Fear flooded Carissa's voice, trepidation gleaming in her eyes visible even in the dim light. "I worry that if he steps out of line, if he continues to rebel, Cobryn might decide to bring us all down."

The idea startled Jacen. Despite his father's current invasion of Wendell, if the people thought Cobryn could not hold one of the countries he controlled, others would rise up. Harith would look to Basium with hope and break their own chains. If Lord Ambrose decided to take up arms against the crown, he would effectively be taking up arms against Cobryn.

"Did you find out anything else about the Jackals?" Bellona questioned, looking between both the King and Queen. Jacen shook his head vehemently but stopped when he realised Carissa had paused and tensed. When she noticed both of them staring intently at her, her shoulders slumped.

"Meliora admitted she's in love with the boy who tried to kill Jacen. That's all I managed to get from her. Miriam thought I should have pushed her further. I don't see how that would have done much good."

"Could Bryce be connected with the Jackals?" Jacen inquired, trying to piece together the puzzle. "It might explain both attempts as work of the group."

"Lord Ambrose ordered Bryce to kill you," Carissa pointed out. "He denied having anything to do with the boy's attempt."

Jacen kept his tone light. "Perhaps a lot of people just want me dead."

It exhausted him, constantly having to watch his back. He was targeted for the crimes his father had committed. It was not the first time—it had happened during the Island Wars as well, when the fallen noble families had made one last desperate attempt to capture him and use him against Cobryn. It hadn't ended well for them.

At least the Island Wars he could understand. He'd had an active, bloody role to play. He had been younger than his wife was now when the Conquest had taken place. Whilst he'd fought in the battle to take Marinel, he hadn't made any of the important decisions. He hadn't wanted to become King of Basium, as he had told his father numerous times before Cobryn had hit him and told him to shut up.

Jacen suspected something more happened in Emlen. Lord Ambrose hid something bigger than just the Jackals. He didn't know what made him think as much, yet his stomach twisted every time he thought of the infernal fortress city.

"We should go back inside." Carissa rubbed her bare arms. "It's getting cold."

Jacen had to agree, although in truth, the chill that came over him had nothing to do with the temperature.

Carissa sat shivering by the fire when Jacen entered their room. She had a blanket wrapped around herself. Despite the fact summer had yet to pass, Carissa seemed cold since their return. He hoped that she hadn't caught a chill, but he had the feeling whatever was wrong, it had less to do with sickness and more to do with what was on her mind. For a moment they stared right at each other before Carissa's gaze returned to the flames.

"The statue that fell in Emlen…" Jacen struggled with finding a way to phrase it that wouldn't sound accusatory. "It didn't fall by itself, did it?"

"No." The word came softly from her lips, almost so softly he thought he hadn't heard it. She raised her hands to warm them over the hearth. He wanted her to elaborate, but the only response came from the logs shifting and the fire crackling.

"So, what did happen?" Jacen persisted.

"I broke it." Carissa bit her lip as she glanced at him. "I pushed it."

Jacen scratched at his jaw. In Isadore, Carissa had claimed she was an Imperium with the gift of empathy. That had been a lie, something he'd suspected for some time, but this proved it. He was hurt she hadn't told him the truth, but now wasn't the time for acidic words. Now was the time to learn what Carissa was determined to keep from him.

"Why?"

It could have been a thousand questions. *Why did you do it? Why did you lie to me? Why are you so frightened to admit what you are?* He wondered which of them she would answer first, what she would take from the single-syllable question.

"Because I am not Imperium."

He sighed, frustration prickling within him like water rising to the boil. "Carissa—"

"I am Maleficium." She rose from the ground, wrapping the blanket around herself like a cloak. She lifted her chin to await his verdict, but concern darkened her eyes. She thought he would be repulsed.

It had been a thought Jacen had never entertained, though he scolded himself for not realising it sooner. Deacon had long suspected magic within Carissa, while Jacen had sensed darkness. How had he been so clueless that he had not combined the two ideas?

"What can you do?"

"Blood magic." Carissa picked at a spot on the blanket. "When I touched your wound, I used your blood to destroy the statue."

A terrible power. Deacon often said blood mages succumbed to homicidal urges and murderous rampages. Jacen did not know much of Basiumite history, but even he had heard of the dreaded Jameson Burnett. Since then, if Maleficium possessed blood magic, they had the sense to keep quiet about it. He understood why Carissa had been so secretive about her abilities.

The silence stretching between them made Carissa uncomfortable. She tugged the blanket closer around herself, violet-blue eyes glistening as she tilted her head to the side.

"Please, say something."

"I'm not afraid." He smiled, wanting to reassure her. Her apprehension made it clear she'd expected him to recoil. He didn't fear her magic. He had seen Deacon's and didn't believe Carissa's could be any worse simply because it was classified as 'dark'. He reached forward to put his arms around her, but she stepped away.

"How can you not be? I am."

"Because I trust you." Months ago, he would not have said those words. She may not say those words. It was the truth—Carissa had saved his life on two separate occasions. Whatever her thoughts and feelings toward him, she cared enough about him to put her reputation at risk. After all, others might have seen her display of magic in Emlen. She'd taken that chance to save him.

"I don't trust myself, not with magic." Carissa shrugged the blanket off, casting it onto a chair where it narrowly missed Soot. The cat meowed reproachfully, darting off underneath their bed. "I only ever hear horror stories. Why should my magic be any different?"

"Your magic saved me." Jacen wanted to close the space between them but was unsure whether she would move away from him again. This time it was Carissa who reached out, wrapping her arms around Jacen and letting him pull her close. She nestled her face in the fabric of his shirt. He smiled and stroked her hair.

It's going to be alright, he wanted to tell her. He wanted to tell her that she was safe with him, that nothing and no one would ever hurt her again. He had the distinct feeling that it would be a broken promise.

Hands squeezed Jacen's shoulders as someone roughly shook him awake. He groaned and rubbed his eyes, expecting Carissa. Deacon stood by his bedside with a candle and a grim expression. Jacen lurched out of the blankets, stunned by his uncle's presence in the dead of night.

"Deacon, what...?"

The older man pressed a finger to his lips. "Get up and get dressed. Now."

Jacen cast a glance over his shoulder. Beside him, Carissa was still asleep, cocooned in the blankets. She was curled up and shivering. Perhaps she was getting sick after all. Deacon gripped his arm, making Jacen turn his attention back to his uncle.

"She'll be summoned too. We need to talk to you first."

"We?" Something must have happened, and it was urgent for Deacon to personally come and wake him at this hour. However, bombarding his uncle with questions would only lead to an irritated response.

He couldn't help but glance at Carissa again. Something happened here, something that Deacon didn't want the Queen knowing. It sent unpleasant shivers running down Jacen's spine.

Deacon waited until Jacen dressed before he led him out into the corridor. By the time his uncle closed the door, Jacen pounced. Grabbing Deacon's arm, he slammed his uncle against the stone wall outside the room, ignoring the way the older man's eyes narrowed.

"You need to tell me what's happening right now." It was not a question. It was an order.

"There has been an arrest." Deacon shrugged his nephew off, continuing down the corridor. The flickering light of the candle faded. Knowing he would be left in darkness if he didn't follow, Jacen strode after him. The clack of his boots echoed through the halls.

"An arrest?" A thought occurred to him. "Has one of the Jackals been caught?"

"Not as such." A little smile played about the corners of Deacon's lips, the sort that made Jacen's palms go clammy. Whatever had happened, it suited Deacon just fine, or he would not look pleased. "An ally to the Jackals, one who has been helping them from within the castle walls."

A cold stone sunk in Jacen's stomach. He tried to think of who could be so foolish. It would never have been Bellona. Could it have been Vida? Jacen liked to think his sister wouldn't be so stupid, though the girl was easily swayed. If Deacon could whisper in her ear so easily, why not someone else? Deacon being satisfied with the arrest, however, ruled Vida out of the equation.

"Who?"

Deacon stopped in the corridor, turning to face Jacen, his hazel eyes alight with a horrible mixture of triumph and anger.

"Miriam Darnell."

THE BETRAYED QUEEN
CARISSA DARNELL

The last time that Carissa had been dragged from her bed in the middle of the night was the Conquest. The idea that something terrible could be happening again made her thrash, made her panic. She considered the idea of reaching for her magic, but decided it was best to wait it out. The darkness lingering in her veins was her last resort. Nonetheless, her heart hammered against her ribcage as two Generan guards—Deacon's men—escorted her into the throne room.

Neither of them said a word to her, despite Carissa's persistent questions. Like stone, their expressions remained impassive. Knowing she wouldn't get a word out of them, Carissa resorted to stubborn silence.

Deacon wasn't the only one there. Jacen stood beside him, arms folded and a terse frown on his face. But someone else shifted in the darkness and Carissa gasped aloud when she saw that more of Deacon's men had brought Miriam here. The soldiers had their hands on the hilts of their swords, as if ready for one of the Darnell women to strike at any given moment.

"What in the name of the goddess is this?" Carissa demanded, infuriated beyond words. She didn't even know what she was so angry about. The combination of her grandmother's presence, Jacen's fury, and Deacon's smug smile made her certain it wasn't anything good.

Deacon glanced at one of his men. Carissa recognised him as Nikkos Adonis. He was lord of one of the Generan cities—Belvedere, if she remembered correctly—and one of Deacon's good friends. His presence here made her nauseous. She swallowed hard and waited for an answer.

"Did you find her?" Deacon asked of his friend.

"No." Nikkos shook his head, glancing at Carissa. "Bellona must have known something was wrong. She rode out of Marinel not half an hour ago."

Deacon sneered. "Guilty conscience, no doubt."

"What are you talking about?" Carissa asked, shrugging free of the men who held her arms, drawing dignity about her like a cloak. "I am the Queen of Basium. I do not appreciate being dragged from my bed in the middle of the night without explanation."

The mention of her friend's name was like a knife to the ribs. Why did they want Bellona? What did they think she'd done? Despite her assertion that she was the Queen, Carissa shook like a leaf, trying desperately to disguise how much anxiety this situation gave her.

"We have evidence to believe there is a plot going on within these very walls to kill the King." Deacon looked to Jacen, who clenched his jaw and remained silent. Carissa wished he would speak, wished he would say this was all ridiculous. "We have received notice that Miriam Darnell is working closely with the Jackals, and that your good friend Bellona Lenore planned to join them, along with her father."

"But that's absurd!" Carissa cried out, looking around wildly as if someone might back her up. Why was her grandmother silent? Why wouldn't Jacen say anything? "Bellona would never… She doesn't want Jacen dead."

"We can't know her aim in wanting to join the growing rebellion." Deacon waved a dismissive hand, glee on his face as he moved over to Carissa. "Yet if she wasn't guilty, why would she run?"

Carissa had no answer for that, and her lack of retort made Deacon's smile widen. When she glanced at Miriam, her grandmother wouldn't meet her eyes. Was it true? Was she really working with the Jackals? Miriam was aware she cared for Jacen and believed he had a good heart; why would she plot to murder him?

"What evidence?" Carissa folded her arms over her chest, trying to ignore the cold seeping into her bones. "If someone has presented evidence, or made a claim, then I deserve to know who."

Deacon peered across the hall, beckoning to someone in the shadows. A tall, slim figure made their way into the candlelight. Jacen turned away like this was something he didn't want to see. Carissa pressed a hand to her mouth when she recognised the accuser.

Vida.

Her expression was nothing but cold, her eyes icy as they raked over Miriam and Carissa. Her mouth twisted into a thin line. There was no denying the look on Vida's face—hatred. Her piercing gaze fixed firmly on Carissa.

The complete change in her friend caught Carissa off-guard. What had happened to the girl that she'd shared mindless court gossip with; who'd braided her hair and helped her choose the best dress for every occasion?

"Vida…" she whispered, shocked and confused.

"Save your breath," her friend said contemptuously. She tossed her blonde hair over her shoulder and looked to Deacon. "Carissa planned to assist the rebellion. Add fuel to the fire. She heard about Cobryn marching on Wendell and knew the time would be now, so she sent for Sidonia to discuss the matter further."

"The attempt on Jacen?" Deacon asked, as Carissa tried to process what her friend said. No, not her friend. Vida was clearly not her friend, not anymore.

"She cares too much about Jacen to have been behind the plot to murder him." When Vida smirked, it was reminiscent of her uncle in a way that made Carissa tense. "That was all Miriam."

It hit Carissa with the force of a punch. Vida lied. She may not have been involved in the sort of conversations that Bellona had been, yet the idea that Carissa reached out to Emlen in secret was completely false. For whatever reason, Vida had fabricated these accusations. Judging by her self-satisfied smile, it was pure spite. Carissa's surprise quickly bled into anger.

"You fucking snake!" Carissa lunged for Vida, cracking a hand across her face. Nikkos hauled her back, but not before the damage was done. Vida reached up to touch her cheek, her face twisting in disdain. The gold wedding ring on Carissa's finger left a welt on Vida's cheek. She bared her teeth yet made no move to retaliate as Nikkos held the struggling Queen.

Carissa wanted to scream at her, to hit her again. She didn't understand why Vida made up these accusations. Worse, she had the feeling that Deacon knew they weren't true—but he would act on them anyway. She turned her attention on the one person who could make a difference. Jacen.

"This isn't true. None of it. You know that."

Jacen glowered at Vida. "I can't speak for Miriam and Bellona, but Carissa wouldn't have expressed interest in joining the rebellion. That's ridiculous."

"Oh, because she tells you everything," Vida said sarcastically. "Just like her magic."

Carissa clenched her hands into fists. Vida would sabotage her relationship with Jacen by playing on her brother's insecurities. She knew Jacen better than most, and she would destroy him.

Jacen frowned. "What are you talking about?"

"The fact that she's a Maleficium." Vida raised her eyebrows. "I've known for months."

The silence that stretched on was awful, Carissa shifting her feet. Jacen looked taken aback that Vida had known Carissa's secret while he'd only just found out. Deacon's eyes lit up and flicked back to Carissa, suddenly interested in the conversation again, and that was what she had feared the most. He would force her to become a weapon.

"A Maleficium?" A hunger danced in Deacon's eyes.

Vida nodded. "A blood mage, to be specific."

"You leave her alone." Miriam spoke up, her voice low and venomous. "It's me who you're accusing of trying to kill the King. Carissa's abilities have nothing to do with my crimes."

"Too true." Deacon turned his attention back on her. "Miriam Darnell, you are hereby arrested for high treason against the crown. Your sentencing will take place over the next few days."

"No!" Carissa struggled against Nikkos, her voice piercing as it echoed through the hall. "I am the Queen and I demand you release her! She has committed no crime!"

None of them listened. None of them paid her any attention. The men marched Miriam away without even a backward glance. Her grandmother made no attempt to fight, head bowed in submission as they removed her from the throne room. Carissa wondered with horror if, of all Vida's poisonous accusations, this one could be true.

"Don't you see, Carissa?" Vida examined her friend with raised eyebrows. "Here you are, plotting away like you have some kind of power. You are, and always have been, a puppet."

Carissa paced her room for hours before throwing herself onto her bed in a fit of tears. How could she have been so stupid, so naïve? This whole time she had thought she gained more ability to speak for herself and her country. Deacon had her on a leash the entire time and proved his point by tightening it. There was only one person who Carissa could rely on to fix this mess.

The door creaked open and Jacen entered the room. Defeat riddled his posture—his shoulders slumped, his eyes tired.

Carissa scrambled off the bed, hardly daring to hope, but knew he was her last chance at freeing Miriam. Bellona was safe—for now. She crossed over to Jacen, gripping his hands, eyes pleading with him to listen to her.

"You have to talk to Deacon. You have to convince him that this is nonsense."

"Miriam confessed, Carissa." Jacen's voice was weary. "She confessed that she plotted to kill me. She said you knew nothing of the plot, and that you hadn't been in contact with Lord Ambrose regarding rebellion, but Deacon doesn't believe it."

Carissa lapsed into silence, releasing Jacen's hands. So, it was true—her grandmother had planned to have Jacen killed. It seemed too rash for a woman like Miriam. Something was wrong. She had to talk to her grandmother and learn the truth for herself.

"Does Deacon want to throw me in the dungeons too?" she spat, temper flaring.

"No." Jacen raked a hand through his hair. "He says that it's clear you have been misled by people like Miriam and Bellona."

"Surely you don't believe this." Carissa wanted her husband to shrug off the accusations. He knew Deacon manipulated others at every turn. She couldn't have said what caused Vida to turn on her so savagely, but it had to do with Deacon whispering in her ear. What had he said, Carissa wondered, that made her former friend become so hateful toward her?

Her body curled in on itself, shoulders dropping. No one would listen to a thing she said—Deacon's word was law. He had allowed her to exercise some freedom and now he had taken it from her. How could she have believed she was in control of a country that Cobryn had taken over, a throne he'd put his son on? Her power had only been an illusion, and now Deacon and Vida proved who truly ruled Basium—and the reality horrified Carissa.

"What I believe doesn't matter," Jacen said, and when she looked at him closely, she could see dark circles under his eyes. "He could claim Miriam attempted to kill you and everyone in this court would believe it—because what happens if they don't?"

"Cobryn never wanted me to have any power," Carissa whispered, clinging to the shred of faith she had that Jacen believed her. "I knew that much… but Deacon…"

"Deacon knew I'd choose you over them." The words were blunt.

"I need to do something." Carissa found herself overcome with indignation and a resolve to take action. "The accusations against my grandmother, against Bellona…"

"Listen to me." Jacen took Carissa's face in his hands, hazel eyes gleaming in desperation. "If you fight this, they will—"

"Kill me?" Carissa sneered. She dared them to try. She didn't fear death, not when she'd watched them execute her family.

"No, but you will wish they had." Jacen tilted her face up, and she saw the tenderness in his expression, the softness of his eyes that showed how much he cared for her, how fiercely he loved her. How she wished it could be enough. "Miriam is alive for now. I'm as powerless as you. The only person that any of them will listen to is Deacon. He's crept into this place over the years like a weed, and he holds all of the cards."

"You'd have me do nothing?" Carissa tore away from him, stung, eyes welling with tears as the sheer hopelessness of the situation washed over her. "I can't be their pawn, Jacen. I won't."

"We need more allies," Jacen insisted. *We.* He was on her side. She should consider this a small victory. Yet she had considered Vida a loyal friend, and Vida had betrayed her, lied about her. As much as she wanted to put her faith in Jacen, she didn't have the luxury of trust.

Carissa remembered Lord Ambrose and the Jackals. It hadn't been her they hated. It hadn't been Jacen, really. It had been everything Cobryn had done, everything his family stood for. Her stance had been less aggressive, but her views were similar. The pieces of the puzzle slotted together now. Carissa knew what she needed to do—she just needed to find the strength and ability to do it.

Deacon would have her under heavy guard. He would take no chances, especially when Bellona had already escaped. Carissa's heart ached for her friend. It was selfish to wish Bellona was with her, but the other girl would make this ordeal bearable. She had Jacen, but it wasn't the same. He was a conflicted man, one whose side she couldn't be certain of. Bellona had killed for her. Bellona was loyal.

Is she? Carissa had been certain of Vida's loyalty, confident in the knowledge that she could trust her best friend with the secret of her magic—and Vida had exposed her as a Maleficium. Carissa wanted to believe in Jacen and in Bellona, but how could she when her world shattered around her?

"I know where to find allies." Carissa's eyes flicked up to meet Jacen's. He frowned and shook his head.

"No. We can't trust Lord Ambrose."

"We can't trust anyone," Carissa pointed out. Was this what it meant to be a monarch? To be watching her back constantly, concerned that those close to her might attempt to overthrow her or use her? Carissa had survived in a court of snakes for years. Lord Ambrose was no more dangerous than Deacon.

Her next move was hers alone to decide. If she lashed out, Miriam would suffer for it. If she did nothing, what kind of ruler did she prove herself to be? She would not remain idle, shutting herself away in her castle and letting the enemy control her country and her people.

Deacon's move was meant to show her that she had no power, that in her own court, though she was a Queen, he pulled the strings. Carissa had attempted to cut the strings, but that had proven no good. She would try a different tactic, one she had been practising before she had grown too bold. She would allow Deacon to think he was the puppeteer, and her the meek puppet.

This time, she would not make the mistake of trusting her friends, or Jacen. This time, her motives would be secret, her cards held close to her chest. She could only hope that her compliance would save Miriam before it was too late. Carissa had watched the rest of her family as they were brutally murdered. She didn't think she would survive it if Miriam was executed too.

If Deacon wanted to play a game, then they would play.

THE WRETCHED KING
JACEN MORROW

"No." Jacen's hands balled into fists as Deacon concluded his speech on what was to be done following Miriam's arrest and Bellona's flight from the capital. "No, absolutely not."

"I don't remember asking a question." Deacon cast an irritated look at his nephew, eyebrows raised at his objection. Vida paced in front of the hearth, eyes flicking to the logs when they crackled—Vida, who had changed into a completely different person with no explanation. Something must have happened for Vida to turn against Carissa with such spite.

"You want Carissa to execute her own grandmother." Words couldn't convey Jacen's disgust at the sheer cruelty of Deacon's plan. "What the fuck is wrong with you?"

"I want her to learn a lesson." Deacon's jaw tightened. "She is still the little girl we put on the throne with our own agenda in mind. You have returned, she has grown up—but Carissa Darnell has no authority. I want to make that plain to her, since she has forgotten."

"She won't do it." Jacen shook his head fervently. He knew his wife well enough to realise that Carissa would endure any torture instead of accepting this fate.

"She will if she believes Bellona's head is next on the line." Deacon's lips curved into a smile. To Jacen's knowledge, Bellona's whereabouts were unknown. She would return to Theron if Deacon's men did not find her first. Carissa had been kept in the dark about her friend, and would no doubt believe that Bellona had in fact been captured.

What sort of monster was his uncle? What sort of person wanted to administer that much pain? Was this truly about controlling Carissa, or was Deacon punishing her for rebuffing his advances? Deacon would achieve ultimate power by marrying Carissa. Since he wasn't able to do that—although, Jacen didn't cross off the option of being murdered by his ambitious uncle—he would pull the strings as hard as he could from the sidelines.

Jacen wanted nothing more than to wrap his hands around Deacon's throat and squeeze, see the panic in his uncle's eyes, watch the colour leave his face. Such an action would be rash and result in retaliation, possibly against Carissa. It was clear that Jacen cared for his wife, but he would have to hide just how much. Deacon would delight in using them against each other.

That was what gave Deacon so much power in the first place—his magic. He had seen Deacon use his abilities on Carissa, and that had just been a threat. His uncle was a powerful Primordial and forgetting that would result in death. Deacon controlled Basium through fear, and even Jacen was afraid.

"Get out." Jacen waved a dismissive hand. If he had to put up with his uncle for a moment longer, he might be tempted to throw caution to the wind and gut him here and now.

Deacon frowned. "Excuse me?"

"I am still the King, and I command you to leave. I wish to speak with Vida alone."

Deacon's eyes flashed with fury, but he turned and swept from the room without protest. Once the door slammed shut, Jacen turned his attention on his sister, who sat silent and resplendent in a chair beside the bookcase. She tilted her head to the side at his attention.

"Why, Vida?" Jacen wanted to demand the truth from her, but it sounded more like a plea. "Why did you do it?"

"I heard you all talking." Vida sounded vulnerable, and there was hurt in her eyes. "About the Gracewood. About what really happened to Bryce Ambrose. All these things you never bothered to tell me about. It was like I didn't matter. I wasn't a part of your little group."

In a moment, the vulnerability was gone, replaced by hard anger. Jacen was baffled at the realisation Vida had done this because she had felt excluded. Her friends and brother had kept secrets from her, and so in spite and pettiness, she had sold out the people closest to her.

"You lied about Carissa and Bellona because you weren't included in the conversation?"

"No, it's more than that," Vida snapped, pushing herself to her feet. "None of you trusted me. You were silent with secrets when I was there. I was treated like I was an enemy. Why in the name of the gods should I trust you?"

"You turned yourself into the enemy." Jacen had no sympathy for her. "You said Miriam wanted me dead, that Bellona would join the Jackals, that Carissa considered allying with Lord Ambrose. You made us your enemies all on your own."

Vida sneered. "You're fortunate I didn't paint them a pretty picture of *you*."

Jacen stepped forward and slapped her across the face. He regretted it the moment his palm connected with her cheek, in the same spot where Carissa's ring had marked her. He had never hit a woman, and he wondered exactly what he was becoming. Striking Vida, ruminating on murdering Deacon. He had tortured and killed during the Island Wars, but he hadn't enjoyed it. Now he lashed out at his own family. They might deserve it, yet that didn't stop him realising the truth—he was no better than them.

Vida raised a shaking hand to touch her face. She and Jacen had received blows from their father when they talked back, when they said the wrong thing, when he was in a dark mood. Jacen swallowed hard, staring at the ground, unable to look at her. He waited for her to leave in a huff, but she didn't.

Vida laughed hollowly. "Go ahead and defend her, *Your Majesty*. Defend yourself."

He didn't. Consumed by guilt, Jacen turned and marched from the meeting room. How was he any better than the family he condemned?

Sidonia Ambrose's arrival was the subject of gossip throughout the court, probably because of Vida's accusation that she came at the behest of Carissa to discuss an alliance. Had she come to sit on the council as a representative, as had previously been discussed?

The first dinner with their guest was a tense affair. Sidonia's presence caused a stir within the city. The young woman was not thrilled about being there, her expression sour as curdled milk. Carissa pushed her food around her plate without touching it. Vida was her effervescent self, offering Sidonia more red wine.

"I must say, I was astonished to receive a summons to the capital." Sidonia's eyes fixed upon Carissa, her expression stern. "Particularly upon hearing news about Miriam's arrest. The last thing I would have thought you'd want is a member of House Ambrose in Marinel."

Jacen went cold. What purpose did Sidonia's presence have in such turbulent times? Jacen assumed that his uncle meant to use her as a bargaining chip, a hostage to guarantee Lord Ambrose's good behaviour.

"Of course we do." Deacon set down his knife and fork, offering Sidonia a charming smile. "We want your family to know precisely how House Morrow feels about them."

Sidonia smiled humourlessly and took another sip of her wine. It was clear that she did not trust any of them. Carissa had gone pale, and Jacen wondered if she would be sick. He watched Sidonia raise the goblet to her lips once more, and it suddenly occurred to Jacen that Sidonia was the only one partaking of the alcohol. No one else had lifted a drink to their lips the whole time.

"We also want you to deliver a message back to your father, Lord Ambrose." Deacon raised his eyebrows as Sidonia coughed, rubbing at her throat. Beside him, Vida smirked, as if she knew something. As if she waited for something.

"What message is that?" Sidonia's voice was hoarse, as if she'd taken some food down wrong and struggled to swallow it.

Deacon's eyes were cold. "That we do not tolerate attempts on our own, or rebellion against us."

Sidonia lurched to her feet, her face contorted in fury and fear. She gripped the edges of the table before collapsing onto the ground. Carissa pushed herself to her feet, violet-blue eyes wide, but Deacon caught her by the arm before she could run to Sidonia. The eldest child of Lord Ambrose convulsed, choking up blood and bile on the stone tiles of the dining hall.

Carissa's scream of horror resonated throughout the room before Deacon clamped a hand over her mouth. Vida no longer smirked. Instead she stared down at Sidonia's corpse, at the young woman's wide eyes staring sightlessly at the ceiling as blood dribbled from her mouth. There was something haunted about Vida's expression and Jacen's stomach coiled at the realisation of what had happened.

Sidonia had been poisoned. Not by Deacon, but by Vida. Jacen was left speechless at his younger sister's actions. Lord Ambrose would never have backed down permanently, not even with the threat of his eldest daughter's life. So, the Morrows would deliver a message far more lethal: death awaited those who crossed them.

"Do you think anyone in this court will care that she is dead?" Deacon hissed, his hand still pressed over Carissa's mouth. He tore his arm back with a yelp. Blood welled on his palm where Carissa had bitten him, causing satisfaction in Jacen. She spat in his face, her whole body shaking in anger.

"You murdered her. Lord Ambrose will have war for this."

Deacon laughed, wiping the saliva from his cheek. "Sweet Carissa, that is precisely what we want. We have given him the perfect excuse to strike, the perfect excuse for us to stamp him down into the dirt. Emlen will be the first Basiumite city to take up arms against the crown, and it will also be the last."

There was no way Jacen could convince Deacon to spare Miriam an execution. Her crimes were considered high treason, and if she avoided death, it would make Deacon look weak, which was something his uncle didn't want. The manner of her death, being executed by her own granddaughter... Carissa would do it, if Bellona was threatened. It would break her.

Jacen rapped his knuckles against his uncle's door. How things had changed within the court of Marinel over the past few days. The nobles had turned to Deacon, recognising him as the true power behind the throne. Carissa's absence was excused as her being grief-stricken at the knowledge that her grandmother would attempt such an atrocity. In this place, Deacon's word was the only one that mattered.

"I take it that Sidonia at least had a proper burial." Jacen's tone indicated his contempt for the horrific murder as he entered his uncle's room.

Deacon rose from his desk, setting down the quill he'd scratched at a piece of parchment with. How could he display such easy disregard for the young woman he'd helped murder just to send her father a message?

"Of course she did. I'm not an animal, Jacen."

Jacen folded his arms over his chest. "No, but you are a monster."

Deacon sighed and rolled his eyes to the heavens as if Jacen was being absurd.

"I'm doing this for the survival of our family," he said patiently, treating

Jacen like a child throwing a tantrum that he had to calm. "Your pretty little wife and her scheming bitch of a grandmother would destroy us."

"For the family," Jacen said mockingly. "You can't truly think that two women could bring us down. Our family has Basium, Harith, and soon Wendell. You just know what you're doing gives you more power. It's got nothing to do with anything else."

"Vida understands," Deacon reminded him, making Jacen's jaw clench as he moved over to the desk to see what Deacon had written. He was curious as to what his uncle was up to, although it could be nothing good. "She knows that Miriam is a poisonous influence, a weed. Ask Carissa what you do with a weed in a garden. She'd tell you to rip it out."

Jacen's blood ran cold as he inspected the letter that Deacon was in the process of writing. It was a written decree—that Miriam Darnell had committed treason, and she was to be executed at the end of the week.

"She'll never sign this."

"She doesn't have to." Deacon's eyes glimmered as Jacen turned to glower at him. "Not when the King could."

It terrified him, the knowledge that Jacen could make such monumental decisions without his wife's knowledge or consent. It was what both his father and uncle had been counting on when he'd been installed as Basium's King. His wife was a figurehead, a means to produce an heir to the throne, nothing more.

Jacen shook his head fervently. "If you do this, they will hate us all the more. You'll encourage them to rise up. They'll want blood for this."

"I know exactly what executing Miriam will cause," Deacon said darkly, his eyes narrowing. "It gives us reason to crush an insurrection the moment it begins. These people seem to have this illusion that they have some control over the way things are in Basium. I will remind them they do not."

"Why do you want Carissa to be the one to do it?" The level of malice in the idea was unfathomable to Jacen. "Pure spite?"

"No, to show them that she is ours now."

Deacon didn't care what all of this would cost. He didn't care how much blood was spilled and how much it would break Carissa to secure their grip on the Basiumite throne. He was a man who thought the means justified the end. Something Vida believed, something Cobryn believed.

"I'll do it." Jacen turned away from Miriam's death marked down in ink, drawing himself up as he faced Deacon. "I'll carry out the execution. I'll sign the damn decree."

For the girl who had been forced to kneel in the gardens while her family was brutally murdered. The girl who had been given a throne and a husband in a matter of days. The girl Jacen was in love with and would do anything to protect and shield from the cruelty Deacon had in mind for her.

Deacon examined him with an unreadable expression. He would never understand something like what he felt for his wife. His uncle only understood power and control. Love wasn't something he had ever experienced.

Another knock on the door. Jacen spun around as Nikkos entered the room, at least giving him the respect of a stiff bow. Jacen did not understand why the man was here other than to support Deacon. Shouldn't he have fought in Wendell with Cobryn, a series of battles Nikkos departed from to come to Basium? Had Cobryn asked him to, or had it been Deacon to summon him from the heat of war?

"Your Majesty. Lord Morrow." His eyes darted between them both, gleaming with triumph. "Cobryn has done it once again. Wendell has fallen."

THE MONSTER QUEEN
CARISSA DARNELL

News of Wendell's fall spread rapidly. The Wendellian King's younger sister, Gretchen, became Cobryn's next wife. The reports sickened Carissa. She had hoped Wendell might be able to drive Cobryn out. Another country conquered was another army Cobryn might use against Basium should they rise against the Morrow family.

Why hadn't they been destroyed like Basium? Why hadn't Harith? Why could their royal families live while Carissa's had been viciously taken from her?

She knew the answer—because her family had openly defied Cobryn, because they had told him 'no' until the very end. Harith and Wendell bent the knee, but Basium never would have.

The narrow stairwell leading into the dungeons was dark, a cool breeze sending shivers down Carissa's spine. The thought of her grandmother being kept in such awful conditions appalled her. It would have been easy to break down in tears at how far they had fallen, but Carissa was a Queen, so she would continue to act like one.

The cells were as dim as the stairwell, the bars grimy, each containing a narrow cot as the sole item of furniture within. Carissa pursed her lips at the conditions. She had not been into the prison in many years, since she had snuck in with Peregrine on a dare, and she made a note to improve its state.

Miriam rose and crossed over to the bars at her granddaughter's appearance, and Carissa reached a hand through like she was drowning and Miriam was the only person who could hold her afloat. Tears stung at her eyes and an itchy lump caught in her throat, but she took a deep breath and held her emotions back.

"Tell me what to do," Carissa pleaded. "Tell me how I can stop this."

"You can't." Miriam squeezed her hand. "You need to make peace with the idea that this is going ahead whether you want it to or not."

The idea of doing this without her grandmother overwhelmed her, and it was the final blow that broke her. Carissa collapsed against the bars, sobbing openly. She'd already lost her family. One of her best friends had betrayed her. Her husband… Jacen loved her, but would that be enough? She could feel a rift forming between them. The relationship they had built cracked at the seams and threatened to come crumbling down.

"My brave girl. Look at me." Miriam wiped her tears from her cheeks, gently cupping her chin and raising her face. "I have been teaching you for many years to hide your abilities. The time for secrecy is over. They know what you are, but they have yet to see your power."

"Oh, I will show them," Carissa spat the words out like they were poison.

"You must be careful." Miriam linked her fingers through Carissa's, brown eyes urgent. "There is something I never told you, child. You are from a powerful bloodline. Dark magic comes naturally to you, do not let it control you."

"Grandmother—"

"Jameson Burnett was my father." The words resonated throughout the dungeon, causing Carissa to stiffen and lapse into silence. The monster from the history tales, the nightmare young children were warned about—he was her great-grandfather. She shook her head slowly, but no lie hid in Miriam's eyes, only guilt.

"I should have said something to you earlier. I was afraid of what you would think of me, that you might become afraid of yourself."

"It was you." Carissa breathed. "You were the one who led him to his death."

She remembered the stories, the ones claiming Jameson's own daughter had been the cause of his demise. She'd led him to his death, luring him into the hands of the King's army. A powerful Imperium—it had been Miriam. That was how her grandmother knew so much about the dark magic Carissa struggled with. That was how she understood what it meant to be a Maleficium, a blood mage.

Miriam's eyes sparkled with ferocity. "Yes."

"Did Grandfather know?"

"That was how we met." Miriam's sad smile broke Carissa's heart. "He was with the soldiers who took Jameson down. The others never remembered who I was, but he did. I claimed to be a distant relative of the man, fearing his parents would never allow us to marry if they knew the truth. But Patrick…he didn't doubt me, not for a moment in all of the years we were married."

So many decades of love and trust between her grandparents, stolen away in mere moments by Cobryn Morrow and his hateful brother. Patrick had been an old man. He had never stood a chance.

"What should I do?" Carissa was painfully aware this would be her last time asking Miriam for advice. She wanted to do something daring, to break her grandmother out of this dungeon and ride for Emlen or Theron. Such actions always had consequences, and they were both too heavily guarded for them to ever make it. Miriam was right—she had to accept this, even if it destroyed her.

"Show them your power." Miriam stated, gripping her granddaughter's hand tightly. "Remind them you are not something to be owned or contained. Use your magic wisely and don't succumb to it. I have faith that you will turn the tides."

Miriam's fervent belief made fresh tears well in Carissa's eyes. She struggled to smile past them. She kept trying to remind herself of what her family would have wanted for her—and yet, what *would* they have wanted? Pain and heartbreak wouldn't have been the answer.

"Did you really do it?" Carissa asked softly. "Did you try to have Jacen killed?"

"No." Miriam shook her head slowly. She did not look insulted that Carissa had asked. "Not that it matters to anyone outside of this dungeon. It's common knowledge I disliked your husband when he first returned, and Deacon has twisted that and used it against me."

Carissa bit down on her lip. She had guessed as much but needed to know the truth for herself. If even she had suspected that Miriam might commit such a crime, she could understand just how easily Deacon had spun his web of lies around the entire court. Even those who had known Miriam since before Carissa had been born would question it.

"Oh, my sweet granddaughter." Emotion thickened Miriam's voice. "I am sorry it came to this. Sorry that I couldn't live to meet your son."

"My…" The statement made Carissa tense, before realisation dawned upon her. "You've seen something."

"You are with child, Carissa." The words were gentle, but Carissa flinched away from them.

It was true that she had been unwell. However, she had attributed missing two bleedings and the nausea to the immense stress she was under. The idea of bringing a child into this nightmare—the coveted son and heir—only made her terrified. Resting a hand on her stomach, still flat beneath the fabric of her dress, she silently promised her unborn baby that where she had failed to save Miriam, she would not fail to save him.

"I don't know how to be a mother," she murmured. "I don't even know how to be a leader."

"Yes, you do." Miriam's brown eyes shone. "You need to trust in yourself. You have been through so much these past few years. Take all that pain, all that rage, and use it to build something better."

Carissa broke down against the bars, pressing her face into her hands as Miriam hushed her and stroked her hair. She was losing her family all over again, and she was just as powerless to stop it as she had been during the Conquest. Her brother with a sword through his chest, her father decapitated, her mother's bloody and lifeless body where she had died protecting Carissa's baby brother…

"I hate them," she snarled the words. "I hate them for what they've done, what they're still doing."

"Look to your allies." Miriam took a step back, releasing Carissa. "Theron, Emlen…you can count on their support."

Carissa wasn't so sure of that, but she didn't say so aloud. She didn't feel as though she had anyone. The world would be a bleak place without Miriam, and she couldn't help but think how utterly alone she was going to be. In that moment, the idea of her baby stopped terrifying her and became a small comfort.

The day of Miriam's execution dawned carrying winter's chill despite being in the middle of autumn.

Carissa's attendance had been non-negotiable, and she'd had no doubt that others would suffer if she did not comply. So, she stood before her people, a powerless figurehead, the puppet they often mocked her as. The swan crown adorned her black hair, though she had never felt less like a Queen.

Vida had departed the capital the day before, returning to Genera for her wedding. Carissa had not seen her in private since her betrayal. She did not want to, for she feared she would lash out at her again, or worse—use her magic to kill her. Jacen told her Vida had done it because she believed she wasn't trusted, that Carissa viewed her as an enemy. She hadn't then, but she certainly did now.

Where one Morrow had departed, another arrived. No doubt drawn in by Deacon's poisonous words and the chance to see the former Queen die, Cobryn arrived with his entourage. Where before he had been accompanied only by Lilith and Ayesha, Cobryn's new wife was with him this time—a woman in her early twenties with features hard as marble and grey eyes cold as stone. Gretchen Dale, the younger sister of Wendell's King.

It was no coincidence that Gretchen would bear witness to this execution. This was a lesson, to show what would happen to her own family if they decided to rise up and shake off their oppressor.

Carissa had witnessed her share of executions in the courtyard in front of the palace. The prisoners were brought past the pillars to the stone platform, usually with jeers and fruit-throwing from the crowd. Their sentence was read out, their last words were spoken—and then they met the executioner's blade, with varying degrees of panic.

Today, the crowd stayed silent. They knew what Miriam's execution meant. Some of their hopes would die with her. The commoners watched the entrance to the palace with guarded eyes. Even the nobility shifted uneasily. She wondered if any of them had spoken up, or if they had succumbed easily to Deacon's gilded lies.

Casting around, Carissa saw no sign of her husband. It was not like him to be late, nor did she think he would be forgiven if he refused to attend the execution.

The great double doors opened with a creak, and two soldiers in Morrow colours led Miriam out into the courtyard. No one spoke as the former Queen, the powerful Imperium, Jameson Burnett's brave daughter, was led down the steps. Then a figure appeared behind the soldiers, and Carissa's breath caught in her throat.

Jacen.

He was clad in the colours of his house, and a sword rested in his hand. Her grandfather Patrick's sword, judging by the swan engraved on the pommel. Carissa stepped forward, but Deacon rested a hand on her arm. Dark circles pressed under Jacen's eyes, and he never once looked toward his wife. He followed Miriam and the soldiers to the platform, drawn in like a moth toward the flame.

Once Miriam stood before the wooden block that spelled her demise, Jacen removed a scroll of parchment from his belt and began to read.

"Beloved people of Basium, your former Queen, Miriam Darnell, comes before you today as a traitor to the crown. Whilst she was given clemency after the Conquest, she abused that gift and instead plotted to take my life. The life of your King."

The words sounded tired and mechanical. Lifeless. Carissa didn't understand why it was Jacen up there reading the sentence aloud. Usually one of the lords of the council would do so, and then the executioner would step forward to carry out the sentence. Carissa could see no executioner dressed all in black, and a horrific thought occurred to her.

Jacen not only dictated the sentence, but he was also the blade that would swing the sword.

"The crime that Miriam Darnell has committed is high treason. The only punishment to fit such a heavy crime is death."

"No," Carissa whispered, moving forward again. This time, Deacon grabbed her arm more firmly. She thought she could stomach seeing her grandmother executed, but by her own husband...

Why was Jacen doing this? Why would he, knowing it would break her heart? She attempted to shrug off Deacon's grip, but his hold was tight as a vice.

"Do you have anything to say?" Jacen asked, turning his attention upon Miriam. He couldn't look her in the eye.

Please, beg for your life, Carissa thought desperately, despite knowing Miriam would do no such thing. *Beg and perhaps they will spare you.*

Instead of responding, Miriam glanced across at Carissa, brown eyes solemn. She mouthed three words to her—*I love you.* Carissa choked back a sob, pressing a hand over her mouth as tears blurred her vision.

Miriam gracefully gathered up the folds of her dress and kneeled, resting her head on the chopping block. Jacen removed the sword from its sheath with a sharp grating sound, raising it above his head so it glinted in the sunlight.

"Jacen, *no!*" Carissa exclaimed, making no attempt to hide her distress. She didn't care how weak she must seem, how desperate. All that mattered was that she could not, would not, witness this waking nightmare. When she attempted to struggle free, Deacon gripped her around the waist to hold her back. Carissa clenched her hands into fists, nails digging into her palms so tightly they stung as she drew blood.

Jacen was pale, his expression grim, as he brought the sword swinging down and cut off Miriam's head in one swift stroke.

Carissa's high, thin scream of anguish and fury resounded throughout the courtyard. Her blood magic, dark and terrible, surged to the forefront of her being—and propelled from her with the force of a hurricane. She reached for it greedily, and let it consume her.

The pillars fractured with a sharp crack and crumbled, and the silent crowd began to cry out and gasp as chaos unleashed. The pillars fell hard, smashing to the ground with sickening thuds. The distressed murmurs and shocked cries ascended into screams of terror, a chorus of the damned. Large pieces of stone fell through the courtyard, crushing nobles and commoners alike. People ran, shouting to one another. Cobryn barked orders to the soldiers, his wives quickly escorted inside.

Deacon released Carissa and stepped back, staring at her with a look of fascinated horror. Carissa whirled on him, wanting to break him next. If she could bring down pillars, it would be easy to break every bone in his body. A dark smile curved the corners of her lips. How sweet it would be to make him suffer for all the pain he'd brought her over the years. She laughed at his shock, the sound high and mocking—and reached out a hand toward him.

Deacon was faster. Throwing his own arms forth, he brought down moisture from the air and transformed it into manacles of ice, binding her wrists in front of her. Carissa hissed and tried to use her power to break through, but Deacon was stronger. He had a lot more practise. Try as Carissa might, she could not fracture the shackles of ice he placed on her.

It was Cobryn that made Carissa's dark magic retreat, that made her pull it back inside her without a second thought. There was a troubled look on the Generan King's face as he stared at her. It was the look of a man sizing up a deadly enemy.

THE GUILTY KING
JACEN MORROW

Jacen was concerned. Carissa had been asleep for almost a day. She was exhausted from her display of magical power—a great and terrible incident that had cost eight people their lives and injured several others. Although Jacen knew his wife hadn't meant to kill anyone, witnessing her raw power firsthand had horrified him. It was the only instance in which he was glad that Deacon had stepped in. If he hadn't…Jacen didn't know what could have happened.

Jacen stood in the meeting room with his father and uncle. Deacon sat at the table, staring at the glass of wine in front of him. Cobryn paced back and forth like a caged animal. Jacen leaned against one of the bookshelves, his posture rigid.

"Did you know?" Cobryn wheeled around, turning on his son. "Did you know she was so powerful?"

"No," Jacen admitted honestly. "I knew she was Maleficium, a blood mage. But what she did at Miriam's execution…"

The memory of the execution made the words die on his lips, made his throat constrict. How should he have expected her to react? He had executed her grandmother without any explanation prior about why. He would hear her screams of anguish until the day he died.

"You decided to keep a snake's egg and you were surprised when the viper that hatched bit you." Deacon slammed his hands down on the table, eyes aglow as he inspected his older brother. "We have a great weapon at our disposal, Cobryn."

"Don't call her that," Jacen spat, pushing himself away from the bookshelf and marching over to the table. "She's not a weapon. She's my wife."

Deacon sneered. "She is whatever we want her to be. With her grandmother dead, who would doubt that Carissa Darnell has the ability to become a creature from nightmares?"

Jacen recalled the coldness in Carissa's eyes as chaos erupted around her, as stone pillars collapsed throughout the courtyard. Seeing his usually compassionate wife so callous had been shocking, to say the least. He was surprised this power had not been displayed when the rest of her family were killed years ago, but he understood that magic did not peak until a mage was of age, or close enough to.

"The girl is with child." Cobryn spoke softly, contemplative—unusual for him. It was the words that made Jacen still. Carissa was pregnant? How was it that he hadn't known? Why hadn't she told him?

"What?" Jacen and Deacon spoke in unison.

"I had one of our medics look her over after the execution. She is possibly three months into the pregnancy."

Jacen raked a shaking hand through his hair. His family pushed for this ever since he had first returned to Basium, but the knowledge that his wife carried his child frightened him. Carissa had not trusted him enough to tell him. After Miriam's execution, Jacen didn't know if she would ever trust him again.

There would be time to explain himself, but that wasn't to say Carissa would listen. Could she love him now? Dread overcame Jacen at the idea that it had been Deacon's plan all along—have Jacen step in to carry out Miriam's execution, effectively tearing apart what feelings he and Carissa had for each other. It would be a clever and devastating move—precisely the sort of move Deacon was capable of.

"So perhaps she will have an heir soon." Deacon folded his arms over his chest, his expression hard as marble. Jacen's heir, not his. Yet another barrier between him and Basium's throne. Paternal protectiveness toward his unborn baby surged at the idea. Whatever the cost, he would keep his child safe from Deacon and his schemes.

"We should hope so." Triumph flared in Cobryn's eyes. Why shouldn't he feel satisfied? He had recently taken Wendell, with Basium and Harith already conquered. Soon, he would turn greedy eyes to the eastern country of Cirocco.

"I will make sure she's taken care of," Jacen insisted. "That she and the baby are kept healthy."

"Good." Cobryn nodded slowly. "Once she has the child, if it's a son… well then, her usefulness will have run its course."

Jacen knew what they meant, and it made him feel cold, as if Deacon had turned his spine to ice. After Carissa's display at her grandmother's execution, Cobryn had become rattled by what she could do. She was needed—at least until she tied her family's line to his. Once Carissa had birthed a son and heir, they would kill her.

News reached Basium of Vida's marriage to Meryn Pyralis. Jacen cared little for it—Vida had proven to him that she could not be trusted, that she was selfish and would do whatever she wanted for her own gain. Once, Jacen would have been saddened he was not present for an event so important to his sister. Now, when Jacen thought of Vida, numbness settled over his heart.

Cobryn summoned his son to the courtyard where Miriam's execution had taken place. He approached his father, who surveyed the damage Carissa's magic had caused. The pillars were slowly but surely being restored. The crimson bloodstains had been washed from the stone.

Jacen swallowed hard, trying to forget it all, but the event was too recent. It wasn't just Carissa's magic haunting him, but his own actions. The sickening sound of steel slicing through flesh as he took off Miriam's head, the metallic scent of blood, the way it had dripped onto his boots. The vivid memories almost made him gag.

"I never saw why I needed to be Miriam's executioner."

"Yes, you did." Cobryn turned to glance at his son. Where there was usually smugness, the self-satisfaction of a man who had just won another country, Jacen saw concern. "Deacon wanted to play you against each other, and you fell for the bait perfectly."

So, it was as Jacen had suspected. His hands balled into fists. He had played the game just as his uncle had hoped, and he had lost any chance of Carissa loving him in the process. Cobryn neither sounded thrilled nor displeased at what Deacon had done. Jacen knew his father well enough to realise he was calculating his options.

"Your wife is a dangerous woman."

"If you'd known about her abilities at the beginning—" Jacen steeled himself, preparing for an answer he would not like— "would you still have let her live?"

"I would have." Cobryn glanced at him, eyes sharp. "But she would have married Deacon instead."

Jacen recalled that Deacon had been the one to subdue Carissa, the only mage in the immediate vicinity who had the ability to. He wondered what she would have become, a broken young Queen subject to Deacon's lack of mercy. If Cobryn thought he had seen darkness in her at the execution…

"What is it you want me to do?" Cobryn had asked him here for a reason, and Jacen found himself once more in the position of loyal son. Carissa would hate him if she saw him now, but he pushed aside thoughts of her and the unborn child she had kept from him.

"It is important your wife has this child." Cobryn placed a hand on his son's shoulder, squeezing hard enough to make Jacen wince. "After Miriam's execution, she may have some…dark thoughts. She may decide she does not want the baby. It falls to you to convince her otherwise."

Jacen didn't know how to respond to that. If Carissa didn't want a baby, he thought she would have quietly taken care of the matter. It was not up to him to force her to carry a child to term if that wasn't what she wanted. This heir was important and yet he dreaded the baby's birth, knowing what it could mean for Carissa. Cobryn viewed her as a broodmare. Deacon was worse since he saw her as a weapon.

To Jacen, this was his wife, the woman he loved. Yes, she had kept her secrets from him, but could he blame her? He had kept a fair share himself of late, all in a ridiculous effort to protect her when he would have been better off being honest. She had every reason to despise him after he executed Miriam.

"She wants the baby," Jacen muttered, before he locked eyes with his father and realised Cobryn searched for something concrete. "If she has doubts, then I'll do my utmost to remind her of the need."

He hated himself for those words, almost as much as he hated himself for falling into Deacon's trap and executing Miriam. It had been the kindest way for Carissa's grandmother to die, though he didn't think she saw it that way.

"My son." A genuine smile curved the corners of Cobryn's lips. Once his father's pride in him would have been something Jacen strived for, so why did he feel empty receiving it now? "You have never failed me, and I pray you never will."

THE MURDERER QUEEN
CARISSA DARNELL

Being held prisoner in her own room did not agree with Carissa. The first few days after her grandmother's execution had involved an abundance of tears. She had barely left her bed. The nausea from her pregnancy made it worse. Carissa found herself with a lack of company, aside from Soot, particularly as she refused to speak to Jacen. Once she was calm, they could have a conversation, and he could explain why he had agreed to execute her grandmother.

Soon, Carissa realised crying and feeling sorry for herself would do little to help her situation. She wanted to be defiant and resilient, but she could not find the strength. Why should she keep fighting when it was so exhausting to constantly be beaten? She found herself having such thoughts often, wondering if it would be easier to simply become the demure puppet the Morrows wanted her to be.

For my family. For those who had died during the Conquest, for Miriam, for her unborn son. That was what drove her, what kept her from giving up. She could not let such sacrifices be in vain, particularly not when Miriam counted on her to rebel and take back power in Basium.

Every part of her being ached for her grandmother. Miriam had been all Carissa had left of her family, a tenuous tie to brighter memories and a happier past. Losing Miriam had meant losing her light, losing whatever peace Carissa had left. No wonder the darkness had come forth. Although guilt-ridden over the destruction her magic had caused, the thought of the damage she could still do terrified Carissa.

"Your Majesty?" It was Eirian, a servant a few years older than Carissa who had been the person she had seen the most since her imprisonment. The young woman crossed the room with a plate of food, setting it beside the bed. "Forgive my bluntness, but you must eat, my Queen. The baby needs nourishment."

The thought of her child that made Carissa reach for the plate. No sooner had she helped herself to the food than two women swiftly entered her room without announcement. Eirian spun to face them, slim body tensing. Carissa recognised them instantly—the wives of Cobryn Morrow, Lilith Marwan and Gretchen Dale.

"Leave us," Gretchen commanded, pale eyes narrowing at the servant woman.

Eirian glanced at Carissa, who nodded. She did not know why these women had come to see her. She was more than able to defend herself if they meant her harm. Whereas she had once reached for her magic with reluctance, it was no longer her secret weapon. She would utilise it wherever and whenever necessary.

The thought of losing control at her grandmother's execution made Carissa tremble with guilt. She had been informed that eight people died, and another dozen injured because of what she had done. Whatever destruction she had caused, she had not meant to kill her own people. It was the Morrow family who she wanted to suffer, yet all she had done was reveal her power.

"Can I help you?" Carissa said, polite but stiff. Of all the people she would have expected to visit her, these women had been nowhere on the list.

"We wanted to see how you were faring." Lilith's voice was soft and melodic, almost soothing. Carissa thought it was the first time she had heard the woman speak. Whenever at Cobryn's side, Lilith remained silent and watchful.

"*You* wanted to see how she was faring," Gretchen corrected, tossing her dark blonde hair over her shoulder. Chin tilted upwards, shoulders held back—a proud woman, regardless of her marriage to Cobryn. Despite her sharp tone, the fact that she had accompanied Lilith anyway indicated that the two women had become close. They shared a husband, and the violence he visited upon them.

"We wanted to speak with you about everything happening." Lilith hesitated, before sitting on the edge of Carissa's bed. "I understand you must be feeling trapped and powerless..."

"I don't think you have any idea how I feel," Carissa responded quietly, no venom in her voice, only exhaustion. She had not asked for these women to come to her, to offer sympathy. She wanted none of it.

Lilith's eyes widened slightly. Gretchen's narrowed as she loomed over Carissa.

"You think you're the only one who's known pain and suffering?" Gretchen demanded, and the words grated against Carissa. Shame flooded through her at remembering who she was talking to.

"I didn't mean that," Carissa said quickly, realising her words had been insensitive and self-absorbed.

"I've heard what sort of man your husband is." Gretchen flashed her a smile, something swift and vicious that didn't reach her eyes. "He is good to you. You may not understand each other, but he has never raised a hand to you in cruelty. Cobryn has done unspeakable things to Lilith and I. Suffering is not a scale, little Queen."

"Gretchen." Lilith placed a hand on her arm, and the younger woman fell silent. Sighing, Lilith turned her attention on Carissa. "It's true that we are not going through the same ordeal. Nonetheless, I thought it may be easier to… become your friend."

The word 'friend' felt foreign to Carissa. Vida had been her friend, and she'd betrayed her. Bellona had been her friend, and she'd fled from Marinel. It gave Carissa cause to be wary rather than grateful. Trying to make more friends seemed like an invitation for more pain. She swallowed the sudden lump in her throat and blinked back tears that threatened to blur her vision.

"You are in a position more advantageous than Lilith and I." Gretchen was certainly the blunter of the pair. "Cobryn might have murdered your family, but he allowed you to sit on Basium's throne."

"Your families also sit on the throne," Carissa reminded her, unsure of where this conversation was headed.

"Yes, but you're a *woman*," Gretchen said pointedly. "We cannot do anything to influence what happens to our countries, but you can with yours. Jacen will listen to you, and Cobryn may just listen to him."

"I don't want anything to do with my husband right now," Carissa responded coolly. Whatever they wanted to convince her to do, it wouldn't work. It would be some time before she was able to speak civilly with Jacen.

"Cobryn won't be satisfied until he has Razmara." Lilith's dark eyes filled with urgency. "I don't want that happening. I want the same as you do—for my country to be free of his reign."

Carissa examined her, the woman who had been married to Cobryn over a decade, who was the mother of his youngest child. Gretchen had her bitterness, Carissa had her numbness, yet it was Lilith and her softness who was the strongest of all of them. How could someone endure so much and still speak so gently?

These women spoke treasonous words. They had risked much to come to her—and it became apparent that belief in Carissa hadn't died with Miriam. Her eyes widened as she glanced between them, realising what they didn't say aloud. *We will bring him down, him and all of those who helped him climb so high over the bodies of our families.*

"Enough hiding and sulking." Gretchen's eyes gleamed, and she offered Carissa her hand. "It's time to fight back."

Carissa took it and grasped it firmly. Lilith placed her hand atop theirs. A silent pact—a wordless vow between three women who had watched their countries burn and had suffered for it. Together, they would find a way to fight back, and this time they would not fail.

She thought of her mother's bloody corpse, the mangled remains of her little brother, her father brutally murdered before her eyes, and a new memory, fresher than the others: Miriam's beheading. All those deaths stung, biting into her like a knife across flesh. Tears welled in Carissa's eyes and spilled down her cheeks.

I will avenge you.

EPILOGUE
SEBASTIAN DARNELL

In the days immediately following the Conquest, Sebastian Darnell wanted nothing more than to lash out in anger and grief at the man who had taken his family from him. He was whisked away to Emlen and raised as a blacksmith's apprentice, renamed Solomon to protect his identity.

Quintin Faustus had been the one who saved him as he stumbled out of the collapsing tunnels. Several of his childhood friends had died down there, and Sebastian had lost his family ring. It had always been too big for him, an heirloom, and his hands were slick with blood that night. For the best, Lord Ambrose assured him—the remains would be too horribly disfigured to identify, and the ring would insinuate that Sebastian had been among those crushed in the tunnels.

The person who Sebastian might have been, had he not lost his family, had died down in those tunnels. The Conquest had chewed up the boy that he'd once been, the pampered prince. It had spat back out a young man hardened by loss, a warrior. A believer in justice, no matter what it took.

Lord Ambrose summoned Sebastian from the smithy and, with the news spreading throughout Emlen, he knew precisely why his benefactor had called upon him. The entire city grieved for the horrific and unnecessary murder of Lord Ambrose's eldest daughter, Sidonia.

Striding into the hall in his stained blacksmith's attire, Sebastian noted Lady Ambrose's red-rimmed eyes. Her remaining children were close by her side. As his father's only son, Jarl would need to remain cautious, for he would be the person the Morrows sought to eliminate next. Meliora's skin paled but there was a steely determination in her eyes. Her expression softened at the sight of

Sebastian, and her lips hinted at a smile.

"My lord. My lady." Sebastian bowed from the waist. Everyone present knew the truth of his heritage, but he had to keep up the pretence at all times. No one doubted the Morrows had their spies everywhere. "I was saddened to hear about the death of Sidonia. Your oldest daughter was everything a respectable young woman could hope to be."

"It was poison, did you know that?" Jarl spoke, teeth baring in a snarl of hatred. "A variety of belladonna. My sister died in agony."

Sebastian remained silent. Having spent the last few years as a blacksmith's apprentice, he was not a boy of witty words. He had offered his condolences, though he did not understand why he had been summoned. Did Lord Ambrose wish him to play a part in retribution? His eyes again locked with Meliora's. The girl had almost been caught in their web of lies and mystery by Sebastian's older sister, Basium's Queen.

Carissa. The name made Sebastian's heart harden. He did not think his older sister was cruel, but she was misguided. Carissa had a crown thrust upon her head the moment their family had been wiped out, yet she had lived a comfortable life since. Sebastian, in contrast, had become a boy of the streets. His older sister had allowed herself to become a puppet for the Morrows while Sebastian fought for freedom.

"Jarl." Lord Ambrose placed a hand on his son's shoulder, stepping forward. "You do not bow before us, Sebastian. You never will again."

The boy froze, violet-blue eyes casting around to see who might have overheard. Lord Ambrose appeared calm despite his grief, and Sebastian didn't think he had slipped up. Using his given name had been deliberate, and hope flared within him. Quintin and Lord Ambrose often spoke of this day—the day they would reveal to Basium that its true King was alive after years of hiding.

"Lord Ambrose?" Sebastian remained cautious. Did Sidonia's death prompt this sudden decision?

"We have received further news from Marinel." Lord Ambrose hesitated, glancing at his wife before looking back to Sebastian. "Not a week ago, your grandmother and former Queen, Miriam, was executed by Jacen Morrow."

Sebastian's entire body tensed. Although he had interacted with Carissa whilst behind the mask, he had not seen his grandmother since the Conquest. He remembered her well, doting but firm, stern but fair. His hands shook as he tried to process the news that cut him like a blade.

"Why?"

"She was accused of high treason." Lord Ambrose folded his arms over his chest. "She was accused of conspiring to murder the King."

Sebastian absorbed this information in grim silence. He could not blame Miriam if that was what she had been doing, though he doubted it. His grandmother was a clever woman, smarter than to be discovered plotting murder. He wondered what Carissa had done, how she had reacted. She was the Queen, after all. Sebastian knew the answer—Carissa had done nothing, and that was why Miriam was dead.

"Was it quick?"

"Jacen decapitated her." Lord Ambrose raked a hand through his thinning hair. He appeared exhausted, as though he had aged years in the space of months. "But what happened after that was more terrifying. In her grief, the Queen displayed a dark and powerful magic, tearing down pillars and destroying much of the courtyard before she was apprehended."

"You mean to tell me Carissa is a Maleficium?" A cold chill ran down Sebastian's spine. He had suspected as much when Farran's statue had almost crushed him, conveniently ending his attempt to murder Jacen. He had seen the wrath in Carissa's eyes that day, yet never voiced his suspicions. His instincts had been correct.

"Your sister is a danger as well as a pawn," Lord Ambrose admitted. "Now that the Morrow family knows what she is capable of, they will use her to instil fear into Basium's population."

"What are we going to do about it?" Sebastian asked. Lord Ambrose had likely discussed this with Quintin, but he was eager to hear their plan for himself. He had been summoned because he was likely a key component.

"We are going to show Basium that she is not their only option." Lord Ambrose smiled tightly, eyes shining with hope. "We are going to give them the King they need instead of the Queen they've been forced to accept."

Sebastian took a sharp breath. He was done hiding behind jackal masks. It had been a brilliant suggestion on Quintin's part—an undisguised jab at House Morrow. The mask had served its purpose, kept him safe over the years, made him a part of something. There had been the knowledge that eventually, he would have to forsake security for his inheritance—Basium's throne.

Jacen Morrow had stolen his crown. But now, Sebastian Darnell would take it back.

That night, under cover of darkness, Sebastian visited Meliora. He didn't know if Lord Ambrose was aware of the blossoming romance between the rightful King and his youngest child, but perhaps the man didn't mind. Maybe he hoped that Sebastian's affection for Meliora meant she would be his Queen.

When he entered her room and clicked the door closed behind him, he noticed Meliora kneeling before a candle on the dressing table, lips forming silent words. He knew her mind was on her sister. Meliora and Sidonia had bickered frequently, but Meliora had been devastated at the news of her older sister's murder. After a few moments, the girl rose to greet him.

"Sebastian." His name came out a reverent whisper, her eyes wide. "You came."

"Of course I did." He raised his eyebrows, head tilting to the side in confusion. "Don't I always?"

"Things are different now." Meliora seated herself on the edge of the bed, brow furrowed. "You are going to be King."

"It changes nothing," Sebastian assured her. They had known this day would come—the day where Sebastian would come out of hiding and take back his country.

He remembered his mother—brave, loving Imogen. She had fought against the Generan soldiers to buy him time to escape. She had not been a warrior. She died violently to ensure Sebastian lived. For many years, Basium thought her death had been in vain. The time had come to show them that it wasn't. Sebastian's heart ached at the thought of his valiant mother. He would be as strong as she was.

"Your coronation is tomorrow," Meliora said, as though he needed the reminder. The idea made his stomach twist unpleasantly. He had prepared for years for this day, but it wasn't enough. Sebastian had had two older brothers. Until the Conquest, he had never considered the possibility that he would be King.

Then there was the fact that Emlen would declare its independence by supporting Sebastian. One day, he would be installed upon the throne of Basium. For now, Emlen would have to be enough.

"I don't know that I am ready." He would only confess his concerns to Meliora. Lord Ambrose and Quintin wanted to see a strong and capable monarch. At sixteen years old, Sebastian felt terribly young and unprepared. Emlen saw strength, but Meliora saw his doubts.

"I don't know that anyone ever is." Meliora shrugged her shoulders. He knew that she did not understand. She did not have the burden of a large inheritance, a country, on her shoulders. She would marry an important man and bear children as was her duty. Despite that, Sebastian relied on her encouragement.

"I will be better than *her*." Sebastian's lip curled at the thought of his sister. It was contempt that came to mind when he thought of Carissa. He did not wish to see her dead or harmed—but she did not deserve the throne, not when she was controlled by her husband's family.

"Come to bed," Meliora insisted. Despite the deep affection between them, they hadn't made love; it wouldn't impact him, but Meliora would be left with the taint of giving up her purity before marriage. For now, passionate kisses and heated touches would have to be enough.

Sebastian crawled into bed beside Meliora, burying his face in her hair and savouring her sweet scent. Sometimes he wished they could be nothing more than this—just a boy and a girl, complete in each other's company. His destiny would always be a wedge between them. He thought of tomorrow, and all he felt was dread.

He reminisced on his childhood, on the happier memories he had shared with Carissa and their brothers. How they had bickered in their younger years, especially when Sebastian had made a mess of Carissa's favourite dresses. Whatever kinship he felt toward his sister had been snuffed out, leaving the certainty that she was the enemy.

Sebastian was uneasy in the formal clothes he had borrowed from Jarl. They hung loose on his wiry form, and the velvet cloak dragged his shoulders down. He wished he could have spent the hour of dawn at the forge working on a new blade, but he didn't know if he would be allowed to do that again. Being a blacksmith's son and apprentice had only been a fictional story, though Sebastian had found a genuine love for the craft. It gave him peace when he was restless.

No peace could be found this morning, only a war brewing as certainly as the storm lingering on the horizon. Dark clouds hung overhead as Lord

Ambrose called for an announcement. The citizens of Emlen filed into the streets before the castle steps, murmuring amongst themselves. Many of them would have heard what happened in Marinel and wondered what their lord intended on doing about it. Not one of them believed the murder of his daughter would go unpunished.

"My people!" Lord Ambrose exclaimed. He was an excellent speaker, a worthy mouthpiece for Quintin and the goals of the Jackals. The nobleman may not be as extreme as the rebels, but especially now, he shared their opinions. "I come before you today with devastating news. Our beloved former Queen, Miriam, has been executed in the capital."

Gasps escaped the crowd, and the murmurs rose in volume. Sebastian waited behind the doors, in the shadows. He could see the people, but they could not see him. By the chatter that came over the crowd, he realised his grandmother had been admired throughout all of Basium. His eyes stung with tears when he realised she would never know he had survived the Conquest.

"I do not believe Queen Carissa to be a cold or cruel young woman." Lord Ambrose clasped his hands. "This was not decreed by her. The Morrow family has control over our young Queen, and for that reason, she will never be our ally. We cannot abide by a puppet."

"She's a Maleficium!" a voice from the crowd called out. "We've seen that she has dark magic. What chance do we stand against that? It isn't as though we have a choice."

Sebastian smiled wryly when he realised Quintin spoke. The man would often stand among the people and voice doubts, allowing Lord Ambrose to further explain the plans they had both agreed to. A clever strategy.

"Oh, we have a choice." Lord Ambrose glanced toward the doors, and Sebastian took that as his cue to make a dramatic entrance. He had wanted to make this a casual event, yet Lord Ambrose had insisted upon the importance of making a show of his survival. When Sebastian stepped into the light, he expected more muttering in the crowd. What he was unprepared for was the stunned silence his appearance caused.

"Lord Ambrose." He inclined his head.

"Everyone believed Sebastian Darnell died during the Conquest, crushed in the collapsing tunnels. Instead, he survived and fled here to Emlen, and has been raised in secrecy ever since, preparing for his ascension. He has lived among the people as Carissa has not. He knows you and you know him."

"Is he to be our King?" Quintin again, voicing what the wide-eyed population of Emlen likely wondered.

"Sebastian is the last male heir to the throne of Basium." Lord Ambrose let this sink in, turning to take something from his wife, something that glimmered in the pale sunlight. "He has more of a claim than his older sister, and today, I intend to acknowledge that claim. I intend to serve the rightful monarch."

Sebastian stepped forward, sweeping the cloak aside and kneeling before Lord Ambrose. His eyes locked with Meliora's as she stood to the side with her mother and brother. She gave him an encouraging smile. Sebastian's knees trembled, though he ignored them. He was no longer a boy hiding in Emlen behind a jackal mask, a blacksmith's apprentice.

Lord Ambrose placed the crown upon Sebastian's head. It had been made especially for him, for this occasion. Identical to the golden swan crown with one exception—Sebastian's crown was jet black. Heavy and uncomfortable, it weighed him down, yet determination swelled within him. This may not have been what he was born for, but like the molten metal he had beaten into a sword, he had been forged into this.

Marinel had Carissa, their Queen and their weapon. Now came the time for Emlen to flex its might and showed off a secret weapon of their own.

When Sebastian rose, Lord Ambrose bent the knee. His family kneeled. Slowly but surely, the entire crowd kneeled.

Emlen had crowned its King.

Pronunciation Guide

People

Bellona Lenore—BELL-OWN-AH LE-NORR
Carissa Darnell—CAR-ISS-AH DARN-ELLE
Cobryn Morrow—CO-BRIN MO-RO
Cyprian Ambrose—SIGH-PREE-IN AMB-ROSE
Deacon Morrow—DEE-KIN MO-RO
Kato Lenore—KAY-TO LE-NORR
Jacen Morrow—JAY-SIN MO-RO
Jarl Ambrose—YAH-L AMB-ROSE
Lilith Marwan—LILL-ITH MAH-WEN
Meliora Ambrose—MELL-EE-OR-AH AMB-ROSE
Miriam Darnell—MIH-REE-AM DARN-ELLE
Quintin Faustus—KWIN-TIN FOUR-STUS
Sebastian Darnell—SEB-AS-CHUN DARN-ELLE
Tiago Benedict—TEE-AH-GO BEN-EH-DICT
Vida Morrow—VEE-DAH MO-RO

Places

Ardelis—AH-DELL-ISS
Basium—BASS-EE-UM
Bao—BOW
Cirocco—SI-ROCK-OH
Fortua—FOUR-CHEW-AH
Genera—JEN-EAR-AH
Harith—HA-RI-TH

Isadore—ISS-AH-DOOR
Marinel—MA-RIN-ELLE
Nicodemus—NICK-OH-DEE-MUS
Seneca—SIN-ICK-AH
Theron—THE-RON
Wendell—WEN-DALL

OTHER

Imperium—IM-PEER-EE-UM
Maleficium—MAL-IF-UH-SEE-UM
Primordial—PRIME-OR-DEE-ALL

ACKNOWLEDGEMENTS

How do I even begin to thank all of the people that have made this book possible?

My alpha readers—Nat and Tracey. Thank you for putting up with Blood of Queens in its rawest form and loving it nonetheless. I poured my whole heart into this story, and it was one of the first novels I've written that I was proud to share. Thank you for making that such an easy choice.

My critique partners—Cass and Jenni. You both had such awesome feedback for me to work with, and your love (and hate) of the characters really fuelled my fire. I also want to thank Cass for my map, it's extraordinary, you've been on this journey with me from the start so you know this world inside out.

My beta readers—Z, Elsie, Julia, Ashley and Lei. Thank you for sticking through while I pestered you for your thoughts and feelings.

My editor—Camilla, thank you for taking this and polishing it so that it truly shines, I am eternally grateful for your suggestions and for making this story flow as it really should.

My cover designer and interior formatter—Celin, I have always marvelled at your creations and so it's been an absolute pleasure being able to work with you on my book. Thank you for creating such a gorgeous cover for my book.

My street team—Ali, Cass, Chloe, Jacqui, Jenni, Lei, Lina, Z and Tracey. Thank you for signing up to either ages of silence or constant bombardment of what's going on with this.

My partner—Chris, I know you aren't heavily invested in the writing world, but thank you for supporting me throughout this and letting me ramble about the world that I've created.

My roommate—Jack, how could I have done this without a constant stream of kombucha?

Also thank you to those reading this now. Every reader counts, and I am so honoured that you've chosen to take a chance on me and this book. It means the world to me.

ABOUT THE AUTHOR

Maddie is an author from Sydney, Australia. She has been reading and writing from a very young age, and is particularly invested in complex characters, healthy relationships, and well-written female protagonists. She's the oldest of three siblings and the owner of two very cute bunnies called Kenobi and Kylo. She has a Bachelor of Arts in Journalism, though she works in administration

Carissa Darnell lost almost everything in the Conquest. Left the sole heir and rightful Queen of Basium following the slaughter of her family, she hungers for vengeance against the Warmonger, who took it all from her. A puppet monarch, she hides a dark and dangerous magic, one that her grandmother Miriam believes she can weaponise against the enemy.

Jacen Morrow is the son of the Warmonger, King Cobryn Morrow of Genera. In the wake of the Darnell family massacre, he married Carissa to keep a hold over her country. He returns to Basium after years spent fighting a civil war back home, but not everyone is accepting of his position as King - least of all his powerful uncle Deacon, who held Basium with an iron fist in Jacen's absence, and whose ambition is near insatiable.

Along with Carissa's best friends, Jacen's sister Vida and feisty heiress Bellona Lenore, the unhappily married couple must work together to save Basium. For resistance rises in the north, and if Jacen and Carissa cannot stop it, war will once again engulf the country—and it could mean the destruction of everything they hold dear.

$19.99

ISBN 978-0-646-83548-8

90000

9 780646 835488